D0401615

MURDER UNDER THE MISTLETOE

An utterly gripping cozy murder mystery full of twists

LIZ FIELDING

A Maybridge Murder Mystery Book 2

JOFFE BOOKS

Joffe Books, London
www.joffebooks.com

First published in Great Britain in 2023

© Liz Fielding 2023

This book is a work of fiction. Names, characters, businesses, organizations, places and events are either the product of the author's imagination or are used fictitiously. Any resemblance to actual persons, living or dead, events or locales is entirely coincidental. The spelling used is British English except where fidelity to the author's rendering of accent or dialect supersedes this. The right of Liz Fielding to be identified as author of this work has been asserted in accordance with the Copyright, Designs and Patents Act 1988.

Cover art by Dee Dee Book Covers

ISBN: 978-1-83526-232-0

CHAPTER ONE

"Mistletoe?" Abby Finch repeated into the phone. She couldn't have been more surprised if Penny Henderson had asked if she had grown another limb.

"Oh, it's not for me." Penny sounded horrified at the very idea. "I'm on the team decorating St Bart's parish hall for Christmas and I suspect that some of the more susceptible members of the senior's lunch club are hoping to find the very eligible Gregory Tatton under their tree this year."

Her tone suggested that they needed their heads testing.

Having inherited her late sister's cottage, the widowed Penny had only recently moved to Maybridge. She'd joined the lunch club to find new friends of her own age but wasn't looking for a new man in her life. Not even the clearly desirable Gregory Tatton.

Abby didn't know the man, but she'd seen him at various events and despite Penny's reaction, she could see the attraction.

"It's a truth universally acknowledged, Penny," Abby teased, "that a silver fox will be hunted down by lunch club widows who are missing the comfort of a man about the house. It's not by chance that the collective noun for widows is an 'ambush'."

"Is it?" Penny was supposed to laugh. "I suppose he is attractively packaged," she admitted, if grudgingly. "I can think of more than one widow who'd like to ambush him in the store cupboard."

"But not you?"

"Believe me, once was enough." Her conviction was loud and clear. "I'm never going to be at the beck and call of another man, even one who's still got a full head of hair and his own teeth."

"Oh?" Penny was a sweetheart, but so hard on men in general that, unable to resist, Abby asked, "You got close enough to check out his teeth?"

And finally Penny laughed. "You know very well that I was a receptionist at a dental practice. I can spot the real thing at thirty paces."

"Well, I don't know if it was his teeth, but Pam Lewis was all aflutter when I saw her a couple of weeks ago after he'd invited her for coffee in the Buttery. To be honest, I was a bit surprised. She must be a good bit older than him. I was under the impression that most men were on dating sites looking for someone younger."

Much younger.

Deserted by her now late husband for a woman only nine years older than Lucy, their seventeen-year-old daughter, Abby was painfully familiar with the concept.

"Apparently not," Penny said. "I was on the end of an invitation to have coffee with him a few weeks ago."

Abby wasn't in the least bit surprised. Penny might be in her sixties but she was smart, attractive and good company, and yet her reluctance to get involved with any man was understandable. She'd had a brute of a father, a useless husband and a sister who'd been assaulted as a girl. Having taken her grandson under her wing and moved to Maybridge, she was making the most of life on her own terms.

"I'm guessing he didn't get any encouragement?"

"None whatever, but the way he smiled and said he'd see me when I was in a more receptive frame of mind made me want to slap him."

"Receptive? That is a bit creepy," Abby agreed.

"And his invitation did just happen to coincide with the settlement of my sister's estate. Call me cynical, but I suspect it was the fact that I'd inherited Molly's cottage that was the attraction rather than my blue eyes." She paused, then added, "And Pam does have that lovely apartment in Spencer Court."

"You're suggesting that's the only reason he's interested in her?" Abby asked, shocked.

"I'm very fond of Pam," Penny said, "but let's face it, she's not the sharpest knife in the box and Gregory Tatton could have his pick."

"If that's his game, he's going to be disappointed." And once he discovered that the apartment would revert to the Finch estate when Pam died, Abby realised, he'd quickly lose interest.

Penny was one of the few people who knew the background to that. "If there had been any danger of him getting his hands on Pam's apartment, I'd have mentioned it earlier. In the meantime, it won't hurt him to be nice to her for a few weeks."

Maybe not. But poor Pam would be hurt and confused and blame herself when he dropped her. Abby wondered whether she should offer a gentle hint.

There would be tears either way. All she could do, she supposed, was to be on hand with the tissues and chocolate biscuits when the inevitable happened. She changed the subject.

"Are you and Cal going to your family for the holiday?" she asked. "Or are they coming here?"

Cal, Penny's eighteen-year-old grandson, was not only signed up as Abby's apprentice on the government scheme but was dating Lucy.

"Neither. Cal's mother has a new man in her life and the two of them will be spending a loved-up Christmas where the sun is hot and the booze is cheap . . ." She sighed. "I learned my lesson the first time, but my daughter is an eternal optimist. It'll end in tears, it always does, because she falls for the same kind of man again and again, but for the moment she's over the moon."

"Fingers crossed for a better outcome this time," Abby said, realising that Lucy must already know that Cal would be in Maybridge for the holiday and was just waiting for the right moment to suggest that he and his grandmother spend the day with them.

This was clearly the right moment.

"If you and Cal are going to be spending the holiday in Maybridge come and join us for the day. Lucy is planning a veggie special so Cal will be well catered for. The rest of us will have all the turkey and pigs in blankets that we can eat."

"Abby . . . Are you sure?"

"Absolutely." Her marriage to Howard was well over but it would be the children's first Christmas since their father died, and it was going to be tough on them. And Penny's late sister Molly had been very much part of the family. They would all be missing her. "The more the merrier," she assured her, "although I can't guarantee that it will be a totally tear-free occasion."

"We've all suffered a loss this year," Penny said sagely. "A few tears are inevitable. Is there anything I can bring? I've a Christmas cake that's just waiting for the icing. And I can make mince pies."

"Oh, perfect. I'm so behind with everything. Have you thought any more about setting up a home-baking service? I'd happily pay for some of your goodies for my drinks party on the Saturday before Christmas."

"It's a project for the new year." Penny seemed to hesitate. "I thought I might ask Lucy if she'd design some flyers for me. I know she's got exams coming up, so I wanted to run the idea past you first. Just say if you'd rather I didn't offer her a distraction when she should be studying."

"We all need a break, Penny." And Lucy, with her heart set on a career in graphic design and marketing, would love the challenge. "Just make sure you're charging enough for your baked goods to cover your costs and make a profit."

"I've already had that lecture from Cal, but you'll be getting mates' rates. Let me know what you want and we'll work something out."

"Thanks. That's a weight off my mind." Then remembering why Penny had called, Abby said, "So, the mistletoe. When do you need it?"

"Tomorrow afternoon?"

"Wednesday?" Abby asked, checking.

"Can you manage that? After the seniors' lunch on Saturday it's non-stop partying at the hall, so volunteers from all the groups that use the hall are coming together to put up the decorations and dress the tree. I'm sorry it's such short notice. Trish only mentioned it five minutes ago."

"Trish?"

"Trish Porter. She's a waitress in the bookshop café?"

Abby tried to recall the woman. "I think I've met her at different fundraisers. Is she one of the hopefuls?"

"I imagine so. She's always fussing around Gregory, making him cakes, knitting . . . I'd sounded her out about the chances of supplying the bookshop café with cakes."

"That's a great idea," Abby said, encouragingly.

"Trish only works there, but she said they do buy in some ready-made stuff from local producers and offered to mention me to the owner. She just called to let me know that he'll look at a price list. Anyway, that's when she asked me if you might have some mistletoe. One good turn . . ."

"Of course. It's not a problem. There's plenty in the orchard up at the Lodge. There are a lot of berries on the holly this year and I've got some seed heads I've sprayed gold in my workshop. I'll bring those too."

"That's generous of you, Abby. I'll let Trish know."

"I'll drop it in at the hall tomorrow on my way home. It'll be after four," she warned. "I'd offer to stay and help with the decorations, but I have to pick up Sophie from school."

It was football practice and her youngest was a keen member of the squad.

As Abby rang off, it occurred to her that she should call Izzy Hamilton and ask if she needed anything from the garden to decorate her home.

She hadn't seen the glamorous young woman who'd displaced her in the affections of her late husband since the christening of the baby girl he'd fathered.

Abby had helped Izzy through the delivery and the pair of them had forged an unlikely bond. While she suspected that Izzy might be regretting her hormone-fuelled post-birth insistence that Abby be May's godmother, the infant was half-sister to her own children, Lucy, Tom and Sophie. They would be able to talk to May, when she was older, about the father she would never have a chance to know.

CHAPTER TWO

The parish hall was a hive of activity and already looking festive when Abby arrived with the mistletoe just after four thirty. She couldn't see Penny, but Abby's neighbour Beattie was decorating one of the windows with her partner, June, who spotted her.

"Hi, Abby! Have you come to help?" she called, drawing attention to her arrival.

"No, I'm on a drop-and-run," she replied, anxious to escape before someone tried to rope her in to help.

Lisa Callaghan, who ran the Brownies, and Fiona Keane, the vicar's wife, were putting the finishing touches to Santa's grotto in a quiet corner, and she quickly crossed the hall to join them, hoping that one of them would stop spraying the roof with artificial snow for long enough to relieve her of her offerings.

"Hi, Lisa, Fiona. Penny asked for this," she said. "Or rather Trish asked her."

"They're both in the kitchen, giving it a thorough clean before the caterers come in on Saturday," Fiona informed her.

"Oh, right. They won't want to be bothered with this, then. Can I leave it with you?"

"Good heavens, Abby," Lisa said, laughing as she turned around and saw what she was carrying. "That's an awful lot of mistletoe!"

"Do you think I've overdone it?" Abby asked. "I thought it would look good in bunches along the beams." Then she grinned too. "The tradition is that you remove a berry every time someone is kissed, which might be tricky if they're up that high. I wouldn't want to be responsible for any injuries."

"Well, in the cause of health and safety, I'm going to pinch a bit to pin over Father Christmas's chair." Lisa was still laughing as she whipped a pair of scissors out of her apron pocket and snipped off a generous spray. "I know some of the seniors will want to thank him properly for his gifts, and they should be safe enough on his lap."

"Really, Lisa . . ." Fiona's snow spray can let out a disapproving noise as she returned to the task of decorating the grotto, provoking more laughter from Lisa and Abby.

"It's just a bit of fun," Lisa insisted. "And I'm sure the vicar won't object. Weddings are good for business."

"A wedding is not business, it's a sacred sacrament," Fiona reminded her rather sharply, as she shook her can and tried again without result. "I seem to have run out of snow and the roof is only half done."

Abby didn't know Fiona well. They'd met at fundraisers where she'd helped out with a plant stall and were on first-name terms, but church tended to be for weddings, christening and funerals in her family.

Clearly Christmas was a busy time at the vicarage and no doubt a lot of the extra work would fall on the vicar's wife, who, unsurprisingly, seemed a little stressed.

"Maybe some of that holly and ivy will help disguise the bald patches," Lisa suggested quickly, and began to raid the bag Abby had brought with her, pulling out long strands of ivy, only stopping as she spotted the gold-painted seed heads and dried flowers. "Oh, I love these! I'd never have thought of spraying hydrangea heads."

"I cut a load of stuff in that dry spell a few weeks ago," Abby told her. "Once they'd dried out, I gave them a quick squirt of gold paint and made up seasonal sprays to give to my clients for Christmas."

"Lucky clients. It's too late this year, but you've inspired me with gift ideas for next Christmas. What are these prickly ones?" Lisa asked, still digging into the bag.

"*Ricinus*. The castor oil plant," Abby told her.

Fiona turned to look. "Isn't that poisonous?"

"I wouldn't advise eating it," Abby agreed, drily. "Especially not the seeds. I was careful to remove them, and painted like this they're safe enough. I was surprised to find them. They don't normally survive from one year to the next, but the last few winters have been so mild that the seeds must have self-set. It's practically taken over one of the beds at Linton Lodge. I'll have to warn whoever buys the place."

Not that there had been much interest so far.

"The weather is crazy. I had roses until the frosts hit this week," Lisa told her. "Maybe the group making table decorations can use these." She looked around and sighed. "Make that the *lady* making table decorations. I don't suppose you could spare half an hour—"

"I'm really sorry, but I have to pick up Sophie."

Lisa sighed. "It was worth a try."

"We're a bit short-handed on Saturday morning," Fiona said. "Is there any chance you could spare some time to help us set up the tables then?"

Abby had planned to do some Christmas shopping on Saturday morning, but she could spare an hour.

"I can be here just after ten," she offered.

"Bless you," Fiona said, looking up at the tree, where the vicar, high on a stepladder, was fixing the last of the lights. "Nigel is so keen that everything is perfect for our seniors."

Before either Abby or Lisa could agree, a man's urgent voice cut through the buzz of conversation. "Don't hang the snowman there, Janet!"

There was a moment of silence as everyone turned to look, and poor Janet blushed. Aware that that they were now the centre of attention, the man laughed and said in a much gentler tone, "Remember what I told you about balancing the colours, Janet? Maybe something red? Try the robin?" he suggested.

Janet, looking at him with a doting expression, said, "Yes, Gregory." And then as he handed her the robin, "Thank you, Gregory."

"The fuss he makes over that damned tree," Lisa muttered, rolling her eyes. "Do you know him? Gregory Tatton?"

"Only by sight," Abby replied.

Tall, slim, with a light tan that set off his lion's mane of silver hair and a smile that showed off his very white teeth, he was the very epitome of a silver fox.

A silver fox who was instructing a little group of women, who had presumably been decorating their homes for Christmas for the best part of half a century, in the art of hanging tree ornaments.

And from Janet's reaction, they were loving it.

"It's the same every damned year," Lisa said. "This is the parish hall not some upmarket hotel. The tree is for the kids, but that man does his utmost to hide the decorations they've made. He didn't even want to use the popcorn chains the Brownies threaded last week."

Since the popcorn was in evidence, beautifully draped around the tree, Lisa had clearly put him right about that. Few people could match her Brown Owl stare when she set her mind to something.

Her own tree was always haphazardly loaded with decorations the children had made over the years. There were even a few that she'd made herself as a child. A bit tatty by now, but every one a precious memory.

"I'm glad to see they're still using those old lights," Abby said, as she watched the vicar fastening an angel in place. "They were on the tree when I was coming to Christmas parties here."

The tree was already swathed in hundreds of small white fairy lights, but the Reverend Nigel Keane was fastening a string of vintage tree lights in the shapes of robins, snowmen, Christmas puddings, angels, gingerbread men and one larger one of Father Christmas himself that went near the top under the star which had yet to be put in place.

"Nigel really shouldn't be up a stepladder with his knee," Fiona said, but—"

"I hope they've been checked," Lisa, less concerned about the vicar's knee than safety, cut in. "The last thing we need is the parish hall going up in flames."

"Nigel is very aware of the safety issues. The lights were checked a couple of weeks ago," Fiona assured a little stiffly. "Christmas is his favourite time of year and he wants everything to be perfect." She glanced anxiously at the grotto. "He won't be happy with this. Not enough snow and this chair has seen better days."

The brocade had been rubbed to strands on the centre of the cushion.

"I've got a red throw that will cover it," Fiona said, "and I might have another can of snow in the vicarage. I'll go and get them now."

"You've been here for hours, Fiona. Make yourself a decent cup of tea while you're there," Lisa called after her as she hurried away. "And put your feet up for ten minutes."

"I need to get going too," Abby said.

She was on her way to the kitchen to leave the mistletoe with Penny or Trish, when high up on the stepladder, the vicar's phone began to ring.

"I've got to take this," he said, fiddling with this pocket as he climbed down.

"Don't worry, I'll finish the lights and I can fix the star at the same time. Just leave the ties on the table," Gregory said, as the vicar hurried to take his call in the quiet of the vestibule. "Now, can I trust you ladies to finish without me?" he enquired, a touch archly.

Abby could hear a chorus of giggles from the group of ladies surrounding him. Beattie caught her eye and raised an eyebrow as if to say, *Can you believe that?* Abby grinned back, and was looking for a spot to leave her bundle when, from behind, someone called her name.

"Mrs Finch!"

She turned to see Gregory Tatton, teeth gleaming in her direction. "Just the person I wanted to see."

CHAPTER THREE

"Edward!" Tatton called to someone half hidden by the tree and who was fixing one end of a *Happy Christmas* banner across the back wall. "Pop up and finish tying in those lights while I relieve this dear lady of the abundance of mistletoe she has so kindly brought us."

"Edward" appeared from behind the tree and Abby realised that it was Edward March, who had taught English and run the drama group at Maybridge High when she'd been a pupil. She thrust the mistletoe in Tatton's direction with a perfunctory smile, and said, "You're welcome, but excuse me . . ." and crossed to say hello.

"Abby!" Edward exclaimed, a smile lighting up his face. "How lovely to see you."

"It's been an age," she said, as they exchanged a hug. "Where have you been? How are you?"

"I'm fine, thanks," he said but, in contrast to the glowing Tatton, he looked far from well.

At school he'd been one of those inspirational teachers who seemed to have a second sense when it came to suggesting books that his students would enjoy, always keen to renew their flagging joy in reading.

He'd encouraged them to write too. And he'd encouraged her to keep a gardening diary for the school — something that had become part of her life. For her own garden and later for those of her clients.

More than one of his students had gone on to become published authors.

He'd taken early retirement a few years after Abby had graduated, but she was shocked by how poorly he looked. There was yellowness to his skin that had nothing to do with the sun. He didn't look as if he should be out, let alone about to climb a stepladder.

"I was so sorry to hear what happened to Howard," he said.

"I got your card," she said. "Thank you."

"How are you managing?" he asked. "How are your children?"

"It's been tough on them," Abby admitted. "And this is going to be the first Christmas without their father."

"That is always the hardest," he agreed, his expression momentarily bleak, "but you'll see them through."

Before she could enquire further, Tatton interrupted them. "Time is getting on, Edward," he said, pointedly, "and I want a word with Mrs Finch."

"I'm on it, Gregory, but for the moment Abby wants a word with *me*," he replied, with a mildness that did not deceive her, and from Tatton's narrowed eyes, he hadn't missed the note of authority that could control a classroom without the need for Edward to raise his voice.

She sensed some unspoken antagonism between the two but she was more concerned about Edward, and not just because he didn't look at all well.

There had been an incident during a rehearsal for a school play when Edward had frozen at the top of a stepladder identical to the one standing by the tree. He'd had to be rescued by a couple sixth-form boys. He'd been taken home by the head and hadn't returned to school for a week.

It might just have been a one-off, some stress in his personal life, but Abby put a hand on his arm. "Leave that," she urged. "Someone else can fix the lights."

He smiled at her, clearly aware what she was doing. "It's okay, Abby. I can do this." Then, turning to Tatton, "I'll take the star and finish the job while I'm up there, shall I? Since we're pushed for time."

"Don't touch it, March!" Abby, taken aback by his tone, turned to stare at him. Tatton trailed off into an apologetic laugh. "The star was my gift to the tree and I always put it in place. Everyone knows that."

Abby didn't give a hoot what Gregory Tatton always did, that had been rude. Ignoring him, she turned back to Edward.

"If you're not doing anything on the Saturday before the holidays, Edward — the sixteenth," she added, "come and have a drink with us. Jake Sullivan will be there and I know he'd love to see you."

"One of our more enterprising old boys. I heard he was back in Maybridge." His smile, in contrast to Tatton's, was the real thing. "It'll be good to see him. I'll do my best to be there."

"Any time after seven," Abby said. "There will be food."

"If you've finished making party plans," Tatton intervened, "I'm going to reward Mrs Finch with a cup of tea and a slice of Trish's delicious cake."

And, hand to her elbow, he urged her away from the tree.

Irritated at the familiarity, and still concerned about Edward, she glanced back in time to see him pick up Tatton's precious star and slip it into his jacket pocket.

He caught her eye and dropped her the barest suggestion of a wink. She coughed to cover the laugh that bubbled up.

Whatever he was up to, she wasn't about to spoil his fun, and before Tatton could follow her glance, she asked, "What's so special about the star?"

Happy to have finally got her attention, Tatton said, "It belonged to my mother. My father bought it for her when they were on honeymoon in Italy, so it's very precious. She always let me put it on top of the tree when I was a boy, but I haven't bothered with a tree since my wife died."

"I'm sorry to hear that."

He nodded. "There seems little point. This year there's an added surprise. I've added an electrical fitting and it can now be screwed into the vintage fairy lights. It will be as if my mother is there, watching over us."

"That's why it's your privilege to top out the Christmas tree?" Abby asked. "Because it's your star?"

"Top out?" Tatton asked.

"It's the ceremony when the last piece is put in place at the top of a building," she explained. "It's called topping out."

"Is it? But of course, you're now on the board of Finch Developments," he said, with what sounded a lot like satisfaction.

It was public knowledge that Abby had inherited a majority shareholding in the Finch family business after the death of her husband, although why Gregory Tatton should find that a cause for gratification was beyond her.

She sketched a smile and glanced back to see Edward step onto the ladder. Despite his assurance that he was happy to do so, he was grasping the rails so tightly that his knuckles were white.

"Isn't there anyone else who could be doing that?" she demanded. "Edward doesn't look very steady."

"Edward is quite capable of deciding whether he's up to the task," Tatton said. Maybe she didn't look convinced because he added, "There are just the last few lights to tie in. Five minutes at the most. Now, let's find Trish and get you that cup of tea and then we can have a little chat."

"She and Penny are busy cleaning the kitchen, and anyway, I really don't have time, Mr Tatton—"

"Oh, please, call me Gregory, Abby — I may call you Abby now that we're friends?"

He didn't wait for an answer but handed the mistletoe to a woman who loitered as if hoping to be noticed.

"Laura, will you take care of this for me? And maybe you'd like to give some thought about where we might hang it?"

There was a hint of innuendo in his voice, and Laura, all pink-streaked hair and pearls, responding in kind, raised an eyebrow. "I know just the place, Gregory."

"Good girl."

Girl?

Abby grimaced but Laura merely simpered. "I wanted to say how much I love your jumper, Gregory. So seasonal!"

"It is," he agreed, looking very pleased. "Trish Porter made it for me. Such a talent."

Laura's smile swiftly faded, and Abby had the feeling that she'd now be working hard to match anything that Trish could do.

That would be difficult. Tatton was wearing a superb Nordic-style sweater intricately patterned with snowflakes. Abby had been looking at them online, thinking that it would make a good present for Jake but, having discovered that a good hand-knitted one cost upwards of £1,000, she'd thought again.

She wondered if Tatton had any idea of the months of work and the skill involved in creating such a sweater? And it wasn't as if Trish was sitting at home all day with her feet up and nothing else to do.

According to Penny, she was working all hours as a waitress in the café in the bookshop, and that was hard work.

"Trish . . ." Gregory said, as she emerged from the kitchen, rubbing her arm across her forehead, clearly exhausted. "A cup of tea and a piece of your wonderful chocolate fudge cake for Abby."

"I'm so sorry, Gregory, I've been working extra hours all this week and I haven't had time to bake." A flicker of annoyance crossed his face and, sounding a touch desperate, she added, "I'll make one for you at the weekend."

Not just a sweater worth four figures, but cake too. She was clearly keen to impress him.

"No tea for me, I'm running late," Abby said, firmly disengaging herself from Tatton's hand, which had again become attached to her elbow. "If you'll excuse me."

She put her head around the kitchen door. Penny had her head in the oven, but she called out goodbye anyway. Fiona had clearly taken Lisa's advice because she hadn't yet returned and Abby headed for the door with Tatton, annoyingly, still at her side.

"I have to confess that I did have an ulterior motive in offering you tea, Abby," he persisted. "As I said, I do want a word."

What did it take . . .

"I'm sorry, Mr Tatton," she said, pointedly sticking to the formality and looking at her watch to emphasize that she was in a hurry. "I have to pick up my daughter—"

"It's about my garden," he continued, as if she hadn't spoken. "I'm afraid I've let it go rather." He pulled a self-deprecatory face and touched his chest. "Like my garden, the old pump is rather tired. We could both do with a makeover."

Abby hesitated.

She might have the financial security of her late husband's estate at her back — when it eventually sold — but Earthly Designs wasn't a hobby.

The business had to be self-sustaining or there was little point. The restoration of the walled garden and fitting out the new studio and workrooms had involved a substantial bank loan. She couldn't afford to turn away work.

"I can't help with the heart, Mr Tatton . . . Gregory . . . but I'd be delighted to discuss how Earthly Designs can help with the garden, but not now. I can't leave a ten-year-old waiting," she said, fishing in her bag for a card and offering it to him. "Give me a call and we can sort out an appointment."

"That's a bit formal."

She frowned, not sure what he meant. "I'm sorry?"

"Now we're friends."

Friends? He hadn't taken the card, and looking up Abby saw what Penny meant about his smile. Beneath that urbane charm there was something oddly suggestive, as if they were co-conspirators with a secret that the rest of the world did not share.

She was about to tell him, politely, that "formal" was the only way she did business, when Edward called out, "I've fixed the last of the lights and the star is firmly in place. Can someone switch them on to make sure that everything's working?"

Tatton spun around, staring with disbelief at the glittering glass star now sitting on top of the tree.

"What the—! No one touches my star! I warned you March . . ."

"Sorry . . . What did you say?" Edward, frowning, fiddled with his ear. "Damn thing . . . It's coming and going today. I think I need a new battery . . ."

Abby hadn't noticed a hearing aid, though they were very small these days. But the school drama group had been Edward's baby. He'd been a brilliant director and had acted with the Maybridge Players. She was pretty sure that he was acting now and, judging by the sniggers, she clearly wasn't the only one . . .

"Arjun," Edward called, apparently oblivious to Tatton's fury, "you're nearest . . ."

In an apparent outbreak of hearing loss, Tatton's furious "Wait!" went unheeded as retired solicitor Arjun Bedi — she was pretty sure that he was one of the sniggerers — plugged in the tree lights and switched them on.

Hundreds of tiny white LED lights began to twinkle, provoking a delighted "Aaaah".

"The fancy lights haven't come on," someone pointed out. "One of the bulbs must be loose."

Edward, who'd begun to descend, heard that clearly enough. "It's probably the star. The fitting seemed a bit tricky."

"The fitting is perfect," Tatton said, outraged.

"Give me a minute and I'll see if I can tighten it."

"Be careful. It's old. And fragile . . ."

Tatton had gone from outrage to anxiety in a heartbeat. Clearly the star did mean a great deal to him.

There was a slight flicker as Edward touched the delicate glass and, after a moment's hesitation, he went up another step to get a better grip. But, as he eased it more tightly into the holder, there was a fizz of electricity, followed by a bang as the fuses blew, and then the hall was plunged into darkness.

There was a shriek of alarm and a little nervous laughter, quickly silenced as something crashed through the branches of the tree and landed with a sickening thud.

CHAPTER FOUR

Abby, heart pounding, terribly afraid, fumbled in the dark to find the torch on her phone and then swung it around until it lit up Edward, lying on his back at the foot of the tree, very still among the bombardment of decorations falling all around him.

"Someone call an ambulance," she yelled, as, slithering precariously on a trail of tinsel, she ran towards him and came to her knees at his side.

"Edward!"

She put her hand on his chest but it was still. She couldn't feel a heartbeat . . .

"Tell them he's not breathing," she shouted as, hands locked together, she began pumping rhythmically at his chest. "Bring the defibrillator . . ."

"I can't see it!"

"We need light. I'll sort out the fuse . . ."

"Unplug the lights before you do that!"

"Keep still, everyone. We don't want anyone falling. I'll sort out the fuse." That was Lisa.

Someone searching the wall with a phone torch said, "It's not there!"

There was a gabble of voices all offering suggestions, but when the lights came on Abby could see that the bracket where the defibrillator had been installed was empty. She kept pumping at Edward's chest until, after what felt like a lifetime but could only have been minutes, the paramedics arrived.

While one of them relieved her, the other powered up their own defibrillator in an effort to shock his heart back to life.

Abby, exhausted, turned to those watching. "Where is it?" she demanded furiously. "Where's the bloody defibrillator?"

The vicar, who'd gone out into the vestibule to take his call and had presumably returned while the lights were out, looked at the empty space on the wall, then looked around. No one had an explanation.

Grim-faced, he went across to where the paramedics were working on Edward.

Lisa meantime had got everyone to move back and, with Penny's help, wheeled one of the display screens used for exhibitions across from the storeroom to give Edward some privacy.

It seemed as if the entire hall was holding a collective breath while the paramedics administered multiple shocks. Then Abby saw the vicar cross himself and knew that it was over. Edward was gone.

"Mrs Finch . . ."

She turned to discover that the police had arrived in the shape of PC Harry Walcott, the young constable who'd stood guard outside her home after her husband's death.

"Harry . . ." she said, a little shakily. "We have to stop meeting like this. People will talk."

He was supposed to smile, but instead regarded her with concern. "Are you okay, Mrs Finch?"

"I've been better," she said as Penny appeared at her elbow bearing a glass of water. Her hand shook as she took it, but her throat, thick with unshed tears, refused to swallow the sip of water and she choked.

"You'd better sit down."

"I can't, I have to pick up Sophie from football practice. I'm already late." She wouldn't have still been here but for Tatton insisting on talking to her. Wouldn't have known Edward was here, wouldn't have witnessed his death.

It would have been Lisa trying to pump the life back into his heart, knowing all the while that it was futile.

"I don't think you should be driving. Give Sophie a call," Harry suggested. "Tell her that there's been an accident. Is there anyone else who can pick her up?"

"She doesn't have a phone . . ." Abby cast around for someone she could call. Jake was away. Cal was on a job on the other side of Maybridge. Megan, Abby's best friend, would be working. There was Dee . . . "Dee? DC Newcombe? Is she on duty? Sophie knows her."

Abby had become friends with the detective following the death of her estranged husband.

"She was at headquarters this morning, but let's try her. Where is Sophie?"

She told him and then, while he made the call, one of the paramedics put a hand on her shoulder. "You should sit down."

Abby turned see that a chair had been placed behind her and she sank into it.

"I'm sorry that we couldn't save your friend. You made a heroic effort."

"But it wasn't enough," Abby said.

"It's likely that the shock stopped his heart," she said, "and he was dead before he hit the floor. He wouldn't have known a thing and there's nothing else you could have done."

Tears welled up in Abby's eyes. "He shouldn't have been up there."

Wouldn't have been but for Tatton. Vile man, all smiles on the surface, but with something dark lurking underneath. No amount of money would induce her to touch his garden.

"Dee is leaving now to pick up Sophie," Harry said. "As soon as she's there she'll give you a call so that you can speak to your daughter and reassure her."

Abby sighed with relief. "Thanks, Harry. I really appreciate that."

"So," he said, pulling over a chair and taking out his notebook. "I'm not going to keep you a minute longer than I have to, but if you could tell me what happened?" He looked around. "What is going on here?"

"The hall is being decorated for a series of Christmas parties. I brought some mistletoe . . ." Laura had dropped it in the confusion when the lights went out and trampled berries were now scattered across the floor.

"Did you see the gentleman fall?"

"It happened so quickly. Gregory Tatton asked Edward to finish fixing the lights."

"Edward?"

"Edward March. He—"

"Officer . . . I'm Gregory Tatton and I'm in charge here—"

Harry looked up. "Oh, great. Can you make a note of everyone's names and contact details, Mr Tatton, so that people can leave? Better if it was before the duty undertaker arrives to remove Mr March to the mortuary."

"But . . ." Tatton pursed his lips in annoyance. Harry waited, pencil poised over his notebook and, swiftly rearranging his features to those of a co-operative member of the community, Tatton said, "Of course, officer."

Abby watched him round everyone up, gravely reassuring. Some of the seniors were understandably upset and he was there with an arm around a shoulder, a hug for the ladies, thanking them for their efforts and checking that everyone had transport home as he ushered them out.

Gregory Tatton was a man who knew how to bend to a situation and show himself to his best advantage, which made his loss of composure over the star all the more surprising. Even so, not everyone was a fan.

Edward might have appeared cooperative, but he'd wanted to tweak the man's nose, even if it meant conquering his fear of heights. And Arjun Bedi had been happy to play along.

What was that all about?

CHAPTER FIVE

"You knew the victim, Mrs Finch?" Harry was on duty and keeping to the formalities. "Edward March?"

"I did. I hadn't seen him in a while, but he taught English when I was at Maybridge High."

"Do you know if he has a partner or family we should contact?"

"He and his wife are divorced but there were two children, Stephanie and Christopher. They were a year older and younger than me, so we were at the high school around the same time, although I haven't seen them in years. They went away to university and not everyone comes back to Maybridge."

The only reason she'd returned, after gaining her degree in horticulture and garden design, was because her mother was too fragile to be left on her own.

"No problem. We'll find them. What about Mr March? Do you know his address?"

"He used to live in Milton Street but he moved after his divorce. I have his address at home, but I imagine Mr Tatton will know it."

"You said that Mr Tatton asked Mr March to fix the lights?"

"Yes. Frankly, I was concerned about him. Edward, I mean. He didn't look at all well and I suggested he leave it to someone else, but he said he was okay."

"What was everyone else doing?"

"Getting on with decorating the hall, mostly. Penny and Trish were cleaning the kitchen." She looked up, but Penny had moved away to provide some privacy while Harry questioned her. "Fiona Keane, the vicar's wife, had gone back to the vicarage to fetch a couple of things and the vicar was taking a phone call in the vestibule. Beattie and June were putting decorations on the windows. Arjun was helping Edward hang a banner on the back wall. Laura had just been given the mistletoe. Actually, Trish had just come out of the kitchen . . ." She hesitated. "There were some other people here, but I don't know all of them."

"Was anyone near the tree?"

"There were some ladies hanging the last of the decorations. They were lucky not to have been hurt. At least . . ." She looked around and saw Janet sobbing into Tatton's lovely sweater.

"So Mr March went up the stepladder. What happened next?"

"Mr Tatton was walking with me to the door when Edward called out to say that he'd finished fixing the lights . . ."

She paused. The sequence of events spooled through her mind like a movie. Edward pretending not to hear, Arjun plugging in the lights, the fizz of electricity, the bang, the darkness and then the awful sound as Edward fell through the tree . . .

"Take your time," Harry said, as she caught at her breath.

"Are you okay, Abby?" June asked. She and Beattie had come over to check on her.

"Yes, thank you. I'll see you in a minute."

Taking the hint they moved away and joined Penny, who was beginning to clear up abandoned mugs and paper cups.

Abby took another sip of water as she gathered her thoughts. "Arjun Bedi was nearest and Edward asked him to switch on the lights to test that they were working. Poor man. He must be feeling dreadful."

"It's not his fault . . ." Harry hesitated. "Don't you normally test the lights before you put them on the tree?"

"Well, yes, and Fiona did say that the vintage set had been tested very recently."

"The vintage set?"

"There are two sets of lights. The new one, with hundreds of tiny white LED lights, and they were fine. The second set is quite old. It's the kind that have bulbs you screw in."

"Really?" Harry was young and had probably never seen them. "Why would they use old lights?"

"They were a bit special. The lights are in the shape of characters. Father Christmas, snowmen, gingerbread men, angels, robins . . . I remember them from when I used to come to children's parties here."

Sophie would be coming to the Brownie Christmas party here next week. Her last before she flew up to the Guides, went to high school and stopped being her baby.

Abby looked across at the tree. It was partly hidden by the screen put up to give Edward some privacy, a stark contrast to the festive decorations, but she could see the lights dangling from the broken branches. A few were lying on the floor and at least one was smashed.

"These old lights are much more temperamental than the new LED lights," she explained. "The bulbs tend to work loose when they're handled, and if only one isn't making perfect contact, they won't work."

"I see. So what happened next?"

Abby was conscious of new arrivals, men in sober suits carrying a stretcher, and she quickly looked away.

"Edward said he'd make sure the bulbs were tight . . ."

"He didn't ask for the lights to be switched off?"

"No. He would have had to have done that for each bulb . . ." And that would have taken time. More than enough for Tatton to order him down and spoil his little game with the star. "He said the star at the top of the tree might be the problem as the fitting had been a bit tricky. The whole string flickered when he touched it and he took a step up to get a better grip, but when he gave it a bit of a twist . . ."

"Take your time, Abby," Harry said, the formality slipping in the face of her obvious distress.

"There was a sort of fizz," she managed. "There was a bang, the lights in the hall fused, then . . . then we heard him fall."

The tree, well anchored, no doubt to comply with health and safety, had remained more or less upright, but the side that Edward had fallen through was wrecked. Tinsel, the popcorn strung by Sophie's Brownie pack towards a badge the previous weekend and the decorations that Tatton had fussed over, lay among the sparkle of glitter, littering the floor.

"Do you think he lost his balance when the lights went out?" Harry asked.

"It's possible, I suppose. Although if he received a shock that might have thrown him. He was lying on his back," she said. "But it was dark before he fell."

"Who called the emergency services?"

"I don't know," Abby admitted. She looked around. Most people had left. There was Gregory Tatton and the vicar, in close conversation at the far end of the hall. Only June, Beattie and Penny had remained to clear up.

"June, do you know who called the emergency services?" Abby called.

"It might have been Lisa," she replied. "Everyone else was pretty much in shock."

Harry made a note.

"I started CPR," Abby continued, "and called for the defibrillator, but it was pitch black in here and no one could find it."

"When the lights came back on, we could see that it was missing," June added.

Harry looked across to where the case was normally fastened to the wall. It was a hefty piece of kit, but it was definitely missing.

"It wasn't here on Monday when we came for the seniors' Zumba class," Beattie chipped in. "I mentioned it to Diana."

"Diana?" Harry repeated.

"Diana Higgins, the woman who runs the class. She should have been here today, helping, but she wasn't feeling well."

"And did she know what had happened to it? The defibrillator?" Harry asked.

"She thought it might have been damaged by one of the boys' groups that meet here."

"Thank you, Mrs . . . ?"

"Miss. Beatrice Sewell. June and I live in the cottage opposite Abby," she said. "I saw you standing on duty outside after what happened to Howard. It's a pity you weren't on duty when—"

"Beattie . . ." Abby warned just as her phone rang. It was Dee's phone, but Sophie was on the line. "Mum? Are you okay?" Her little girl sounded very shaky.

She wasn't alone, but Abby said, "I'm absolutely fine," her voice a lot steadier than the rest of her. "There was an accident here in the hall and I had to stay and help. Are you home?"

"Yes. Lucy's making me Nutella on toast."

"Don't have too much, you'll spoil your supper. I'll be there soon. Love you."

She had a quick word with Dee, who told her that she'd stay until she got home, then turned to Harry. "Are we done?" she asked. "You know where to find me."

"I've got everything I need. Are you going to be all right to drive?"

"Yes, I'm fine now."

"We'll be in touch if we need a formal statement."

Penny had disappeared, but June and Beattie were there. "Do you two need a lift?"

"Yes, please. We came by taxi but it's hopeless getting one at this time of day and Edward had offered to run us home . . ." The words caught in her throat. "Oh dear."

"Why don't you go and wait in the car," Abby suggested, handing June the keys. "I'll find Penny and see if she needs a lift too."

She was in the kitchen and, having washed the dishes, was searching for a broom.

"I'm taking June and Beattie home. Do you want to come with us?"

"Thanks, but I'm on my bike. And someone sensible needs to stay and clear up after they've taken Edward away."

"You're a star. Come and have a bite of supper with us when you're done," Abby suggested. "You won't want to be on your own."

"I won't be alone. Unless Cal and Lucy are doing something?"

"Not on a school night," Abby said, "but I'll text him and tell him to come straight to us when he's finished work. So that's sorted, you're coming to us, okay?"

She thought Tatton had gone, but he and the vicar were in the vestibule, apparently waiting to lock up. She warned them that Penny was still there, clearing up, and the vicar thanked her warmly for her efforts.

Tatton just smiled and said, "I'll be in touch, Abby."

CHAPTER SIX

"I'll give you a call in the morning," Dee said, too busy to stop and talk when Abby arrived home.

Having waved her off, Abby told the children what had happened — it would be in the paper soon enough — but she kept it to the barest details. They were shocked, but as they didn't know Edward, they were more concerned about her.

After supper she didn't have the heart to nag about homework and waved them all off to play Nintendo in the den, leaving her and Penny sitting at the dining table, finishing the wine she'd opened. Once they were on their own, she raised her glass.

"To Edward."

"To Edward," Penny said, then sighed. "It should have been Gregory Tatton. The fuss he made about his precious star."

Abby took a breath, then voiced what had been nagging at her.

"If I hadn't arrived when I did it would have been him," she said, and the thought that she was in some way responsible for Edward's death sent an icy finger rippling down her back. Not that she wished that fate on anyone, even Gregory

Tatton with his sly smiles and innuendo. He could get in touch all he liked, but he was going to have to find someone else to sort out his garden.

Penny shook her head. "Edward's death was nothing to do with you. If Gregory hadn't made such a performance about the star, Edward wouldn't have wanted to . . ." She stopped.

"What?"

Penny shrugged. "I was going to say tease him, but Gregory Tatton isn't a man you'd tease. He smiles a lot but he has no sense of humour."

"Edward winked at me when I saw him take the star, but why take it at all? Was there something going on between them? I wondered if it was because he was such a hit with ladies."

Penny shook her head. "Not Edward. He was polite but distant. He spent all his time with Arjun and that retired decorator chap, David Hogg. But I only joined the lunch club when I moved here few months ago. I'm not up to speed on all the political undercurrents."

"Tatton was just about to go up the tree himself when he spotted me and made a huge point of thanking me for the mistletoe, but I thought it was the ladies who wanted it?"

"That's what Trish Porter told me."

"Well, he clearly knew I was bringing it, but what he really wanted was to ask me about a makeover for his garden."

"Really? Why wouldn't he just call your office for an appointment?"

"I suggested that but 'now we're friends'," she said, putting the words into inverted commas with her fingers, "he said we didn't have to be that formal."

"Oh, right." Penny didn't sound surprised.

"I assume he wants a discount or to avoid paying VAT," Abby said, "or am I missing something?"

"The man who was keeping his garden tidy had a stroke, back in the summer. Maybe he's hoping to recruit you into his army of helpers. Just pop around and tidy his borders, cut his grass when you have an hour to spare. Now that you're 'friends'," Penny added, repeating the finger quotes.

"You're kidding? Why would I do that? I only spoke to him for the first time today."

Penny said nothing.

"What?" Abby demanded.

"As you know," Penny said, "my instinct is to distrust anyone with a Y chromosome, but it's a fact that he has a way of getting people to do things for him. Knitting sweaters, making cakes . . ."

And taking care of his garden? Penny's unspoken question hung between them.

"Warning duly noted, but Earthly Designs is a business. He can smile and say we're friends all he likes. If he wants his garden sorted, he'll get the same rate and pay the same as everyone else."

* * *

When Penny and Cal had left and the children were upstairs in their rooms, if not asleep, Abby retreated to the privacy of her home office and called Jake Sullivan on Zoom. He was away on business in Rome but he'd been one of Edward's students and would certainly want to know what had happened. And besides, she was really missing him. Since his return to Maybridge last summer they'd been seeing each other but, so soon after Howard's death, it had been complicated.

Her marriage to Howard might have been well and truly over, but her first thought had to be for the children.

"I'm really sorry to hear about Edward, Abby," Jake said. "He was a great teacher."

"He was. It's such a shame that he had to retire early."

"Was it bad health?"

"I imagine so. I haven't seen much of him since he gave up the Maybridge Players. I was shocked when I saw him today. It was as if all the colour had been leached out of him."

"He's been ill?"

"Heart, I'd say, if nothing worse. He really shouldn't have been up that stepladder." Abby paused and suppressed a sob. "He wouldn't have been if I hadn't arrived with the mistletoe."

"You can't blame yourself for that, Abby, and I seem to remember that he had a problem with heights. Didn't something happen with the curtains during a school production?"

"They got stuck during the dress rehearsal for *Joseph*. He went up to fix them but froze," she said. "It was a week before he was back at work. And weirdly, it was Howard who was one of the boys who got him down, although I've no idea why he was there. Theatricals were definitely not his thing."

"He came to watch you rehearsing as the seductive Mrs Potiphar," Jake said. "As did we all. Maybe we could do a little role play when I get home? We could imagine that the houseboat is a gilded barge on the Nile . . ."

"Stop it."

"Inappropriate?"

"Totally. Ask me again when it's warmer."

"Oh, Abby . . ." He gave a little sigh. "Edward must have got over his fear of heights."

"Not entirely. His knuckles were white as he was climbing up the ladder, but he was up for a bit of mischief." She told him about the business with the star, and Edward pretending to be deaf.

"Why would he do that?"

"Who knows? Maybe he was just fed up with Tatton's 'I'm in charge' manner," she said. "I can't say that I took to him myself. How's Rome?" she asked, keen to change the subject.

"Cold," he said.

"It's cold here too."

"But it's home, not an impersonal hotel room."

"It looks pretty swanky to me and it's warm, unlike your houseboat, which is going to be cold and damp. Text me when you know the time of your flight home and I'll go fire up the heating."

"Abby, Abby . . . You fire me up. When can I see you?"

"Come to supper as soon as you get back. Tom wants to pick your brains on something IT related."

"I'm happy to have my brain picked," he said, "but that wasn't what I meant."

"Jake . . ." She sighed. "It's less than three weeks to Christmas. Every minute of my life is accounted for."

"You have to eat and sleep. I'm going to have to talk to your kids about dating you. Lunch breaks in the houseboat are fun, but they are no substitute for waking up next to you."

Tempting as that was, she had a seventeen-year-old daughter in the throes of first love.

Cal was treading on eggshells because he worked for her, but he was eighteen, and she knew from experience how quickly things could go from holding hands to out of hand at that age.

At any age.

"I lost a lying, cheating husband six months ago, Jake, but they lost a father they loved." Once to the young, beautiful and politically connected Izzy Hamilton and then again when he was killed. "You shouldn't be wasting your time on a woman with so much baggage."

"It's my time," he said. "I'll waste it however I like. Speaking of which, keep your diary clear for Christmas Eve. I have seats for the Maybridge Players' *Cinderella*."

"*Cinderella*?" Abby laughed. "You want to take me to a pantomime?"

"Well, I thought the kids might like to come too, but that's up to you."

"Sophie may want to go, although I'm not sure that she'll think it's cool being seen going to the panto."

"She's ten!"

"Ten going on sixteen," she said, with a sigh. Today's drama had brought on another tantrum about her lack of a phone. "And Tom and Lucy would probably think it totally beneath them."

"Ask them. You might be surprised. I have ten seats in the front row," he said, "so they can all bring a friend. I assume that will be Cal in Lucy's case."

She sighed. "You assume right."

"He's a decent lad. Be grateful that they're under your eyes. It could be some bad lad at school planning to make her night at the prom."

"Like you made mine?"

For a moment neither of them spoke, then he said, "Tell them that there'll be ice cream in the interval."

Abby rolled her eyes. "Supposing they're up for it, it only makes eight."

"Megan and a plus one?" he suggested. "Or those two mad neighbours of yours. Or Penny and a friend. It'll be a proper Christmas evening and we'll have supper out somewhere afterwards."

It occurred to Abby that Jake, brought up in care, would never have experienced that kind of seasonal family fun. The evening was something they could give him. A thank-you for all he'd done for them.

"Ice cream won't cut it," she told him. "You'll have to buy us all light wands."

"Light wands, sweets, popcorn . . . Name it and it's yours."

He raised an eyebrow and they both knew that he wasn't talking about theatre treats. For a moment they both just looked at one another, then she shook her head. "You have no idea what you're letting yourself in for," she said, "but we'll come back home for supper."

"I wanted you to have an evening out of the kitchen before the big day."

"That's kind of you, but I have no intention of spending Christmas Eve in an overcrowded restaurant with harassed staff trying to cope. I'll put something in to slow-cook while we're out. You and the kids can clean up afterwards."

And then he'd go back to the houseboat to wake up on his own on Christmas Day?

She swallowed. Why did life have to be so damn complicated?

CHAPTER SEVEN

Just before eight the following morning, Abby was staring at the calendar, checking what everyone needed for school, when Detective Constable Dee Newcombe rang.

"Dee . . ." Abby said, tucking the phone under her ear and, satisfied that she was on top of everyone's sports kit, began to butter her toast. "Thanks again for yesterday."

"I'd say anytime, but it's not something you'd want to repeat and I'm not always available. How is Sophie?"

"She seems fine . . . Hang on . . ." Toast in hand, she went to the bottom of the stairs. "Last call," she yelled, then, "Was she upset when you got there?"

"Anxious. Better once she'd spoken to you."

Sophie was the least resilient of her children and she felt a pang of guilt for putting her through that. "I'll keep an eye on her."

"What about you?" Dee asked. "Who's keeping an eye on you?"

"No one. Jake's in Italy but I'm planning on having a pre-Christmas open-house evening on the Saturday before the holiday. A chance to thank all the friends and neighbours who've been here for me since Howard's death. That includes the local constabulary, so I'm hoping you and the DI will be able to come. You'll all get an email invitation in the next day or two, so look out for it."

"Thanks, Abby. I look forward to it."

"There'll be one for Harry and Elvis too. I was glad Harry was there yesterday. He's got a cool head for one so young."

"Yes, he's a good man. He told me what happened. Very unfortunate."

"He talked to you? Are CID interested?"

"No, it's a straightforward accidental death as far as I'm aware, but Harry mentioned that you did CPR on the victim. That must have brought back unpleasant memories."

"I didn't sleep much to be honest," she admitted, no explanation needed. Dee knew what happened when Howard was killed.

"Can you take the day off?" Dee suggested. "Go for a walk, maybe."

Tom took the uneaten toast from her hand, devoured it in two bites and, without a word, poured half a pack of cereal into a bowl.

Abby moved away as he began to slosh in the milk, putting more bread in the toaster. "The paramedic suggested that the shock could have stopped his heart. Will there be a post-mortem?"

"Yes, the coroner is involved, and Harry did take the precaution of asking forensics to take a look at the lights. Have you any idea who was responsible for them?"

"All the decorations are kept in the storeroom in the church hall for everyone to use, but Gregory Tatton did mention that he'd had an electrical fitting added to the star so that it lit up."

"Well used, then, and since it's the church hall, I imagine the vicar is ultimately responsible."

"Oh, no. Poor man." Edward's fall was impacting so many people. Had Christopher and Stephanie been told over the phone? Or would they have had a policeman at the door? Then she remembered something. "Was Edward wearing a hearing aid?"

"Is it important?" Dee asked.

"Probably not."

"Abby?"

She explained how she thought that Edward was winding Tatton up by pretending to be deaf.

"Was there some animosity between them?"

"Well, Tatton is a bit pompous. Maybe Edward wanted to take him down a peg," she said, grabbing the toast and dropping it on a plate as Lucy waltzed in with Sophie stomping at her heels.

Without a word Abby reached for the Nutella — the spread that never failed to sooth the grouchiest of children — and mouthed, "Get a move on."

"Have you made a statement?" Dee asked.

"Not a formal one. Do you want me to include that?"

"I don't suppose it's important, but it wouldn't hurt to mention it."

Abby checked her phone calendar.

"I've got a meeting with a client in the office at nine, but we should be done by ten. Tell Harry I'll be in the new studio in the walled garden any time after that. It'll be an excuse to put my fancy new coffee maker through its paces."

"Oh, I think Harry is going to be much too busy keeping the town safe for Christmas shoppers to make house calls. I'll see you there."

Dee had been there, at her side, since that first awful day and had become a friend. Smiling, Abby said, "I'll get out the good biscuits."

* * *

Abby's client had left, having signed up for her design, when she heard a car pull into the small parking area she'd newly created. There was a tap on the door and she called out, "Come on in, Dee." But as she turned from her drawing board, she saw Gregory Tatton walking through the door.

"That's a warm welcome, Abby."

39

"Mr Tatton . . ." Her smile seemed to freeze in place. "I was expecting my next appointment and she'll be here at any minute," she said, looking at her watch. "I'm afraid I don't have time to talk about your garden this morning. I did ask you to call and make an appointment."

"I thought we'd agreed that you'd call me Gregory."

"I'm afraid that yesterday is all a bit of a blur," she replied, determined to keep any contact with him formal.

"It's a dreadful business. The special lights are ruined and poor mother's star is smashed into a thousand pieces."

Abby stared at him in disbelief. Was that all he was concerned about? Some old fairy lights and a Christmas tree star? A man had died . . .

"Have you spoken to Edward's family?" she asked. "I don't have contact details for them.'

"I'm sure the police have that in hand."

"I can't imagine how awful that must be," Abby said, determined that he shouldn't dismiss it as if it was nothing to do with him. It had everything to do with him. "To have a policeman turn up on your doorstep with such bad news."

"I will of course arrange a collection for whatever charity they choose. And I'm sure some of the old birds will want to attend the funeral, although I don't imagine it will be before Christmas."

Unable to hide her shock at his callousness, she said, "That's dreadful." And she paused before she added, "After such a loss, to have that hanging over you while everyone is celebrating."

"No doubt. In the meantime, I've managed to gather a small crew of volunteers to help replace the tree and one of our members has kindly donated new lights," Tatton said, disregarding her concern for Edward's family. "Although of course we'll never be able to replace the vintage ones. Or the star."

She took a breath. Clearly there was nothing to be gained from labouring the point. The man had an empathy bypass.

"Is the Christmas lunch going ahead?" she asked.

"The caterers were booked and paid months ago and the gifts have been bought."

"Gifts?"

"My little contribution," he said, with a self-congratulatory smile. "I always play Father Christmas."

Abby had a bizarre image of the ladies sitting on his knee while he asked them what they wanted in their stocking before kissing them under the mistletoe. She suppressed a shudder.

Why on earth couldn't they see through him?

"Is that why you're here?" she snapped, all out of patience. "Do you need more mistletoe?"

"Thank you, but no," he replied, apparently impervious to her disapproval. "Your contribution was so generous that we have salvaged more than enough. I came to give you this."

He took an envelope from his pocket and placed it on her desk.

"You've made a note of what you hope to achieve in your garden?"

"You could say that."

She'd already made up her mind not to work for him, but having experienced his inability to hear the word "no", she said, "I'll look at it later, but there will have to be an initial survey before I can advise on planting." Relieved to hear a second car arriving, she added, "I won't be able to do anything before the new year."

"Tomorrow would be convenient," he said, as he reached for the door, leaving her open-mouthed as he completely ignored what she'd just said. "I'll expect you at ten o'clock."

"When hell freezes over," Abby muttered at his retreating back.

CHAPTER EIGHT

"Who was that?" Dee asked, after having been bowed through with great ceremony by the departing Tatton.

"The man who should have been up the ladder yesterday," Abby replied sharply.

Dee raised a questioning eyebrow.

"Obviously I don't wish that anyone fell to their death, but there is something about a man who will not listen . . ." She shook it off. "Forget him. Come and sit down."

"This is very different from the last time I was here," Dee said, looking around the recently decorated studio. The shelves lined with books and box files. The racks of pens, pencils and paintbrushes and the drawing board with the design she'd just signed off. "Very smart."

"Thank you. Do you have time to look around?"

"Let's get business done first," Dee said, taking a notebook from her pocket. "I read the pathologist's report. As you suspected, his heart was in a bad state but did you know that he'd been diagnosed with terminal cancer?"

Abby gasped, totally shocked. "He looked bad, but I had no idea . . ."

"His doctor confirmed that Mr March knew that he was on borrowed time. And no, he wasn't wearing a hearing aid. Do you want to go through that part again for the statement?"

"It's so stupid." Abby shook her head, sad that such a lovely man, already suffering, should have died in such a way. "Gregory Tatton insisted that he would affix the star. It had sentimental value, he said. He told Edward to leave it to him, but Edward pretended not to hear. He wiggled his ear and said he needed a new battery . . ."

"You said you thought there was some tension between them."

"On the surface they were civil enough, but Tatton's manner was a bit . . ." She struggled to put it into words. "It was more like he was giving an order than a request." Abby shook her head. "Honestly, I didn't take to the man so I might be overthinking it, but I sensed that there was some antagonism between them."

"You're suggesting that Mr March took the star to wind him up?"

"He winked at me when he realised I'd seen him take it. I played along, making sure Tatton didn't see what he was doing. If I hadn't done that . . . If he'd seen, made him bring it back down . . ."

"How well did you know Edward March?" Dee asked.

"I used to go backstage to see him whenever he was in a Maybridge Players production and we always stopped for a chat if we met in town. He'd ask about Howard, the children. He was one of those stand-out teachers that you never forget. It was such a tragedy that he had to retire early."

"Clearly you don't know the background to that," Dee said.

Abby frowned. "It happened when I was away at college. I understood that he'd had health issues. His heart, presumably."

"Not then. It was before my time but one of the older officers remembered the scandal."

"Scandal?"

"Edward March was caught in a compromising situation with the mother of one of his pupils. They were making use of a chaise longue in the props room. She'd been helping out with the costumes."

"No . . ." Abby said, unable to believe it.

"I'm afraid so."

With a sigh of regret for a fallen hero, Abby said, "I remember that chaise longue. It was used in a school production of *The Barretts of Wimpole Street* . . . I played Elizabeth's maid . . ."

"You were fond of him," Dee said.

"He was a great teacher and I'd have said it was out of character. On the other hand, although Edward wasn't especially good-looking, there was never any shortage of mothers eager to help with the drama productions."

"It might just have been one of those stupid lapses of judgement that you immediately regret," Dee said, "but the woman's daughter was in the play and, after a lunchtime rehearsal, she went back for something she'd left behind and there they were . . ."

Abby's hand flew to her mouth. "No . . ."

"The girl fled to her father's office in a shocking state, and when she told him what she'd seen he turned up at the school and made a huge scene that was witnessed by most of the school, as well the parents arriving to pick up their children."

"He abandoned his daughter in his office in order to confront Edward? Or did he take her with him?" Abby couldn't imagine which would be worse.

"That poor child . . ."

The adults would learn to live with what they'd done, but Abby could only imagine how it must have affected her. To see her mother like that was shocking enough. But afterwards, after her father's scene at the school gate, to have to go into school aware that everyone knew. Maybe wishing with all her heart that she'd kept quiet . . .

Dee shrugged. "Facebook was barely going back then, but Maybridge High pulls in children from a wide area and news travels fast in the country. Edward March was suspended, of course. He was named in the divorce proceedings, his wife left him, his children disowned him. His career was in ruins."

"What a mess. Clearly the affair didn't lead anywhere."

"No. It sounds as if was no more than a fling. Reaching out for comfort maybe, if his marriage was at a low ebb," Dee suggested. "Did you know his wife?"

"By sight. Their children were at the school, so she came to events, but they were in different years to me."

"How are your children coping with the loss of their father?" Dee asked.

"Up and down. Tom's uncomplicated. He takes out his feelings on whatever ball he happens to be kicking or hitting at the time. Lucy is totally focused on getting the grades she needs for uni and she has the doting Cal as a distraction. It's Sophie who's hurting."

"And taking it out on you?"

"Better me than at school." Although there had been a couple of incidents when she'd been summoned to the head teacher's office, mostly to ask if there was anything they could do to help.

After Dee had taken her statement, they took a walk around the old walled garden that had been part of the Linton Lodge estate.

The sky was a vivid blue, but there was still frost sparkling on the roof of the long row of workshops and storage rooms built against the east wall of the garden, and rimming the edges of the goldheart ivy.

Their breath clouded the air as they walked around the raised beds. They were already filled with the perennials Abby had divided in the autumn, and the cuttings she'd taken from the Lodge garden which she struggled to keep in check.

It was a time-consuming responsibility until a buyer could be found. Her accountant kept telling her that she should be charging her hours to the estate. But half of it was hers and the other half would be going to Howard's four children. Her own three and the baby girl Izzy had given birth to soon after Howard's death . . .

The *Cornus* cuttings were glowing red and there were buds on the long row of *Helleborus niger* she'd potted up as Christmas gifts for friends and clients.

"I love the dark green paintwork and your gold Earthly Designs logo on those big entrance doors," Dee said. "Very classy."

"Jake commissioned the logo and font. A gift to mark a new beginning."

"For the business or for the pair of you?" Dee asked. "How is that going?"

Abby shook her head. "It's early days."

"Hardly. You've known him since you were at school."

"It's early days for the children."

Dee put her hand on Abby's arm, a wordless acknowledgement then, looking around said, "You've done so much. I can hardly believe this is the same place I saw back in the summer."

"I have the wonderful Eric, who I borrowed from Finch Developments, to thank for that."

"One of the perks of being a director?"

"I still had to pay the going rate for the job," Abby said.

"Of course. I didn't mean to imply . . ."

"Sorry. I didn't mean to jump down your throat. It's just that there have been one or two comments."

Abby knew that most people would have assumed that she'd waltzed in and commandeered whatever staff and materials she needed. It was, after all, what Howard would have done. But Earthly Designs was her own company. She'd created it, and its survival and growth depended entirely on her.

They'd reached the glasshouse. "Gosh, this is beautiful," Dee said.

"Restoring it was one of the biggest jobs. I now have automatic sprinklers, electric-operated windows and a ground-source heat pump."

"Eric did all that?"

"Not the electrics. Everything had to be rewired for the tech and that requires a professional, but Eric gutted the workshops, retiled the roof and installed skylight windows to maximize the light. And he project-managed the entire job for me. He kept everything running so smoothly and on time — I don't know what I would have done without him."

Dee listened patiently while Abby waxed lyrical about the solar panels, the water retention and circulation system and a dozen other innovations to make things run as sustainably and efficiently as possible.

". . . so the energy bills are about half what they could be." Abby caught Dee covertly checking her watch. "Sorry. I must be boring you."

"No," Dee protested, kindly. "Really. The transformation from the neglected garden I saw a few months ago is truly impressive."

"And expensive. I need to grow the business if I'm going to pay back the bank loan."

"It must have helped, though. Having something to focus on."

"It's what I always wanted," Abby admitted, "but to be honest, even after going through all that pain in the last year, it does feel a bit selfish to have so much."

"You can't change what happened," Dee said. "You're getting on with your life, which is a good thing for both you and the children. You should be proud of that. Allow yourself to enjoy what you're creating here. And enjoy the life you so nearly lost."

Abby shivered at the memory, knowing how close she had come . . . Dee was right, she knew. The family had been through a lot. Losing Howard first through the pending divorce, then his death. But the children had gained a half-sister. And she hadn't given up on finding Howard's mother, who had been missing for nearly forty years.

"Thank you, Dee. It will come. In another couple of months I'll be so busy that I won't have time to think, let alone dwell on the past. Several classes of gardens have been added to the Maybridge Show for next year and I've submitted a design in the Back to Nature class."

"Show gardens like at the Chelsea Flower Show?" Dee asked.

"On a much smaller scale. Chelsea has a much longer lead time and I'm still waiting to hear if my design has been accepted."

"I'm sure it will be. They'll want to showcase regional talent."

Abby laughed. "I appreciate the vote of confidence, but you haven't got all day to listen to me witter on and I promised you coffee."

"And biscuits," Dee reminded her as they returned to the warmth of the studio.

"I have home-made shortbread and tiffin."

"Home-made? When do you have the time?"

"I don't. Penny hasn't just inherited her sister's house, she's taken over her role of supplying me with baked goods. For the sake of my waistline, I suggested she start up a home-baking business," she added as she passed the tin to Dee. "She's keen to go ahead and has already arranged to have her kitchen inspected."

Dee helped herself to a chunk of shortbread and took a bite. "She'd do a roaring trade at Headquarters with these."

"Lucy's going to design her some flyers. I'll suggest Penny drops some off."

Dee downed her coffee, grabbed another piece of shortbread and headed back to work, leaving Abby staring at the thick cream envelope that Gregory Tatton had left on her desk.

All that was written on it was "Abby" in an elegant copperplate script.

She didn't usually take pains to be formal in business, but this felt oddly intrusive in much the same way that he'd taken her arm and insisted they were friends.

She gave herself a mental shake, picked up the envelope and thumbed open the flap but, as she took out a single sheet of the same heavy cream paper, an old black-and-white photograph fell on the desk.

Frowning, she picked it up and saw that it was a photograph of two young girls, one fifteen or sixteen years old maybe, the other a little younger who, with a sinking heart, she recognised. Turning it over she read *Jean Barnes and friend at St Michael's Children's Home.*

Frowning, she turned to the note.

Dear Abby,

Our chat was tragically cut short yesterday, so I was unable to give you this photograph for your family archive.

My mother knew Jean Barnes, who often talked about her life at St Michael's Children's Home, which I believe was generously supported by the Finch family. She also told my mother about her time working for your husband's grandfather at Linton Lodge back in the late 1950s. When Jean died, she left my mother a cross which was given to her by Mrs Ruth Finch as a parting gift.

I noticed that Pamela Lewis wears one just like it, which she told me was also given to her by Mrs Finch. I'm sure Pamela is the younger girl in the photograph, although I didn't ask her. She has never mentioned that she spent time in the children's home and I didn't want to embarrass her.

I'll expect you at ten tomorrow when we can have that informal chat about what you can do to update my garden.

Yours most sincerely,

Gregory Tatton

CHAPTER NINE

Abby sat for what felt like an age staring at the note, remembering the names of the girls to whom Ruth had given both a silver cross and a little money when they moved on. She was sure that one of them had been called Jean . . .

She read the letter again.

On the surface it seemed a chatty note about an old connection to the family. But reading between the lines, the threat was clear. A suggestion that he knew things that could harm her family.

A threat that would go away if she put his garden to rights?

No . . .

She was being ridiculous.

She couldn't believe he could use this as a way of getting his garden sorted. Damn it, she'd been through that kind of emotional blackmail with Howard . . .

She picked up the photograph. *Jean Barnes and friend.* Jean might not have said much, despite what he implied in his letter. But once he'd realised that the younger girl was Pam Lewis . . .

Was that why he'd been making a fuss of her? Taking her out so that he could dig for more information?

Pam wouldn't have told him what had happened to her, but it was no secret that she'd worked as cook and companion to Ruth Finch in her final years. But Tatton knew that the cross she wore had been gifted by Ruth and, after the publicity following the discovery of the bones of a long-dead baby in the grounds of Linton Lodge, it wouldn't take much of a leap of the imagination to come to some very unpleasant conclusions.

How much did he really know and how much was pure guesswork?

Not for the first time, Abby fervently wished that she'd just covered over the bones and tried to forget that she'd ever seen them.

Too late for that.

Pam was vulnerable, and with flattery and sweet talk she'd be butter in the hands of a man like Tatton.

She clicked on her contacts and was about to hit Pam's number when she changed her mind. The phone was no use. Like Tatton, Pam could shut out what she didn't want to hear.

She would have to talk to her face to face, and twenty minutes later Abby was parking outside Spencer Court just as Pam emerged, hair freshly styled, wearing a pink coat and just a little too much make-up.

Opening the car door, she called out to her, "You look very smart. Is that a new coat?"

Pam, delighted with the compliment, smiled. "I bought it in Broads, but I can't stop, Abby. I'm on my way to meet Gregory for lunch."

Her face was lit up with excitement and Abby so wanted to be wrong. After so much misery, it would be wonderful if Pam could find a little happiness.

"I need a quick word, Pam."

"Now?" Pam replied, clearly anxious to be on her way.

"It's important. Come and sit in the car out of the cold."

Pam sighed. "Okay, but it will have to be quick," she said, climbing into the passenger seat. "I mustn't be late or Gregory gets cross."

"You've seen him more than once?"

Pam blushed. "Yes. We had coffee at the Buttery. With warm cinnamon buns . . ." She sighed. "Then on Tuesday he suggested a walk by the river, so I said I'd make a little picnic to take with us. I made smoked salmon sandwiches. He told me they were his favourite. But the butter was hard and I was late . . ."

"And he was cross about that? That's not kind," Abby said.

"He was sorry when I explained and he asked me out to lunch today to make it up to me. We're meeting at the new Italian restaurant on the Quays," she said, proudly.

That was a very expensive apology, Abby thought. Exactly how cross had he been?

"I should go," Pam said, getting agitated. "I can come and see you later."

"This won't take long. The thing is, Mr Tatton has given me a photograph." Abby brought out the picture. "I think one of the girls in it is you, and I wondered if you remember the other girl. It says her name is Jean Barnes."

"I don't like photographs," Pam said nervously. Then, as Abby continued to hold it out, she finally looked at it and nodded. "Yes, that's Jean. She was my best friend when we were at St Michael's, but I never saw her after she left. Do you know where she is? I'd love to see her again."

"Gregory Tatton gave this to me for the family archives. It seems that his mother knew Jean. He still has the cross Jean left her. She said that it was given to Jean by Ruth."

Pam frowned. "Jean is dead?"

"I'm afraid so. But she talked to Mr Tatton's mother about what happened to the girls at Linton Lodge. He seems to believe that you were there at around the same time," she added, fingers mentally crossed. He hadn't actually said that, but he'd implied as much. "Because you have the same cross."

Pam fingered her cross nervously. "Gregory said his mother had one like mine and I told him that Mrs Ruth gave it to me on her deathbed. But why didn't he show me this photograph? He should have told me he knew Jean." She looked up, suddenly aware what that meant. "Is that why he's been asking questions about Mrs Ruth? Because he knows . . . Is he going to tell people?" she asked, her voice rising in panic.

"No," Abby said, quickly, wanting to reassure her. This wasn't about Pam, it was about manipulating her. "But I do wish you would talk to someone about the past, Pam. A counsellor could help you—"

"I don't need help! I just want to forget."

"I know." She put an arm around her and Pam leaned against her, tears streaming down her face so that her mascara began to run. "I'm really sorry to have upset you. You know I will do everything I can to protect you."

"Like Mrs Ruth."

Ruth Finch hadn't been protecting Pam. When she'd found her, just released from that awful institution, and discovered what had happened to her, her only concern had been to control the situation.

She'd taken her in and provided her with a home for the sole purpose of protecting the political career of her adored nephew, Howard Finch — serial adulterer, the man Abby had been married to for seventeen years and the father of her children.

But Pam would never hear a word against Ruth. "Yes, like Mrs Ruth. Did Mr Tatton ask you about Linton Lodge when you had coffee with him? Or on your walk?"

She shook her head. "No . . . He talked about the lunch club. He's arranging trips out and asked where I'd like to go and then, when he'd walked me home, he said how lucky I was to have such a lovely place to live. He asked me how long I'd lived there. I explained that Mrs Ruth had found it for me and left it in her will that I was to live there until I die. That's right, isn't it?"

Abby sighed. "Yes, that's right, Pam."

Tatton's interest had clearly been piqued by the fact that, Pam, a pensioner with learning difficulties, could afford a high-end apartment overlooking the river.

And once he knew how, he had clearly asked himself why.

So where had the photograph come from? It seemed a little coincidental to have found it among his mother's things.

"Gregory knows what happened, doesn't he?" Pam said, by now thoroughly distressed.

"He only knows that you were in the children's home, Pam. Not the rest."

"He'll know. If Jean talked to his mother, he'll know . . ."

Pam was undoubtedly right. Lunch today, with several glasses of wine to loosen her tongue, would be Tatton's final attempt to wheedle out any last bits of information that she might let drop.

"I can't see him, Abby. I don't want to see him."

"You don't have to do anything you don't want to, Pam. Why don't you go back to your flat, send for your favourite take out, put your feet up and watch a movie on the telly?"

"But if I don't turn up, Gregory will come here to find me," she said, her voice rising as she began to panic again.

"That won't happen," Abby assured her, "because you're going to send him a text to say that you've come down with the stomach bug that's going around. It comes on very suddenly."

"Will he believe me?"

Not in a million years, Abby thought. "Why wouldn't he? He'll probably send you flowers."

Pam was a source of information and he'd want to keep her sweet while she was still useful.

Pam instantly brightened. "Okay." She took out her phone and carefully tapped in "*Cant come. Sick*" followed by a vomiting emoji. "That should do it!"

CHAPTER TEN

"Yesterday a man fell dead at your feet and today you get a blackmail note? You're having quite a week, Abby."

Megan West, Abby's best friend and local estate agent, had answered her distress call and, since it was lunchtime, had brought comfort food in the shape of some seriously good sausage rolls from the Buttery along with a very welcome hug.

"You can say that again."

"Let me see the note."

"Am I overreacting?" Abby asked when Meg had read it. "Maybe he's just a man who can't take no for an answer."

"Is that what you're hoping?"

"Of course I am. The very idea that he's threatening me, however subtly, is ridiculous."

"Is it? Really?" Megan scanned the letter again then looked up. "Tell me, Abby, what would you do to avoid all that ancient history involving Howard's grandfather being made public?"

Just thinking about it made her feel nauseous but she put on a brave face. "If Pam had been prepared to make a complaint, it would already be out there. If that's what she'd wanted, we would have coped, and I'm not about to submit to being bullied into giving this man's garden a makeover to hide from the truth."

"You really think that's what this is?"

"Penny warned me that he has a way of getting people to do things for him. Maybe this is how he does it."

"Hinting that he knows stuff people would rather keep hidden?" She took in a long breath. "That certainly covers this note. It's carefully worded, but he's telling you, in the most subtle way, that he knows what went on at Linton Lodge back in the day. *I'll expect you at ten tomorrow* . . . Reads like, *Ignore me at your peril.*"

"So I'm not imagining it?" Abby asked.

"I think you should take this to Dee."

"And say what?" Abby got up, pulling her fleece more tightly around her as she paced the floor of her studio. "She's a friend, but she's a police officer first. If I went to her with this, told her that it's an attempt at coercion if not downright blackmail, she'll want to know what it's about. And Pam's name is right there."

"Is that a problem?"

"I swore to Pam that I'd keep her secret until she was ready to talk to someone about it. She's been through enough. I won't expose her to protect myself."

"She's not ready, I take it?"

Abby shook her head. "I tried again, today, but she just says that she wants to forget about it."

"Counselling would help with that," Meg said thoughtfully. "I know someone who would be perfect. I'll have a word, see if she can suggest something."

For a moment neither of them said anything.

"Have you got time for a walk?" Abby asked.

Megan glanced at her watch. "Half an hour."

Abby threw open the door and they stepped into the earthy, frosted scent of the walled garden and took the public footpath through the estate woods to the river, where they watched two small children feeding peas to the ducks.

"Is it all in my head?" Abby asked, after a while. "Am I just feeling guilty because deep down I was happy to keep Pam's secret?"

"You've nothing to feel guilty about, Abs. It all happened long before you were born, and the guilty are dead. All you can do is protect the living. Pam and your children. Have you talked to Jake?"

"He's in Rome," Abby said. "Negotiating some big business deal."

"He could be negotiating for the World Cup," Meg replied, "but if he thought you were in trouble—"

"He'd come galloping to the rescue. I know."

Turning up at exactly the right moment with whatever she needed, whether it was a pizza and a glass of wine, a shoulder to cry on or just a hug.

It was his superpower.

"But?"

"I don't want him involved."

Megan's look suggested that she was making a mistake, but she let it go. "So what are you going to do?"

"I could send Tatton a polite note, thanking him for the photograph of Jean, which, if the records show she worked at Linton Lodge, I will be happy to add to the family archives, but repeating that I have no space in my diary until after the holiday. I could offer him a couple of appointments in January and enclose the Earthly Designs leaflet so that he'll have some idea of how much it's likely to cost."

"As if you've completely missed the threat? Maybe that would work if you hadn't talked to Pam. When she didn't turn up today he'll assume you were behind it."

"Now he's got my attention he won't need Pam," Abby said. "The mouse is wriggling under his paw . . ."

It was Megan's turn to shudder. "You're right. Why would he let it go?"

"He won't, at least not while he thinks I'll buckle. But putting him off would buy me some time," Abby pointed out. "What can he do?"

"If I were him, I'd drop a little gossip into the ears of people who know you. *Wasn't Mrs Finch wonderful when poor Edward fell? Leaping in to do CPR? I wonder if she did that for her husband? Such a tragedy, but they are a tragic family . . . You know, a friend of my mother's worked at Linton Lodge when she was a girl. She knew Pam Lewis. Ruth Finch was so generous to her . . .*" Megan stopped, realising that Abby was staring at her in open-mouthed horror. She continued gently, "The real monsters do it with a soft voice and a smile, but the thing with bullies is to stand your ground. Once they sense weakness . . ." She left Abby to draw her own conclusion.

"He won't do anything while there's still a chance that I'll do what he wants."

"No, but he hasn't given you much wriggle room. He wants you on the backfoot with no time to think, and if he's serious, he won't be able to resist showing you who's in control."

Abby wanted to dismiss it, insist that Meg was making too much of things, but her reaction to him had been visceral. And recent events had shown her exactly what an outwardly respectable man, a pillar of the community, was capable of.

"You're suggesting that I should go tomorrow?" Abby asked, less than thrilled at the suggestion she should leap to Tatton's command.

"It might be a good idea to play for time while we find out more about him and figure out what to do. But not on your own." Megan thought for a moment. "His letterhead said River View, Kingfisher Lane . . ."

Abby frowned. "I don't know it."

"It's on the other side of the river. I sold a house in Kingfisher Lane a couple of months ago. On the river side of the road the gardens have access to the towpath. Very desirable. Is he divorced or a widower? Time to dig out your sleuthing hat, Abby."

"It's woolly bobble hat weather, Meg. Not exactly gumshoe cool."

"Then next time you talk to Jake ask him to bring you a Borsalino fedora from Rome. Humphrey Bogart wore one in *The Maltese Falcon*," Meg said, as her phone pinged. "I have to go but I'll run a search on his house, see what info I can pick up. Just promise me you won't go on your own tomorrow."

"Well, in the interests of probity I'll need to measure up his garden, and for that I'll need someone to hold the other end of the tape measure. It's Cal's college day, but I'll see if I can borrow Eric."

"The gorgeous man with iron girder shoulders who sorted this place out? His mother works for me. Lovely family. Let me know what happens."

* * *

Jake zoomed that evening from Rome.

"Is there anything you want me to bring you back from Italy?"

She thought about Meg's suggestion of a hat and immediately dismissed it. "The sun?" she suggested hopefully. The weather had closed in that afternoon, a dreary drizzle washing away the frost sparkle and lowering the light level to dim. It was only the middle of December and she was already tired of winter.

"Damn it, Abby, I wish you were here."

"So do I," she said. And she meant it.

"That was heartfelt."

"It's been a grim week," Abby admitted.

"Want to tell me about it?"

"Not particularly. Cheer me up."

Jake spent the next few minutes telling her exactly what he could do to make her feel better and she was still grinning when Tom burst into the study. A tall, energetic fourteen-year-old, bursting was the only way he knew how to enter a room.

"Was that Jake?" he asked. "Has he gone?"

"It was," she admitted, thankful that her son hadn't burst in a couple of minutes earlier, "and he has."

"Damn . . . I wanted you to ask him something."

"Language! And you can ask him yourself when he gets back."

"That's no good. I was going to ask him if he'd get me an Italian rugby jersey. Not a copy made here. The real thing. I can pay for it."

Abby was about to say that she'd ask him next time she spoke to him, but she had a better idea.

"Why don't you send him a text?"

"Would that be okay?"

"Why wouldn't it be? He took you to an international at Twickenham, so you're sports buddies. If you ask him, I'm confident that he'll scour Rome for one." Then, choosing her moment, "Oh, and while I think of it, he's asked us to keep Christmas Eve free. He's booked tickets for us all to go to the pantomime."

"A pantomime?" Phone in hand, Tom's grin faded. "You've got to be kidding. That's just for kids."

Pretty much the reaction she had anticipated.

"Actually, it's for the whole family," she said, "and it's a plus-one invitation so you can bring Grace. We're going to have supper here after the show."

He blushed at the name of his first girlfriend. "I can't ask her to a pantomime. She'll think I'm a dork."

Abby thought that the sweet, shy girl who adored her son would sit through anything if Tom asked her but she'd let him work it out for himself.

"It's up to you but tell the girls, will you? Lucy can bring Cal and there's a seat for Penny if she wants to join us."

He went off to tell his sisters the bad news and began her countdown from ten. She'd reached three when the door banged back as Sophie hurtled into the room. Fourteen-year-old boys burst, ten-year-old girls hurtled . . .

"It's not fair! Tom is taking Grace to the pantomime and Lucy has Cal!" And Sophie, in her rage, had forgotten to be too cool for something as childish as a panto . . .

"Why don't you ask Cara?"

"I would if I had a phone. Daddy said he would give me one for Christmas," she said defiantly, and stomped off.

Abby sighed and called Cara's mother to arrange it, then she went through to the kitchen, where Lucy was sitting at the table surrounded by books with Patch, their calico kitten, curled around her neck. Princess, Sophie's kitten, came and circled her feet, mewing for attention.

"Where's Sophie?"

"She's in the den, sulking about not having a phone," Lucy said. "Except it's not really about that, is it? It's Christmas without Dad."

"I know. It's going to be really hard . . . for all of you."

"Jake's trying to help. Taking us all to the pantomime."

"Yes . . ." Abby had thought he was doing it to reclaim something for himself, but of course he was doing it for her children.

She nodded. "Will you be okay for half an hour? I'm going to pop over the road to see June and Beattie."

"Take your time. Cal's coming round in a minute. We'll make some popcorn and let Sophie choose a movie."

"Thank you." Then, "Really. Thank you."

Abby scooped up Princess and took her to Sophie. "I'm just popping over the road. Lucy is about to make popcorn."

She got a scowl but the kitten was gathered in, purring as Sophie buried her face in her thick fur.

CHAPTER ELEVEN

"We're just having a glass of sherry," June said, leading the way into the oak-beamed living room, where the wood burner was throwing out very welcome heat and their Christmas tree was providing a festive glow. "Beattie, a glass for Abby. She needs something cheering after yesterday."

"Not for me," Abby protested. "I've got a ton of work to do, I just wanted to make sure you weren't having nightmares."

"Oh, we're fine. Obviously it's a tragedy, but poor Edward has looked like walking death for months and we'd all like to go like that. No lingering," she said. "Help yourself to Penny's cheese sables."

The golden cheesy biscuits had walnut halves embedded in them and Abby, unable to resist, bit into one while Beattie, who took no notice of her refusal, fetched another wine glass.

"These are so good," Abby said. She was definitely putting them on the list to give Penny for the drinks party. "Have the police been to see you for a statement?"

"Harry called in this morning. Not that there was much we could tell him." Beattie lifted the bottle from an ice bucket and poured out a generous measure. "It's a Manzanilla Pasada," she said. "Try it."

Abby obligingly sipped, and groaned appreciatively as the ice-cold sherry slipped over her tongue. "My word, that's good. I always think of sherry as brown and sweet but this is wonderfully dry and delicate."

Satisfied, Beattie continued, "Harry just wanted to know if anyone had checked the lights before they went on the tree."

"And did they?" Fiona Keane had insisted that they'd been checked over by an electrician, but it was still a wise precaution.

"I've no idea. The taxi was late and the vicar had started fixing them to the tree by the time we arrived." She turned to June. "Who was already there?"

"Trish had taken the afternoon off work because Gregory had asked her to help," June said, picking up the thread. "I doubt she could afford to lose the money but she can never say no to him. Lisa Callaghan and Fiona Keane were decorating the grotto, and as I said, the vicar was fixing lights on the tree."

"There were a couple of women from the young mothers' group," Beattie reminded her. "Karen White — Piercy as was. I know her because she used to come into the library with her mother. I didn't know the woman with her. Tiff someone?"

"Tiffany Loakes," June reminded her. "But she left long before Edward fell."

"That's right. She had to pick up her youngest from school." Beattie took a sip of her sherry. "I heard the vicar ask Gregory to finish off the lights. If you hadn't come when you did, Abby, it would have been him who'd got his chips."

"Beattie!" June gave her a pointed look.

"Oh, no! I didn't mean it was your fault," Beattie said, mortified. "I imagine the wiring had worn thin and all that tugging about while Nigel got it the way he liked it, well, it was the last straw."

"What was Gregory so eager to talk to you about?" June asked, tactfully changing the subject.

Since Abby was there on a bit of a digging mission herself, she was happy to tell them.

"He wants some work done on his garden."

"Oh, well, anyone would love to have their garden given the Earthly Designs touch if they could afford it."

"Can he?" Abby asked. "Afford it? Only, when I asked him to call my office to make an appointment, he suggested that, as a 'friend', we should have a less formal arrangement, which was a bit of a cheek considering it was the first time I'd spoken to him."

"I don't know how he does it," June said, pulling a face, "but people can't seem to do enough for him."

"Oh?" Abby caught her breath. She knew about Trish, but leaning forward, she asked, "Like what?"

"It started when Elaine died — and when I say people, it was mostly the women. A man on his own must be in need of a woman to cook for him, iron his shirts, pick up his shopping . . ." June could do an impressive eye roll. "It's the twenty-first century, for heaven's sake."

"Gregory mentioned heart problems," Abby said, "although he looks very fit."

"His heart? I thought it was his blood-pressure. And his back . . ." The eye roll was followed by an exaggerated shrug.

Clearly she suspected that he was putting it on for sympathy.

"The healthy glow is down to regular visits to a tanning salon run by Christine Jenkins' daughter," Beattie said. "Christine is a member of the lunch club, so he's probably managed to wangle a generous discount. Far be it from me to gossip but she's just one of a handful of lunch club ladies who have their heart set on becoming wife number three."

"Three?" Abby asked.

"His first wife died in a car accident." June topped up her glass. "She was on her way to visit a friend near Bradford-on-Avon and lost control going down Brassknocker Hill. She went straight through the traffic lights, over the junction and off the road."

Abby winced. "It's a thirty-foot drop there."

"We didn't know him then, of course," Beattie said, holding out her own glass for a refill. "He was already married to Elaine when we met him."

"What did he do, before he retired? Do you know?" Abby asked. "Only, I wondered about the fitting for the light. Was he an electrician?"

June shook her head. "He was something high up in accounts at County Hall. He's the lunch club treasurer. Elaine was the secretary. A sweet woman, if a little vague at times. I suspect Gregory wrote the minutes for her. He seemed devoted."

Abby was surprised. She hadn't known him very long, but already couldn't imagine Gregory Tatton being devoted to anyone other than himself. She took another biscuit and sat back. "What happened to her?" she asked.

"They were on holiday in Greece, or was it Turkey . . . ?" Beattie turned to June.

"It was both," her partner obliged. "They were on a cruise. It was a tour around ancient sites led by that woman on the television. The one with the low-cut dresses. By all accounts, they were in an amphitheatre. Elaine stopped to look at the view and Gregory called to her to keep up. There were steps, hundreds of them, centuries old. It seems that she stumbled, lost her balance and fell."

"Poor woman," Abby said, with a shudder. Then, because she wasn't getting the sense that either June or Beattie were fans of Gregory Tatton, she asked, "Would you say that he's generally impatient?"

"Impatient?"

"He was pretty sharp with Edward yesterday when he didn't scramble to finish the lights. And Pam told me that he'd got very irritable with her when she was late . . ."

"She kept him waiting?" Beattie sucked her breath through her teeth. "That's no way to keep a man like Gregory interested."

"I'm surprised he was taking an interest in Pam," Abby said, casually. "I thought these foxy older men were all looking for something much younger."

"Maybe he's drawn to older women," Beattie suggested. "Elaine was older than him."

"Was she? A bit of a mother complex, do you think? He made such a fuss about his mother's Christmas tree star," Abby said.

"It's more likely that he's drawn to their property port-folios and widow's pension," June said, rather more bluntly. Pretty much what Penny had suggested.

And Abby wondered if his first wife had been older too. Divorced or a widow, flattered by the attention . . .

"What happens when someone dies abroad?" she asked. "Was there an inquest into Elaine's death?"

"There was," June replied, looking thoughtful. "There were written statements from other guests on the cruise. Several of them mentioned that she appeared a little unsteady after lunch, and although no one had seen her drinking any-thing other than water there was a substantial amount of alcohol in her bloodstream . . ."

"Her sister insisted she didn't drink," Beattie reminded her. "She made quite a fuss about it."

"She had a sister?" Abby asked.

"We never met her. Gregory said she was just trying to stir up trouble because she wasn't mentioned in Elaine's will. Apparently there had been a falling out," June said. "Sadly, when Sandra Monkford offered to sort out Elaine's clothes for the charity shop, she found a load of empty vodka bot-tles hidden in the bottom of her wardrobe. Not that I ever saw Elaine drinking anything stronger than orange juice at lunch."

"It's what she added to it that accounted for the vague-ness," Beattie said. "And her fall."

Or what someone else added to it.

The thought dropped, unbidden, into Abby's head.

"Sandra still goes round there every morning with a croissant from the Buttery and does a little housework," June said, provokingly, as if aware that Abby's interest was more than idle curiosity.

"She's one of the people who likes doing things for him?"

"When I suggested he was taking advantage, she told me that it was a privilege to help him because he does so much voluntary work."

"Really?"

"Oh yes. He's a volunteer hospital driver," Beattie said. "He takes people to appointments. And he helps out at one of the charity shops in town."

"Which one? I've never seen him in any of them."

"Oh, not behind the counter. He picks up donations and helps with house clearances. And Sandra lives with her son and his sour-faced wife," June went on, while Abby was still considering the information-gathering opportunities that would offer him. "She's probably glad to get out of the house. Although if she's hoping to make it permanent, she has plenty of competition. Wendy does his laundry and Linda Bradley does his shopping."

"Paul Jefferson was doing his garden until he had a stroke and David Hogg repainted his kitchen after there was some kind of disaster. What was it, June?"

"A fire of some sort. I think he said his toaster exploded?"

"He seems to be very high maintenance," Abby said. "He must have a very good pension if he can afford all that help."

"Oh, no," Beattie said, straight-faced. "He doesn't pay anyone."

"You're suggesting that all these people do it out of the goodness of their hearts?" Abby asked.

"More like hope," June said, with a shake of her head, clearly thinking they were crazy. "Well, probably not David, but Paul's gay. He might have harboured a *tendresse*."

"But surely Tatton paid for the kitchen restoration. His insurance would have covered that."

Or maybe he'd made some excuse about forgetting to renew and then, having produced a convincing estimate and invoice on his computer, he put in a claim.

"How long has this been going on?"

"Let me see. When did Elaine die . . . Three, or was it four years ago?" Beattie looked at June for confirmation.

"It was just after we had that do for your retirement, so nearer three. The gardening started later. He apparently had a bit of a turn," June explained, "and needed someone to cut his grass for a few weeks. I don't know how Paul got involved, but he must have been happy to do it, because he was still going round there twice a week until last summer when he had a stroke."

"He just has to ask, and people seem to fall over themselves to help him. Whatever he has when it comes to ironing, I wish we had some of it," Beattie added with considerable feeling.

"You're not unattached with a nice house and decent pension," June pointed out. "He's not stupid. He knows he wouldn't get that kind of attention if he settled on one woman."

"He plays the field?" Abby asked.

"He's charming to everyone, keeping them all hoping, although he has the occasional flirtation when his work crew need bolstering."

"He did have a close call with Maisie Goodyear a few months ago," Beattie reminded her. "She was banking on a proposal on that Venice trip."

"Oh, rather more than that, I suspect. When he was going on about how romantic it would be, she was imagining it was going to be their honeymoon, while what he had in mind was a try-before-you-buy week away."

"He took her to Venice?"

"That was the plan, but poor Maisie ate a dodgy prawn two days before they were due to go. Instead of a business-class flight to Venice it was an ambulance dash to A&E for her. Do have another of those sables, Abby," June urged, picking the bottle out of the ice bucket to top up her glass.

"No . . . really . . ." But she was wasting her breath as her glass was refilled.

"It's just a drop and this is a bit special. We treat ourselves to a bottle occasionally from High Spirits in Market Square, but it doesn't keep for long once it's opened."

Not much chance of that at the rate these two were quaffing it.

"So the Venice trip had to be called off?" Abby prompted.

"Yes and no. Maisie missed out, which was tough since we later heard that she was the one who'd paid for it all," Beattie told her. She enjoyed a good gossip.

"We heard that second-hand from Ryan in High Spirits, so maybe we should take it with a pinch of salt," June warned.

"Why would he lie?" Beattie demanded. "According to Ryan, Gregory had picked one of the most expensive hotels and then persuaded Maisie to upgrade to business class, complaining that he'd be cramped in cattle class."

"Why shouldn't she fly business? Her husband left her very comfortably provided for. As I say, pinch of salt. But as it was all booked and paid for, Gregory went by himself."

"There were a few mutterings that he should have cancelled and waited for her to recover," Beattie added, mutinously.

"According to him there were insurance issues," June said. "She was covered because she was sick, but he wasn't."

"What did Maisie say?" Abby asked.

"Oh, she wasn't around to say anything."

Abby, another sable that had somehow found its way into her hand halfway to her lips, froze, horrified. "She died?"

"What? Oh, no. She was very poorly for a few days but as soon as she was well enough to be discharged her daughter took her home so that she could take care of her."

"But what about when she came back?"

"She didn't. A week later there was a 'for sale' sign up outside her house and the vicar had an email from her daughter asking him to pass on her thanks to everyone for their good wishes. Maisie was still very weak and the family had decided she would be safer living with them."

"Safer? That's an odd thing to say. Was she becoming a bit forgetful?"

"Not at all. She was bright as a button. If you want my opinion," Beattie said, "the family were afraid that Maisie would marry Gregory and leave everything to him."

Not for the first time, Abby thought. "Where did she eat the dodgy prawn?"

"You seem very interested in Gregory Tatton, Abby," June said. "Is there something on your mind?"

"No . . . Well, maybe. He does appear to be a bit of a user."

"You're not suggesting that having got her to pay for everything, he thought he'd have a better time on his own and fed her a past-its-sell-by-date prawn sandwich?"

"That doesn't make sense," June said. "He'd have been much better off marrying her and pushing her into a canal before she could make a new will."

"June!" Beattie said. "That's a shocking thing to say."

Abby, who'd been thinking much the same thing, decided that it was time she left. Saying that she had to get back to the children, she thanked them for the sherry and wished them goodnight.

CHAPTER TWELVE

Eric Braithwaite, six foot three, dreadlocked and reassuringly large, arrived at Earthly Designs the following morning on the dot of nine thirty.

"The boss said you needed me this morning, Mrs Finch. I hope there isn't a problem?"

His voice, honed on a noisy building site was, like his physique, on the large side.

"No, everything is working perfectly, Eric," she said, rubbing her fingers against her temple. Her head was throbbing, possibly as a result of the sherry she'd put away with June and Beattie, or the very late night at her drawing board. "My problem is rather more delicate. I hope you don't mind me asking for you, but I have to go and see a potential client this morning. Cal is at college today and to be frank, while I've met him briefly—"

"It's okay. I understand."

"I'm probably being overly cautious."

"No way. You should trust your gut. My mum works for an estate agent and Miss West won't let any of the women who work for her go on first visits alone."

"It was Miss West who insisted I had company today," she told him. She looked at those wide shoulders, hoping she had an Earthly Designs T-shirt large enough for him.

River View was a modern detached house set back from the road behind a high copper beech hedge that needed a good trim. She drove through the gates, pulled up by the front porch and wasted no time in taking her workbox from the back of her van and handing it to Eric before pulling on her green overalls with their smart new logo. That done, she took a deep breath and headed for the front door.

"Abby. So prompt," Tatton said, with a satisfied smile. Then he caught sight of Eric, who had been standing slightly to one side, half hidden by the porch. "Who is this?"

"Eric Braithwaite. He'll be assisting me today."

"Is that necessary? I thought you were just going to have a look around and then we could decide how to proceed."

"I've had to move appointments around to fit you in today, Gregory." Using his name was a struggle but she wanted him to think she was entirely relaxed about this, even while her fingers were mentally crossed at the lie. "Once I've taken some photographs, measurements and soil samples, I'll let you have some ideas and rough estimates, although that won't be before the middle of January. If you do decide to go ahead, we can arrange a meeting to discuss your budget and a likely timescale."

As she took a step back, ready to get on with it, Gregory Tatton put out a hand as if to take her arm and stop her but Eric cleared his throat and stepped a little closer.

Tatton's hand dropped to his side. "I just wanted a chat today, Abby."

"Until I've seen your garden, Gregory," she said, forcing herself to keep smiling, "and can assess what needs doing, that would be a waste of both my time and yours. Meanwhile, everything you need to know about my terms is on my website or on my flyer." She took one from her bag and offered it to him. "I'm here today purely as a favour," she said, lifting her wrist and pointedly checking her watch. "And I do have to be at the police station at eleven thirty."

"The police station?"

"To sign my statement about poor Edward's fall." Her face ached with smiling as she lied through her teeth. And this time she didn't bother to cross her fingers either mentally or physically.

"Didn't I see a policewoman in your office yesterday?"

He was *challenging* her?

"I believe the preferred term is police officer, but yes, DC Newcombe arrived just as you were leaving. Edward's fall isn't a matter for the CID, of course, but Dee's a friend. She knows that I attempted CPR on my husband when he was attacked," she said, putting it out there, facing him down, "and she was concerned that I might need support."

The slightest twitch of an eyebrow was the only betrayal of his annoyance. His smile never slipped.

"Most distressing," he agreed. "Maybe you should have taken today off."

"Maybe I should, but you are not the only person who wants the job done yesterday," she said, allowing an edge to creep into her voice.

He looked at Eric. "I didn't realise you had more than that boy working for you."

He'd been checking out Earthly Designs? She tried not to feel threatened by that, reminding herself that it was perfectly normal behaviour if you were considering engaging a company for expensive work.

"Eric is a valued member of my team," she explained. "The creation of a garden requires a great many skills, including building work. If you should require a gazebo, a retaining wall or raised beds, then Eric is your man."

"Absolutely," Eric agreed. He didn't need to flex his muscles, his voice did the work for him.

"I see. Well, I'm disappointed that you're taking this line. I thought we understood one another, Abby, and I'd set aside half an hour for you today to settle things."

Settle things? Forget cutting out the tax man. She really had been elected to his band of "helpers".

"Half an hour?" she repeated, making effort to appear calm even though her heart was racing. "If you believe that half an hour is all it will take, then I'm afraid you have seriously underestimated the time, and probable cost, involved."

"It may cost a lot more than you imagine, Abby." And there was the threat, out in the open. "However, you have a reprieve. Edward's death has set back preparations for the seniors' lunch and I have to source a new tree and replacement decorations. This way," he said, taking a bunch of keys out of his pocket and heading around the side of the house, where he unlocked the side gate and held it open for them. "You can make a start and I'll see you at your office on Monday morning, Abby. Ten o'clock. Without the bodyguard. Make sure you shut the gate when you leave."

He didn't wait for a response, but turned and walked away, leaving her with her mouth flapping and still holding the flyer.

She'd been threatened and every instinct was to run, but it wasn't going to go away. She had to put a stop to it.

"Are you really going to design a garden for him?" Eric asked, once he was out of sight.

"Let's just say I'm going through the motions," she said, opening her workbox and taking out her digital camera. "And I don't have an appointment at the police station."

"He twitched when you mentioned that."

"Yes," she said but without any degree of satisfaction. It hadn't stopped him. He must believe he was untouchable.

Abby could see the question hovering on Eric's lips, but before he could ask why she was even thinking of working for the man, she said, "How are you at taking photographs?"

"I can point and click."

"Good enough." She handed him the camera. "If you could go around the borders, overlapping slightly so that I get everything, I can get on with taking soil samples."

"Mrs Finch . . ."

"Eric?"

"If you do have to come here again, give me a call. And I can be there on Monday."

"Actually, I have a class of thirty reception school children coming for a nature walk on Monday," she said, finally finding something to smile about. "I doubt he'll linger."

Eric grinned. "I'd like to see that. And what you said about being a valued member of your team. Will you ask for me if you need any building work in the show garden you've designed?"

"You will be at the top of the list, Eric. In fact, if my design is accepted, I will need a construction team. How would you feel about bossing it up?"

His grin was all the answer she needed.

CHAPTER THIRTEEN

Abby had finally got around to sending out invitations to her drinks party, scheduled for the Saturday before Christmas, when Megan rang to ask about her visit to Tatton.

"I arrived all set to measure up his garden but he wanted me inside for a little chat to settle things."

"Settle things? He said that?"

"He couldn't have made it plainer that if I didn't do what he wanted, I'd be sorry. He actually said any attempt at delay would cost me more than I could imagine."

Abby recounted all that had happened. "The funny thing is," she finished, "according to Beattie and June he was devoted to his second wife."

"Second wife?"

Abby gave her chapter and verse of what had happened to both his wives.

Megan was silent for a moment then said, "One wife dying in an accident is a tragedy, two looks like carelessness. Or maybe careful planning. I haven't forgotten about looking into the background to his house."

"I'm not sure what that will tell us," Abby said, "but at least he'll be too busy playing Father Christmas at the seniors' lunch to have another go at me there."

"You're helping out at the lunch?"

"Just setting up the tables beforehand."

"Do not," Megan warned, "accept sweets from strange men in red coats and false beards."

"Thanks for that," Abby replied, shuddering as they said goodbye.

Then, remembering that she was going to call Izzy Hamilton, she did just that.

"Abby . . ." Izzy sounded surprised to hear from her. "What can I do for you?"

"Nothing at all. I just wondered if you needed any festive greenery. There are plenty of berries on the holly at the Lodge and there's mistletoe too, if you'd like some."

"May and I are going to be staying with my parents over the holiday, but I'll ask them if they could use some. And thank you for the invitation to your drinks party."

"Bring May with you," Abby urged. "I'd love a cuddle with my goddaughter and the children would love to see their baby sister." Half-sister sounded so harsh. "We can tuck her up somewhere quiet with Sophie and her friend Cara. It'll give you a chance to relax."

She had her fingers crossed when she said that. Sophie had been a regular Wednesday Adams throughout the christening and the party that followed it.

※ ※ ※

Megan's advice was unnecessary. Abby wasn't about to hang around to witness Tatton doing his Father Christmas performance with or without the mistletoe, the remains of which were now hanging in a large bunch from the centre beam of the centuries-old hall.

She had only agreed to help set up the tables as a favour to Fiona Keane. As soon as she was finished she would be off.

Inevitably it took longer than she'd anticipated.

Each table had to have a seasonal centrepiece that someone had spent a lot of time making from the holly, ivy, gold flower and seed heads she'd provided.

There were glasses, cutlery and napkins, and place names bearing coloured dots to indicate the dishes that had been chosen in advance.

A team from the caterers followed behind her, placing bottles of wine, baskets of bread, butter and the chosen cold first course.

She'd anticipated that Tatton would have arranged to have Pam seated next to him, but she was on a table at the opposite end of the room.

Had Tatton lost interest now he'd got what he wanted from her? Or had Pam asked to be moved? He didn't seem like the sort of man who'd take kindly to being the one dropped.

Unfortunately, since he'd appointed himself master of ceremonies and was directing operations, Abby was unable to avoid him.

"You are such a treasure, Abby," he said, coming up behind her as she ticked off place names against the table plan — and putting a hand on her shoulder, as if to remind her that she was the mouse under his paw. "Have you heard if Pamela is well enough to attend?"

It was a challenge, but she'd been on her guard, waiting for something of the sort.

"She called a couple of days ago to ask me to pick up some stuff from the chemist — there's a twenty-four-hour bug going around." The man was turning her into a serial liar. "I'm sure she'd have let whoever is organising the lunch know if she couldn't make it. Excuse me . . ."

She waited for him to move out of the way. He just smiled. "I have another little task for you, Abby. As you can see, we've had a last-minute donation of chocolates."

She registered for the first time the impressive pile of clear plastic boxes he was holding beneath his arm.

"Very festive." Each box contained a neat row of chocolates individually wrapped in jolly red-and-gold crackers. They would make perfect table decorations. She'd seen them in the window of the new chocolate boutique that had opened in Maybridge. "And very expensive. Someone has been extremely generous."

He shrugged. "They were left on the table in the entrance," he said. "Presumably it's the owner of the shop hoping to drum up some Christmas business."

"They didn't hand them over in person?" she asked, surprised. "Or at least leave a message on something with their logo? I'd have thought they'd want everyone to know where they'd come from."

"Someone in a rush," he suggested, and since she made no effort to take them, he had to remove his hand from her shoulder to put them on the nearest chair. Abby resisted, with difficulty, the urge to step back. "I'll pop in to thank them before I come up to see you on Monday," he added, making the point that he didn't give up.

"You'll be competing with the reception class from St Michael's Primary School who are coming for a nature walk through the Lodge gardens on Monday morning," she warned him, "although if you want to join us, an extra pair of hands is always welcome." She didn't wait for a reply, but instead glanced at the chocolates. "Someone has been thoughtful enough to do a taste test."

She raised a questioning eyebrow in his direction.

He smiled, as if amused by her attempt to embarrass him.

"I'm a bit of a chocolate addict," he confessed, matching her eyebrow and raising it to a naughty-boy grin. "In case you were wondering what to buy me for Christmas."

Abby, wishing she'd kept her eyebrow where it belonged, said, "All those chocolate fudge cakes can't be good for your arteries, Mr Tatton. Maybe you should suggest Trish turn her baking skills to something healthier. Flapjacks, perhaps? Oats are good for the heart."

"I appreciate your concern, but I'm in no danger of a heart attack."

"The bad heart is like the bad back?" she suggested. "Just a useful ploy?"

The grin faded, but in the same annoyingly urbane and self-assured tone he said, "I thought we could add a chocolate to each of the place settings."

"We?" Refusing to be intimidated, she challenged him. "Surely you mean me?"

"There are more than enough to go around. Leave any left on the table in the grotto."

Thankfully, just then Fiona arrived. "The catering manager wants a word, Gregory."

"Can't you handle it?" He was enjoying himself and annoyed at being interrupted.

"If I could," she snapped, "I wouldn't have had to come and find you."

"As you see, I'm in demand," he said, as Fiona, looking harassed and at the end of her tether, spun away. "I'll see you later, Abby. There's a gift for each of the helpers in my sack and one of them has your name on it. I think you'll appreciate it."

How could he say something so innocuous and make it sound like a threat?

"The caterers?" she prompted, since he seemed to be waiting for a response and the one that was hovering on the tip of her tongue was not going to help.

She held his gaze until he turned and walked away, but her fingers shook as she set down the last of the place names and started to go around with the chocolates.

There were quite a few left and she made a festive pile with them on the table in the grotto, which would be given plenty of use at the various children's parties in the run up to the holiday.

Lisa's sprig of mistletoe was in place above the shabby chair but the grotto was still short of snow and Fiona's throw had not materialised. Not that it mattered, once Tatton was enthroned no one would see it.

All morning she had been avoiding the replacement tree, but now she turned to look at it, twinkling with its new set of tiny fairy lights, and stood for a moment, remembering Edward.

Fiona joined her.

"I didn't want another tree," Fiona said. "I wanted to cancel the lunch. I'd have cancelled Christmas if I could."

"Tricky if you're the vicar's wife, I'd have thought," Abby sympathised.

"Yes, but this lunch just days after . . ." Fiona shook her head. "It was too late to cancel, of course. People have paid for their Christmas lunch and they wouldn't get a refund."

"Being together today will be a chance for you all to raise a glass in Edward's memory," Abby suggested.

"I suppose so." She dug in her pocket for a tissue and blew her nose. "Ignore me, Abby. It's just that Nigel is seriously stressed. He's responsible for the church hall and he's convinced they're going to blame him. It's making him a bit, well, short-tempered."

"That's understandable. Did anyone actually check the lights before they went on the tree?" Abby asked. Seeing Fiona's look of panic, she quickly went on, "I assume that the fitting Mr Tatton had made for the star was certified by a professional electrician?"

"I don't know. Do you think that could have been the cause?" Fiona asked, looking marginally more hopeful.

"The police have it in hand but I'm sure the coroner's verdict will be accidental death," Abby said.

"Yes . . . Yes, of course. I'm sorry, I haven't been sleeping since it happened. And of course, Nigel too . . ." she added.

"And he keeps you awake." Abby nodded sympathetically.

"I'm really grateful for your help today. I'm usually overwhelmed with offers from women wanting to make a good impression on Gregory, but they were all at the hairdresser's this morning, glamming themselves up."

"Now that Maisie is no longer in the picture?" Abby prompted. She mentally crossed her fingers yet again. "I was going to send her a Christmas card, but I don't have her daughter's address."

"Poor Maisie. She was so looking forward to Venice, but maybe it was for the best. Gregory seems to be somewhat careless with his wives."

"Careless?"

"I didn't know Flora, of course, but Elaine . . ." She shook her head. "Her sister came to see us after the inquest. What was her name? Eve? Something like that. Anyway, she was adamant that neither of them had ever touched alcohol. Their mother had been an alcoholic and they'd had a pretty grim childhood from all accounts . . . Of course she hadn't seen Elaine since her marriage. I had the impression there had been a serious falling out." She shook her head. "Sorry, you want to send Maisie a Christmas card. Her daughter's email address will still be on the system if that would help?"

"That would be perfect. The children are all about the environmental impact so we're sending e-cards where we can and making a donation to a homeless charity."

"Yes, we're doing that too. Nigel suggested it a few weeks ago in the morning service notes. Linda Bradley wasn't happy. She owns the card shop in Ship Street, next to the ice cream place, but what can you do? The charities are desperate . . ."

"I heard she does Gregory Tatton's shopping," Abby said. "I suppose if she's working in town . . ."

"Convenient," Fiona agreed. "I'll send you the address after lunch but let me get you a glass of fizz before you go. You certainly deserve one."

"Thanks, but I'm driving." And anxious to escape while Gregory was busy greeting the arrivals, she added silently. She glanced across to where he was making sure they all had a glass of Prosecco or orange juice instead of leaving it to the caterers. Acting as if he really was hosting the lunch that they had paid for. "I'll just slip out the back way."

Safely behind the wheel of her elderly Volvo, Abby checked her phone for messages.

There was a text from Tom telling her that he'd gone to a rugby training session he'd forgotten to mention, and one from Lucy, who, having walked Sophie to her dance class, had gone into town to pick up a book she'd ordered and met up with some friends.

So much for the chores she'd left them to get on with while she was elsewhere being a "treasure".

She supposed she should be grateful that Tatton hadn't called her a "girl".

Ugh . . .

CHAPTER FOURTEEN

Abby had a text from Fiona late that afternoon, thanking her again for her help and giving her the promised email address for Maisie's daughter.

She'd asked for contact details on the spur of the moment. Now she wondered how the woman would react to a note from a total stranger asking about her mother's relationships with Tatton. Click delete? Block her?

It had been a stupid idea, and having sent a quick thanks to Fiona, she concentrated on the more mundane task of feeding her offspring.

Megan called in on her way home that evening. "I'm sorry I haven't been back to you sooner about Tatton's house, but there's something going around and we're short-staffed."

"Have you only just finished?" Abby asked. "Can I get you something to eat?"

"No, can't stay long, I'm going out this evening. But I'd love a cup of Earl Grey."

"A date?"

"No," she said, a little too quickly. "It's a work thing."

Abby led the way into the kitchen.

"This looks very festive," Meg said, pointing at the newly installed fairy lights around the garden doors.

"I try to put it off as long as I can and, frankly, I'm a bit off fairy lights, but the children got the decs down while I was out and these were already up when I got home," Abby said, dropping a teabag into a mug and pressing the button on the kettle. "Frankly, I'm dreading the trip to the Christmas tree farm tomorrow."

"That's going to be hard on all of you."

"That's the thing about Christmas," Abby said. "It's all about memories. Everything you do after a death is a reminder that this year is different." If her grandmother hadn't been living with them to create some semblance of normality, there would have been no Christmas for her the year after her dad had been killed by a sniper's bullet.

And the year her mother had died, Howard, seeing how hard it was going to be for her to deal with the festivities, had taken them all to Disneyland Paris.

Maybe that's what she should have done . . . Not Disneyland, but somewhere.

"I wish there was more I could do to help," Megan said.

"You're coming for lunch on Christmas Day. Come early and you can prep the sprouts. I'd suggest you bring that not-a-date work person you're going out with this evening, but I'm not sure how much fun it's going to be."

"It's very quiet this evening." Megan, refusing to rise, looked around. "Where are they all?"

"Cal's band have their first gig and Lucy's gone to support him. Tom's in the den playing games with one of his mates and Sophie's having a sleepover with Cara. There are lemons," she said, "or do you want milk?"

"Lemon, please. I'm cutting every calorie I can so that I can get into last year's dress for the company Christmas party," Megan said, taking one from the bowl and finding a knife to slice it, while Abby made a second cup.

Once they were settled at the dining table, Meg took out a notebook.

"Okay. This is what I've found out so far. According to the sales sites, the ones that tell you the last time a house was sold and the price paid, River View hasn't been on the market since it was built in 1987, when it was registered to Robert and Flora Major."

"Tatton's first wife was called Flora. He must have inherited it from her."

Megan looked up from her notes. "I wonder if Elaine had a property that she brought to the marriage?"

"It seems likely. He asked Penny out just after it became common knowledge that she'd inherited her sister's cottage. And he wanted to know how Pam came to live in Spencer Court."

"So, there's a pattern in his behaviour."

"Penny reckoned that the mistletoe was a lure being trailed by seniors' lunch club widows on the pull. Apparently, he's overwhelmed with domestic help from those eager to become the third Mrs Tatton."

"I'd say they're wasting their time unless they're well-endowed with property. Why would he saddle himself with just one woman if he has a little harem of helpers eager to make his life comfortable? I imagine he gets more than his kitchen floor scrubbed while they're down on their knees."

"Thanks for that," Abby said, shuddering. "I'm going to have that image in my head whenever I look at him."

"You'd better remember it. Everything you've told me, and every word of that note, suggests a man who enjoys controlling people. It might start with something simple like laundry, but it will escalate . . . It might be wise to have a word with Freddie Jennings," Megan suggested. "He knows what went on at the Lodge, and as your solicitor he should have advance warning so that he'll be prepared if the manure does hit the fan."

"Yes, I'll do that."

"In the meantime, back to Gregory Tatton. A man who wants his every need catered for and is prepared to use emotional blackmail to get it." She tapped her pen against her chin, looking thoughtful. "The question is, are you the only one? The general assumption is that all these people are making his life easy out of the goodness of their hearts . . ."

"You're suggesting that he knows something about them that they'd rather didn't become public? What on earth could Trish Porter have to hide? Any of them, come to that."

"We all have secrets, Abby. I wonder what they all did before they claimed their bus pass? Teaching, nursing?" Megan offered.

Teaching . . .

What happened to Edward had been very public. She had been shaken by that revelation but it may not have been his only indiscretion. Although what Gregory Tatton could hope to gain from Edward was a mystery. Edward wasn't fit enough to do anything physical. Divorce and early retirement couldn't have left him with much in the way of assets. Besides which, blackmail was a crime. She didn't think Tatton would risk that.

Could it really be just about taking pleasure in knowing people's secrets, getting off on the power it gave him?

"Abby?"

"Sorry, I was thinking . . . Well, Sandra Monkford gets his breakfast and does some cleaning. I've no idea what she did before she retired, but Linda Bradley, who does his shopping, runs the card shop in town."

"Maybe Linda's cooking the books?"

"It's possible, but how would he know?"

"Maybe she has two card readers. One for the tax man, one for her. He might have spotted what she was up to . . ."

"I suppose it's possible, but a garden makeover is a big step up from doing his shopping."

"He'll take what you're in a position to give," Megan said. "And you have a lot more than most," she added, pointedly.

Abby groaned, realising exactly how much trouble she was in. "He was smirking as he congratulated me on inheriting a controlling share in Finch Developments. I'll bet he's already planning an extension . . ."

"Shit, Abby. He must be salivating. Tell me, who actually asked for the mistletoe?"

"Penny said it was Trish Porter, but he was ordering her around on Wednesday and less than pleased when she admitted that she hadn't had time to make his chocolate fudge cake this week."

"This week?"

"It sounded as if she makes him one every week." Abby heard herself say it and shook her head. "No one is going to blackmail someone for a weekly chocolate fudge cake."

"Forget the cake. It's not about the cake."

"No." And Abby shuddered, thinking about the hours that Trish must have put into that sweater he'd been wearing. "It's all about control."

"Tatton used Trish to bring you into his orbit in order to establish a connection. He insisted on talking to you despite your need to pick up Sophie, and that's classic sociopathic behaviour. What did he say to you today when you were helping out with the lunch? He did speak to you?"

"He told me there was a present with my name on it in his sack," Abby said, remembering how pleased he'd looked. "I'd always planned to leave before the lunch started so, thankfully, I missed that particular treat."

"If he didn't send it home for you with Beattie, it contains a message and he wants to watch you open it. You've got a door camera, so make sure you can see who's there before you open it, Abby. This is your private safe space. Whatever you do, don't let him in here. And keep the side gate locked."

"You're giving me the creeps, Meg," she said, stirring the lemon around in her tea.

"Not me, him. But let's not worry about that until it happens. Right now we need to find out everything we can about him. Where he came from, what family he has, what he's been doing all his adult life."

Abby swallowed. "Okay."

"As I said, the Land Registry records show that River View was jointly registered in 1987, the year it was built, to Flora and Robert Major. Then in 2005 the name is changed to Flora Tatton."

"Was she divorced or widowed?" Abby asked.

"I'm afraid the Land Registry doesn't offer that information, but Flora didn't add his name to the deeds when they married, which is interesting."

"Maybe she had children by her first husband who she'd want to inherit. Anyway, he must have had a place of his own before they were married."

"Good point," Meg said, making a note. "The sensible course of action would be to hold on to that property and put it on the letting market. I'll make some enquiries, although he might have sold it after Flora died, when the registration of River View was changed to Gregory Tatton."

"So she either left it to him or she died intestate."

"Does it matter? There was no suggestion of foul play when she died?"

"No . . ."

"But?" Megan asked, picking up on Abby's doubt.

"If she'd died intestate he'd have inherited everything. If there were children from her first marriage, it would be interesting to know what they thought of their stepfather."

"You could search for birth certificates, but I doubt he'd choose a woman who was burdened with offspring who might cause trouble."

"I wonder if that's why he let Maisie go?"

"Who's Maisie?"

"She was expecting wedding bells," Abby explained. "They planned a week in Venice, which Maisie paid for, but she got food poisoning and couldn't go. While Tatton was whooping it up on the Grand Canal, her children swooped in and whisked her out of harm's way."

"Well, whether Flora had children or not, the registration of River View changed in 2017 when he married Elaine."

"He added his second wife to the deeds?"

"Yes. It makes sense unless there's a good reason not to
. . ." They exchanged a glance, well aware that Abby had a very good reason not to have added her late husband to the deeds of the house she'd inherited from her mother. In the

event of divorce, he would have owned half of it and with his philandering ways that was always a possibility . . .

"It would suggest that Elaine wasn't quite as vague as people seemed to think," Abby said.

"Vague?"

"'Sweet but vague' is how Beattie and June described her. After she died, the family discovered a secret stash of vodka bottles in her wardrobe. Although her sister told Fiona Keane that neither of them drank because their mother had been an alcoholic."

"She has a sister?"

"Yes, although she hadn't seen her since her marriage to Tatton."

"That makes sense. The first thing that controlling men do is cut you off from friends and family."

"And it's entirely possible that he was the one topping up her orange juice with vodka," Abby said. "All those uneven steps in ancient ruins . . . I wonder if there was a substantial life insurance policy? We need to talk to her sister."

"Do you have her name?" Meg asked. She was already whipping out her phone as Abby shook her head. "Elaine's death would have been covered in the *Maybridge Observer*, I'll bet the article is still online. Here we are."

Abby moved next to Meg as she scrolled down the page. "There's not much here. It was Elaine's second marriage, she'd been divorced . . . Here. Yvonne Thompson. Her sister's name was Yvonne Thompson." Meg looked triumphant, then glanced at the time and gave a yelp.

"Sorry, but I have to run. Remember, check before you open the door to anyone, Abby. Don't ever let Tatton inside your house. And lock your side gate."

CHAPTER FIFTEEN

Abby waved Meg off, but she was trembling as she closed her door and leaned back against it.

The more she heard about Gregory Tatton, the less she liked. If nothing else, he pressured people and for some reason they buckled.

Ignoring the temptation to pour a large glass of wine, she went to her computer and searched the internet for Flora Tatton.

The *Maybridge Observer* obligingly provided a photograph of the horrendous crash scene. No one else was involved, the conditions were good and the speculation was that her brakes failed, although the car was too badly damaged to check.

It said that her husband was shattered. There was no mention of children by her first marriage.

After that she searched for the report about Elaine's death. The original story apparently made the front page but told her nothing she didn't already know.

The inquest verdict of accidental death had not been sensational enough to make it beyond page five, but it did tell her that it was Elaine's second marriage, that she'd been divorced and that her sister's name was Yvonne Thompson.

Abby wondered what had broken up that marriage and where her first husband was now.

As with Flora, apart from her sister's insistence that she didn't drink, there was nothing to suggest it was anything but a tragic accident.

But Megan was right.

Gregory Tatton wasn't a man any sensible woman would get involved with. It would certainly be a mistake to underestimate him.

She sent texts to Lucy and Tom warning them that there had been a spate of break-ins to garages and sheds and she was locking the side gate so they would have to use the front door.

Then, as an added precaution, she grabbed a torch and went down the garden to ensure that the gate leading to the lane at the back of the house was securely bolted.

* * *

Christmas tree Sunday had always been a family occasion. Going to the farm, choosing the tree, which was always too big, then mince pies or gingerbread men and hot chocolate in the farm shop.

The rain had cleared, the sky was a clear, pale blue, the deep frost was sparkling and their breath smoked in the morning air. It should have been perfect, but everyone was quiet, remembering other days like this, and it wasn't just Sophie who was struggling.

Abby was remembering the first Christmas she'd done this with Howard when she was pregnant with Lucy. The tree they'd chosen, the decorations they'd bought to make it their own.

And all the years since.

The good ones, and the years when Howard had been playing away when she'd had to put on a big smile and play happy families for the children.

Today there was less excitement, less laughter, no demands for a bigger tree. It was all much too polite as they walked on eggshells, afraid of saying the wrong thing.

And then, as they waited in the queue for the chosen tree to be wrapped, Tom said, "Do you remember the year the tree fell off the car when we were coming down Hunters Hill and a lorry ran over it?"

Lucy laughed. "I remember Dad getting out of the car and yelling at the driver . . ."

"And he yelled back at Dad for not securing the tree properly."

Sophie, who couldn't have been more than four years old at the time, put on a gruff voice. "Who needs a tree so big that it blocks the damn road?"

"And Dad said, 'I do, and don't damn well swear in front of my children!' And then they both laughed and he helped Dad put it back on the car and they wished each other a happy Christmas," Lucy said.

Well, he had been running for election to the county council that year, Abby remembered, and every vote counted . . .

But glad that they were talking about him she said, "You three were all in the back of the car, giggling and repeating 'damn, damn, damn . . .'"

"You wanted to go back and get another tree because the top had been run over but Dad insisted it would be fine with a bit of tinsel."

"It took more than tinsel. You had to tie in a bit of cane to straighten it so that the angel stayed on top, and then all the needles fell off the bits that had been run over."

"They fell off everywhere," Abby said. It had been nothing but twigs long before Christmas Day.

"You complained so much about the mess, Mummy," Sophie chipped in, "that Daddy got out the vacuum cleaner every morning and cleared it up, which you said was a Christmas miracle."

Talking about the year of the bald Christmas tree unleashed a whole load of memories and, by the time the tree was strapped to the roof of the Volvo and they went inside for the hot chocolate and spiced ginger latte, they were all pitching in with memories and laughing.

It was what they needed. To talk about Howard. Remember the good moments. It was something she needed to stop shrinking away from, afraid of upsetting them, even with Sophie. Especially with Sophie . . .

Back home, Abby and Tom found a pot large enough for the tree and drenched it.

"We can't take it inside and decorate it until the pot's stopped dripping," Abby said, and hoping to build on the good mood, "Does anyone fancy a trip down to see the Christmas market?" It was new this year, an initiative by the chamber of commerce to bring people into the town. "I've still got some shopping to do. What about you, Sophie? What are you going to give Cara?"

She shrugged. Back in her shell.

"I'm going to get a giant hot dog with everything on it," Tom said.

"What are you thinking of buying Grace for Christmas?" Abby asked.

He blushed. "I don't know. I don't know what girls like."

"I'd suggest something soft," Lucy said, "but she's already got you."

Abby rolled her eyes. "What are you getting Cal?"

"A vintage Bowie T-shirt. Stick with me, kiddos," Lucy declared, "I'm the Christmas present queen."

"Great. And there are loads of really good food stalls. We could all get some lunch out."

Lucy whispered something to Sophie. She shrugged but nodded and it was a done deal.

Market Square was crowded, the Salvation Army were playing carols by the Christmas tree, and the air was full of the scent of mulled wine and exciting spices from the pop-up food stalls. They wandered around for a while. Each of them chose a new decoration for the tree, Abby bought some hand-made candles, and they ate whatever took their fancy.

Then Tom spotted some mates and said he'd see them all later.

"I have to go to High Spirits to place an order for the party and then I'm going to the bookshop for some last-minute presents," Abby told the girls. And for a reviving pot of tea. It had been a long week. She also hoped she might have a chance to talk to Trish.

"We've still got a few things to buy," Lucy said. "We'll go home when we're done."

"Okay. Stay close together and watch your purses in this crowd."

High Spirits was an oak-beamed, double-fronted shop that, like most of Market Square, had been there since Tudor times. Her late husband had been a regular customer, using it for business and political parties, and the manager greeted her by name.

"Mrs Finch, what a pleasure. What can I do for you?"

"I've got a list, Ryan . . . I'm having a drinks party on the sixteenth so I need spirits, mixers, beer, some of those posh soft drinks, and I'm hoping you've got a quaffable wine that won't break the bank?"

He took her list. "No problem. I've got some good special offers on for Christmas that will suit. And we're doing a very good non-alcoholic gin?"

"Oh, that's a good idea. And maybe some non-alcoholic beer too."

"Will you want glasses?"

"Oh, yes. Thanks for reminding me."

"Jason will be delivering on Wednesday afternoon. Is that convenient?"

"If I'm not there, Beattie and June will take it in. In fact, can you add a bottle of the sherry they buy from you." Which was their Christmas gift sorted.

"The manzanilla?"

"Yes, I think that's what they said. You probably heard that there was a horrible accident in the parish hall? They were there and they plied me with it when I went across to make sure they were okay."

"I heard all about it. David Hogg was there and really upset. He said that the poor man who died shouldn't even have been doing the lights. Well, you were there. You'd know."

David . . . "He's a painter and decorator?" Abby said, as if she knew him.

"That's right. He ran his own business until he retired. Still does a bit if you need something doing. Hattie, who runs the travel agents next door, is his daughter."

"Well, he's right about what happened. Gregory Tatton was sorting out the lights, but he asked Edward to finish them off for him. Do you know him?"

"Tatton?" He rolled his eyes. "Ghastly man. He had David painting his kitchen after he'd set fire to it. When he sent in his bill, Tatton said he thought he was doing it as a friend. Some friend. And the callous way he swanned off to Venice leaving poor Maisie Goodyear at death's door when she'd paid for everything . . ."

"I was told that she'd paid," Abby said, "but it seemed unbelievable."

"Believe it. Hattie gave us chapter and verse. Tatton was all flattery, insisting that she deserved to stay in a five-star hotel, fly in business class. Naturally, she assumed he was paying for the trip — eye-watering amounts for five days — but it was Mrs Goodyear, all starry-eyed, who handed over her credit card. Poor Hat was really shocked."

"And then she was too sick to go. Poor woman."

"If she'd been poor," Ryan said, darkly, "he wouldn't have been interested. Maisie's daughter came in to settle her account, which was pretty steep. Apparently Maisie had confessed that the cases of wine she'd bought — really good stuff — were for Tatton. She was furious, and I thought she was going to tell me to send him the bill, but once she'd got all that off her chest, she settled up. I did suggest she get her solicitor to send the receipt to Tatton with a request for reimbursement."

"I wonder if she did?"

"Probably not. If he'd said it was a gift, as I suppose it was, there was nothing anyone could do about it. Now, the manzanilla? Do you want to take it with you, or do you want us to deliver it with the rest of your order?"

CHAPTER SIXTEEN

The Bookshop on the Bridge lived up to its name. The bridge crossed the River May as it curved along the edge of the town, and the bookshop was perched on the corner as it turned into Ship Street.

Like Market Square, the building had been there since Tudor times, the surviving remnant of a much older bridge, lined with shops, that had been damaged beyond repair by a flood more than a century earlier.

As she stepped inside, Abby saw the vicar was impatiently watching his wife, book in hand. "Stop fussing about, Fiona. I've found what I came for and I need to get on."

"I thought I'd buy this for Gary," she said, clutching a paperback copy of the latest bestseller.

"Put it back," he said.

"But   "

"When was the last time your cousin sent you as much as a Christmas card? Put the money in the charity box and pray for him while I go and pay for this."

"Yes, Nigel." She put the book back obediently, but she seemed to be struggling.

"Are you okay, Fiona?" Abby asked.

"Oh, Abby, I didn't see you there. Thank you . . ." She sniffed. "I was so fond of my cousin but we've lost touch and now Edward . . ." Seeing her husband returning with his purchase, she quickly turned on a smile. "I was just thanking Abby for her help yesterday."

The vicar glanced at her, smiled and nodded. "Very kind, Abby, but if you'll excuse us . . ." And with that they were out of the door.

Abby raised her eyebrows at his abruptness, but it was a busy time, everyone was a little stressed. And right now she needed to get some gifts herself.

The shop was spread over two floors with window nooks where browsers could sit, and floor cushions in the children's department for weekly storytelling sessions.

While the entrance was at street level with departments for fiction, biographies, maps and gifts for readers, the descent to the lower floors was via a curving flight of stairs lined with craft and cookery books to a floor where you could find pretty much everything else.

The beams were a hazard to anyone over six feet tall, but it was a booklover's delight and the Orangery café, a more recent glass-fronted addition at river level, tempted even those who never read anything more challenging than the instructions on a microwave meal to go in for coffee, lunch or a very fine afternoon tea and, in the summer, sit on the deck and watch the boats, swans and ducks passing by.

Abby, having browsed the shop for gifts and stocking fillers, headed down there for the much-needed pot of tea.

Trish was wiping down a table and smiled when she saw her. "Hello, Abby. This table is ready."

"Thanks, Trish. How are you? How was the lunch yesterday?"

"The food was good," she said. "Obviously we were all very sad about poor Edward, but we raised a glass to his memory."

"Even so, it must have shaken up those of you who were there."

"Well, yes, but you were amazing. The way you dived in to try and save him. I wouldn't have known what to do."

"Maybe Mr Tatton could organise a first aid demonstration for the lunch club," Abby suggested, taking the opportunity to mention his name as she put her basket on a chair and removed her jacket and scarf. "He seems to be good at that sort of thing. Did they ever find out what happened to the defibrillator?"

"What? Oh, no. Gregory thinks one of the rowdier youth elements that use the hall is responsible. Have you been grabbing some last-minute presents?"

"Well, that was the idea, but I saw Daisy Dashwood's autobiography and that will be going in my own Christmas stocking." She picked it out of the basket. "It's been on my wish list since it was published. I try to catch her gardening programmes when I can. Did you know that she comes from Maybridge?"

Trish didn't answer. She was staring at the copy of *A Case of Royal Blackmail* by Sherlock Holmes that Abby was buying for Megan as a bit of a joke, and the colour seemed to have drained from her face.

Abby, seeing her reaction, picked the book out of the basket. "Have you read this? I thought this might amuse a friend, but I'm going to put it back. Blackmail is such a vile crime. It must seem like a life sentence for the victim."

"I don't read," Trish said quickly. "I knit . . ."

"Of course. Mr Tatton told me that you'd knitted the lovely sweater he was wearing on Wednesday. With the snowflake design."

She swallowed, coloured. "Yes . . ."

"I was thinking of buying one for a friend, but the hand-knitted ones are so expensive. It's understandable. The skill and the time involved. I don't see how you can make it pay."

"Oh, I don't . . ." Trisha stopped. "I don't knit for money. Gregory saw the one Sandra asked me to make for her grandson. She paid for the wool . . ." She didn't finish. She'd didn't have to.

Tatton had seen what Trish could do and he'd wanted one. And what Tatton wanted . . .

A weekly supply of cakes and an expensive sweater — she doubted that Tatton had paid for his wool — would bite deep into the pension of a woman who still had to work to make ends meet, not to mention the hours and hours of her time.

"Have the police been to see you yet?" Abby asked.

Trish physically jumped, and Abby, feeling guilty, put a hand on her arm. "Good heavens, you're shaking. Have you been working all day? Sit down for a moment."

"I can't . . ." She looked nervously towards the kitchen, but then subsided onto a chair. "It's been an awful week. Poor Edward . . ."

Abby looked around and caught the eye of a young waitress. "Trish isn't feeling too good. Will you bring us a pot of tea and a couple of toasted teacakes?"

"I can't—" Trish began but Abby brushed aside her protest.

"I insist."

"Don't worry, Mrs Finch," the girl said. "It's quiet for the moment. I'll cover for her."

"Thank you . . . It's Hannah, isn't it?" Abby said. "You're in Lucy's year?"

She smiled, delighted to have been recognised. "I'll get your tea."

"I'm sorry, it's been a long day," Trish said. "And that young policeman who was at the hall came to take a statement from me. It's stupid but they always make you feel so guilty, don't they?"

Abby agreed. "That moment when you see a police car in your rear-view mirror and you panic. Are your brake lights working? Did you miss a red light?"

Hannah arrived with the tea. "The teacakes will be ready in a minute."

Abby gave the pot a stir. "I hadn't seen Edward for a while," she said. "I was shocked to see the change in him. Frankly, I was surprised Mr Tatton asked him to climb a ladder."

"He just wanted to get everything done," Trish said, but she was looking at her hands. "Gregory is so good at organising everything."

"Even so, he can't be looking forward to the inquest."

"Inquest?" Trish repeated, startled into looking up. "But it was an accident."

"Even so, there'll have to be an inquest to establish what happened. Is this strong enough for you?" Abby asked as she poured the tea.

Trish nodded.

"The coroner will be sure to ask who was responsible for the lights, although from what I saw it seemed to be Mr Tatton's star that caused the problem. Milk?"

Trish nodded again. "I didn't see anything. I was in the kitchen."

Was she? Abby thought back. She'd definitely been in the hall when Gregory had asked about the cake.

"Mr Tatton didn't seem at all happy that Edward had put it in place."

"He did tell him not to do it," Trish pointed out.

Abby paused in the act of pouring the milk and looked up. "You heard him from the kitchen?" Trish coloured and Abby, pretending not to have noticed anything amiss, said, "Edward didn't hear him. Or do you think he was just teasing Mr Tatton? He was making quite a fuss about his star."

"More fool him," Trish blurted out. "If he'd done as he was told, it would have been Gregory who'd got the shock."

The milk splashed into her tea and Abby's hand shook as she put down the jug. It wasn't just Trish's outburst. It was that several people had said the same thing. If the lights had been tampered with, logically he must have been the target . . .

Abby glanced at the book in her basket, the one that had caused such a reaction from Trish.

Blackmail. Financial or emotional, it was all about secrets.

So what was Trish so desperate to hide that she'd succumb to the kind of pressure that Tatton was now attempting to use on her?

"I get the impression that people tend to do what Mr Tatton tells them. In this case, thanks to Edward, he had a lucky escape." Abby suddenly remembered the Christmas foliage Trish had asked for through Penny. "Was the mistletoe a success?"

"Gregory seemed pleased."

"Gregory?" Abby stirred her tea. "I thought it was the ladies who'd asked if you could find some."

"Oh . . . Well, no. He wondered where to get some and then suggested that you might have some at Linton Lodge. Penny came in for a pot of tea and I know her grandson works for you, so I asked her."

"I'm surprised he didn't tell me that when he came to my studio on Thursday."

The white lies were becoming epidemic.

"He came to see you?"

"He had a photograph he thought I might like for the Linton Lodge archives, but I'm pretty sure that it was just an excuse to get some kind of deal on a garden makeover. 'Now we're friends' was the way he put it, although Wednesday was the first time I'd spoken to him."

"He wants you to work on his garden?" Trish's look became speculative.

"He wants to talk about it, but I've told him I can't do anything before Christmas."

"Once he's made up his mind on something, he doesn't like to be kept waiting."

"Was that how it was with the sweater?" Abby asked. "I suppose he wanted it for the holiday season."

But Trish was saved from the need to answer by the arrival of the teacakes, which put a halt to conversation while they relished the pleasure of biting into the crisp, buttery fruit buns.

"Thank you, Abby," Trish said, standing up and grabbing a tray from a nearby table, gathering up the plates the minute they were finished. "That was a treat, but if I don't get to work . . ."

"Me too. You'd think," she said, as she wound her scarf around her neck and put on her jacket, "that it would be quiet in the gardening world at this time of year, but it's when people have time to look around and think about the changes they'd like to make. I'm afraid if Mr Tatton wants Earthly Designs to remodel his garden, he'll have to learn a little patience. You know what they say, *Live as though you'll die tomorrow. Garden as if you'll live forever . . .*"

Trish stared at her for a moment, then stuttered her thanks and practically ran back to the refuge of the kitchen. But that was okay. Abby now knew that Megan was right. Tatton had used the mistletoe to engineer their meeting. And he'd used Trish as his cat's paw.

Trish, who knitted and baked for him and who, if she wasn't very much mistaken, was afraid of him.

CHAPTER SEVENTEEN

That evening the children decorated the tree until there was barely a glimpse of green, and went wild with tinsel, wrapping it around everything, including the kittens. Abby left them to it, shutting herself away in her office, and asked herself again: what could Trish Porter be so desperate to keep hidden that she was compelled to knit and bake for Gregory Tatton?

She must have reached retirement age to belong the seniors' lunch club, even though she was still working. But had she always been a waitress?

And where did Tatton get his information?

She was beginning to have the strongest doubts about his mother's friendship with Jean. It was far too convenient that he should know everyone else involved, and a serial blackmailer would always be alert for the possibilities.

Had Howard's murder and the consequent publicity suggested that there might be something in it for him? Had he been digging for information that would be useful should an opportunity arise?

According to Beattie, Tatton had worked at County Hall in the accounts department, and financial services would touch everything that happened in the county.

The Register Office was there with records of births, marriages and deaths going back for who knew how long. And the archives of institutions like St Catherine's, where Pam had been illegally shut away for so many years.

They had responsibility for fostering, the care system, education. He could have found the photograph of Jean there and recognised Pam.

Abby sat back in her chair.

Was it that simple? Did he use the County Hall computer system to trawl though the records, putting in the names of people he knew and waiting to see what popped up?

Edward's suspension must be on record somewhere, although that scandal had been public enough. Maybe there was more that hadn't come out at the time . . .

Well, two could play at that game.

She typed *Gregory Tatton, Maybridge* into the search engine on her computer and hit enter. There weren't many links, but he'd been a public servant and he came up as an accounts officer in Finance and Support Services at the county council.

Bingo . . .

There were links to the newspaper reports on the deaths of Flora and Elaine that she'd already seen, but there was no social media presence. There was surprisingly little online for someone who was so active in the community. But not for someone who preyed on the vulnerable and needed to keep a low internet profile in case a victim came looking for him.

Was that what had happened?

Where had he come from? Was he local or had he moved to Maybridge when he married Flora? If so, where had they met?

She'd wondered how Maisie's daughter would react to a note from a total stranger asking about her mother's relationship with Tatton. But having heard Ryan's gossipy tale of her fury over the cases of wine, she decided it had to be worth getting in touch.

She checked the details which Fiona had obligingly supplied, and wrote:

Dear Heather James,

You don't know me, and I'll totally understand if you choose to ignore this email, but I've been helping out at the seniors' lunch club in Maybridge.

My neighbours Beattie and June, who know your mother, told me a little of what happened to her and, as I now find myself in a slightly awkward situation with Gregory Tatton, I wondered if there was anything you'd be comfortable sharing with me, in confidence, about your dealings with him.

She added her phone number and signed off.

CHAPTER EIGHTEEN

Abby had just dropped Sophie and her friend Cara off at school the following morning and was climbing back into her car when she received a text from the chair of the Maybridge Show.

Lady Hamilton was happy to inform her that her show garden design had been accepted. She added her congratulations and informed her that the *Maybridge Observer* would be getting in touch for an interview.

At last some good news, and with her heart beating just a little faster than normal, she rang the Finch offices. She was going to need all of Eric's skill, and after the holiday she was going to have to go to the abandoned area of the quarry to organise the removal of the stone that had been the inspiration for her design.

With that arranged, she headed up to her studio, eager to look over the details of her design and start making lists before the children arrived for their nature walk.

It was a madcap couple of hours, although thankfully some parents had come along to help keep the little ones from wandering off and getting lost.

They ticked off the insects they saw and the birds they hadn't scared away. They collected leaves to identify and make prints of when they were back at school, and they gathered acorns, beech mast and horse chestnuts, and finally left with tree seedlings she'd potted up for them, with instructions on how to care for them so that, when they were big enough, they could be planted out in the school garden.

It was midday before she had a chance to listen to the messages on her answering machine. She was certain that one of them would be from Tatton with some innuendo-laden demand for immediate attention and she was right.

He'd left one on Saturday evening.

"Abby, my dear, you didn't wait for your gift from Santa but I'll drop by with it on Monday afternoon."

Well, that explained why he hadn't turned up that morning.

She was about to haul herself out of the chair to make sure the gates were locked, when there was a sharp rap on the door and she practically jumped out of her skin.

"Abby?"

Not Gregory but DC Dee Newcombe. Relief practically overwhelmed her for about a second before she realised that this wasn't a social call.

"What's happened?" she asked, rising to her feet, throat in mouth. "The children? Cal?"

"No!" Dee was quick to reassure her. "It's nothing like that. I'm here because Gregory Tatton was found dead at his home this morning."

"What?" Abby sank back onto her chair. "But I saw him . . ." She stopped. If Dee was involved, it wasn't going to be something as simple as a heart attack.

"When was that?" Dee asked.

"On Saturday. I saw him at the seniors' lunch club when I was helping to set up the tables. What happened to him?"

"We're waiting for the results of the post-mortem but I thought I'd better warn you that we're treating his death as unexplained."

Warn her?

"There was an open bottle of whisky that had been knocked over when he fell, along with the glass. There were quite a few chocolate wrappers too."

"That's awful," Abby said. Whisky and chocolate? Had he vomited, choked? "Who found him?"

"A woman who does some cleaning for him. Sandra Monkford. Do you know her?" Dee asked.

"Just to pass the time of day. Someone told me that she takes him a croissant every morning and does some cleaning."

"When he didn't answer she became concerned, looked through the window and saw him lying on the living room floor."

"Poor woman. What a terrible shock."

"She rang the emergency services, but they had to break the door down to get in," Dee said. "He was still dressed in the Father Christmas costume he'd been wearing on Saturday, so he'd been dead for at least thirty-six hours."

"That's awful," she said, and meant it. Whatever he'd done, it was a horrible way to die. Then, frowning, "He went home from the lunch in his Father Christmas costume?"

"Mrs Monkford suggested that he was quite . . . merry."

"So who took him home?"

"No one had brought their cars because they knew they would be drinking, so he called a taxi. Mrs Monkford said that he was waiting outside for it when she left."

"Oh, right."

"He had his Santa sack with him, containing the gifts he'd been given. He'd been opening them before he died. Gloves, hand-knitted scarves, some impressively expensive cologne as well as several more bottles of wine and spirits. And of course the chocolates."

"How is Sandra?"

"Shaken," Dee said. "One of the officers who'd gone to the scene called her daughter-in-law and she came and drove her home."

"I'm glad she's not alone . . . But why are you here, Dee? What has it to do with me?"

"He was holding a package when he died. It looks as if he'd leaned forward to take it out of the sack and that's when he fell."

"Did he hit his head? Twist his neck?" Abby asked, still grappling with the fact of Tatton's death.

"It doesn't appear so, but the package he was holding had your name on it. And the last call he made was to you."

Dee held out her phone with a photograph that showed a small package, wrapped in red tissue, tied with gold string and with a label bearing the name *Abby Finch* in the same copperplate script with which he'd written the letter.

"Oh . . ." Abby swallowed. "He told me he had gifts for all his helpers, but it was never my intention to stay once I'd set up the tables."

"So he took it home with him?"

"Well, yes. Obviously." She swallowed again. "He left a message on my answering machine to say he'd call in with it today. I thought it was him when you knocked."

"Can I hear it?"

Abby played the message.

"I don't understand why he didn't give it to someone to pass on," Dee said, once she'd heard it. "Your neighbours were there, according to Mrs Monkford."

"The thing is, he's keen . . ." Abby swallowed. "Was keen . . . for me to do some work on his garden. Maybe he thought I'd put him to the front of the queue if he came bearing a gift." Recalling Megan's warning that it would be a message of some kind, she felt a flicker of alarm. "Did you open it?" Of course they had or why would Dee be here. "What was it?"

"It was a second-hand paperback copy of *Crooked House* by Agatha Christie." Her voice rose in the faintest suggestion of a question. "Not something likely to encourage you to put him to the top of the waiting list."

"No . . ." But it had definitely been a message and Abby wondered where he'd found the book. Perhaps he'd come across it when doing a house clearance for that charity and slipped it into his pocket.

"He'd inscribed it to you."

"Oh . . ." There was a hollow, sick feeling in her stomach, but she forced herself to ask, "What did he write?"

"A nursery rhyme. The one about a crooked man living in a crooked house."

She showed her a photograph of the inside cover of the book. Beneath the rhyme he'd written, *I can't wait for you to straighten my garden, Abby*. It was all in the same handwriting, so there was no possibility that the rhyme had been written by a previous owner.

"I haven't read it, have you?" Dee asked.

"A long time ago," she admitted. "I certainly won't be wanting that copy. You can put it in the nearest bin."

"Not until we've established the cause of death."

That sounded ominous. "He did mention to me that he'd had some kind of heart incident, but I didn't get the impression that it had been more than a warning. He looked fit enough, although I'm not sure his diet was that good. He told me himself that he had a fondness for chocolate. I believe he had someone make him a chocolate cake every week, which can't have been good . . ." Abby could hear how defensive she sounded and stopped.

"We're checking his medical records," Dee said.

"Of course. Is there any chance that it could have been food poisoning?" Abby asked. "Have any of the other lunch guests been taken ill? He can't be the only one who lives alone. Oh, my God, Pam . . ."

"Reverend Keane and his wife are contacting everyone who was present," Dee said quickly, "but there are no reports of anyone else being taken ill."

"Thank goodness for that."

"It seems that he arrived home, used the bathroom, possibly had a glass of water — there was a used glass in the kitchen sink — and then settled down with a bottle of whisky that someone had given him. There was a bottle bag by his chair."

"Who was it from?" Abby asked.

"Is that important?" Dee regarded her with an impenetrable expression for a long moment. "There was no gift tag. Someone had no doubt reused the bag. There were some cards, so I imagine one of them came with it. And as I said there were chocolates and chocolate wrappers, although there was no sign of a box."

"Were they the ones that look like mini crackers?" Abby asked.

"Why would you think that?"

"When I was helping set up the tables before the lunch, Mr Tatton gave me several boxes of those chocolates and asked me to put one at each place setting. There were a few left over which I put on the table by Santa's grotto for anyone to help themselves. It wouldn't surprise me if he took them home with him."

"A few? How many is that?"

"Well, there were five boxes containing ten each but he'd opened one and taken a couple to taste. He said he had to ensure they were up to standard." Dee frowned and Abby hurriedly continued, "I'm not sure of the exact amount left over."

Dee checked her notebook. "There were nine wrappers."

"That seems a lot. I could check against the seating plan?" Abby offered.

"That would be helpful. And at least I now know why your fingerprints were on all the wrappers we found."

Fingerprints?

"What? How?" Abby demanded.

"We have yours on file," Dee reminded her. "Did Mr Tatton buy the chocolates?"

Abby gave her a long look. "He told me that they'd been left for the seniors' lunch. He assumed that they were from the new chocolate boutique promoting their Christmas specials. Le Petit Chocolat? They're next door to Knickerbocker Gloria. I noticed some in their window. I'm sorry, Dee, I'm not thinking . . . Would you like some coffee?"

"No time, I'm afraid, but we will want statements from everyone who was in the hall on Saturday. Someone from uniform will contact you."

CHAPTER NINETEEN

Abby's hands shook as she punched in Megan's number.

"Hi Abby! Congratulations!"

"Sorry?"

"The list of designers who'll be creating gardens at the Maybridge Show next spring is on the *Observer* website this morning. Your name is at the top of the list. I left a message. I thought that was why you were calling."

"Oh, no, I haven't seen that yet . . ."

"Of course, you had the children this morning. How was school?"

"Fine. They were lovely, but Meg, Dee was just here. Tatton's dead."

"Dead?" Megan repeated. "I'm not exactly sorry to hear it, but how? What happened?"

"I don't know," Abby said, but she had a mental image of the scene Dee had described in her head. "Possibly a surfeit of whisky and chocolate. He'd been lying there since Saturday evening and for the moment the police are treating it as an unexplained death."

"Who found him?"

"The woman who takes him a warm croissant from the Buttery every morning for his breakfast and does a little cleaning for him."

"Every morning? That's a bit self-indulgent. You don't get much change from three pounds for one of their almond croissants."

"Assuming that he paid for them." Abby repeated what Ryan had told her about his treatment of David Hogg and Trish's admission that Tatton hadn't paid her to make his sweater. "It did cross my mind that Sandra might be another of his victims, but I may be jumping to conclusions. According to my gossipy neighbours, Sandra lives with her son and daughter-in-law and was happy to get out of the house for an hour or two."

"Oh, well, I can help her with that. If she wants to get out of the house so desperately that she'd clean for free, tell her to come and see me. I wouldn't expect her to buy me pastries and she'd be paid top rate for the job. Can you get me her contact details?"

"Meg!"

"Am I being a bit insensitive?" she asked.

"A bit?" Abby sighed. "No, you're being honest, but the last call Tatton made was to leave a message on my answering machine saying he'd call in this afternoon. And my fingerprints were on the wrappers of the chocolate he'd been eating just before he died."

"What?"

"I'd put them out on the lunch tables. Plenty of people saw me."

"Okaaaay . . . That's a bit unsettling but why would it matter? Unless . . . Ohmigod, do they suspect that he may have been poisoned? Was there anything else he'd been eating or drinking?"

"There was an open bottle of Scotch that was knocked over when he fell."

"If he'd been drinking and stuffing himself with chocolate he might have vomited and choked," Meg said. "It seems a bit soon to be checking for fingerprints."

"It's not just my fingerprints, Meg. When Tatton died, he was clutching the gift he'd been planning to give me at the lunch on Saturday." And she told Megan about the book and the inscription.

"Shit . . . You must be totally creeped out. Did you say anything to Dee? About how he'd been hassling you?"

"No."

"But you're worried that his death might not be down to natural causes."

"People keep saying that it should have been Gregory on that ladder. He told me himself that he always fixed the star, and I can't get past the feeling that the shock was meant for him."

And there was the missing defibrillator.

If the lights had been tampered with in an attempt to injure Gregory Tatton, might it have been removed in order to prevent his resuscitation?

"You're suggesting that, having missed the first time, whoever fiddled with the electrics has had another go?" Megan asked.

"Isn't that the fate of blackmailers?" Abby said. "When a victim gets desperate, they hit back. If he'd bothered to read Agatha Christie instead of using her to send me a message, he'd have known that."

"But who? How, if you weren't a trained electrician, would you know how to make a light fitting lethal? Or get at Tatton's precious star?"

"There's probably a video on YouTube," Abby said. "And the lights are kept in the storage cupboard at the hall. Once Tatton had converted the light fitting, he probably returned it to the cupboard. The vicar might know."

"So," Megan said, "anyone could have got at it in the last couple of weeks, but that must rule out anyone who was there that day, or they'd have done something to stop Edward."

"No one knew Edward had taken the star except me," Abby said, unhappily. "Tatton told him to leave it. That he was going to do it. Everyone heard that. Even Trish Porter, who said she was in the kitchen."

"It's not your fault, Abby," Megan said, sounding concerned.

"No. It's the fault of whoever planned this and didn't foresee the chance of someone else getting hurt."

For a moment they both silently contemplated what would drive someone to such lengths, then Meg said, "Is it that easy to poison someone? I wouldn't know where to get my hands on anything lethal. Can you even buy rat poison these days?"

"You don't need rat poison. Any garden will provide you with the means to kill someone," Abby informed her. "Laburnum, oleander, foxgloves, monkshood, the castor oil plant. Those are all deadly and most people have at least one of them in their garden. I've got them all here at the Lodge. And that's before you get to the wild stuff. Deadly nightshade, hemlock, and some very nasty fungi . . ."

"The castor oil plant?" Meg asked. "Is that a real thing?"

"*Ricinus communis*. You've heard of ricin?"

"Well yes . . . It was the poison that killed the defector who was jabbed with an umbrella a few years ago. Why would anyone have that in their garden?"

"It has lovely leaves and attractive seed heads," Abby said, "but according to the book I have on poisonous plants—"

"You have a book? Get rid of it!"

"Learning which plants are poisonous is important, Meg. When I was at college we took a trip to the Duchess of Northumberland's Poison Garden at Alnwick—"

"She has a *poison* garden?"

"It's famous. Look it up on the web if you don't believe me. Three grams of ricin would be fatal."

"That's not much is it?"

"The thing is," Abby explained, "I cut a load of the seed heads, dried them and painted them gold for Christmas decorations. And I delivered some, along with the mistletoe, to the parish hall on Wednesday."

"That's why you're so worried."

"They were used in the table decorations. Which I put in place."

"Abs . . ."

"I made sure there were no seeds left inside. I wanted those to plant for next year."

"But whoever was there would know that they came from the Lodge," Megan pointed out. "And there's a public footpath through the woods. Anyone could slip into the garden and help themselves."

"I suppose so, but it's actually quite common. I saw some on the roundabout by the supermarket and none of this information is secret, or difficult to get hold of." Abby's head was beginning to throb. "It's getting your victim to take it that's the problem for a would-be murderer."

"They would need something tempting and strong tasting to deliver the fatal dose. So was it in the whisky or the chocolate?"

"He'd have noticed if the whisky bottle had been opened."

"Not necessarily. It is possible to remove a metal cap without cracking the seal."

"Is it? How do you know that?"

"Once, many years ago, when I was the junior who typed up the house details, a boss who'd been very mean with the Christmas bonuses went home with a bottle that contained something other than the very pricey single malt he'd been given by a grateful client."

"Oh, that's bad."

"Appalling," Meg admitted, "but I was just a naive and shocked onlooker and I left as soon as I could find another job with less typing and the occasional opportunity to conduct a viewing. But let's not get ahead of ourselves. Tatton might simply have overindulged and choked. There might have been a fault with the wiring. Just bad luck. Do you know if the police have got around to looking at the lights?"

"I don't know. As you say, all these departments are backed up and there was no suggestion that it was anything but a tragic accident."

117

"Dee didn't mention the coincidence?"

"There was no reason to connect it with Edward's death. That was a uniform matter, an accident. She only came to see me as a friend after that. There was no reason for her to have read my statement."

"But if we're right, and Tatton has been blackmailing people, surely it must have crossed his mind that the accident with the lights was aimed at him?" Megan pressed.

"You'd have thought so, but his only concern seemed to be that his precious star was smashed."

"And yet now he's dead."

"He'd had a good lunch, he'd been drinking, stuffing himself with chocolate and goodness knows what else . . ." Abby sighed. "I'm probably letting my imagination run away with me."

"Well, whatever it is, you can forget what he knew, or thought he knew, about what went on at the Lodge fifty years ago. You're off that particular hook."

Which was, Abby thought, a very strong motive for murder.

CHAPTER TWENTY

Abby, well aware how quick Jake was to pick up that something was wrong, had been letting his calls go to voicemail and sending him brief texts rather than her calling or zooming.

Tonight, with some genuinely good news to share, she finally rang him, but before she could speak, he said, "Okay, what's wrong?"

"Nothing," she said. "What makes you think there's something wrong?"

He didn't bother to answer.

"No, really, I'm sorry I haven't called you. It's a crazy time of the year and I've been rushed off my feet, but I do have some exciting news. I heard this morning that my garden design has been accepted for the Maybridge Show."

"Congratulations. Not that I doubted it for a moment, or that you'll get a gold medal or whatever they're awarding," he said. "That's the good news, now tell me what's wrong."

"Jake, it's been a tough week . . ."

"Is this about Edward March's death? Is something bothering you about that?"

"Wasn't being there enough?" she snapped, and immediately regretted it. "I'm sorry, but yesterday was the annual trip to the Christmas tree farm, then putting up the decorations . . . The holidays are always emotional and this year is particularly hard for the kids. Everything they do is the first time without their dad."

"Do you think that Howard would have been there for them this year?" Jake asked. "I imagine he'd have been busy doing all that with Izzy and his new baby."

Abby sighed. "You're right, of course. The children would have been upset and angry with him, but now he's dead and you can't be angry with someone who's dead . . ."

"So they're angry with you?"

"Tom and Lucy are old enough to understand. It's Sophie I'm worried about."

"I should be there with you."

"No." She swallowed. "No, Jake. This is something we have to get through by ourselves . . ." Hearing the hurt in the silence that followed, she explained, "It's not the right moment for them to see me with someone else. Not like that."

"What about the panto? Do you want me to stay away from that, too?" he asked, not quite managing to hide the edge in his voice.

"Of course not. The panto is a great idea. Howard always ducked out of going, so there are no painful memories."

"And Christmas Day?"

"There are going to be loads of people here for lunch."

"In other words, I'll be lost in the crowd?"

"No . . ." She stopped, because maybe, in inviting all and sundry, that was precisely what she was doing. "You don't have to come if you'd rather not," she told him. "I imagine you've had any number of glamorous invitations."

"Do you want a list?"

"A list? There were that many?"

"Well, there was the invitation to spend Christmas and the New Year on a Caribbean island—"

"You're kidding."

"Then there was the Norfolk country estate, with the added thrill of slaughtering pheasants by the dozen on

Boxing Day. I could have gone to Dublin to stay with some friends and I've even had a pity invitation from my ex and her husband who've rented a Scottish castle with their friends for the holidays."

"Please tell me you'd pass on the pheasant slaughter."

"Definitely not my idea of a good time, even if I knew one end of a shotgun from the other."

"And you declined the Caribbean to spend Christmas in Maybridge?"

"Sun and tinsel?"

"I could be tempted," Abby replied, with feeling.

"Really? I'll ask you next year and see what response I get, but the thing about Christmas, Abby, is not where you are, it's who you're with. And despite all temptations, I choose an evening at the panto with you and the kids followed by a day of mayhem and almost certainly tears."

Abby felt such a rush of warmth and longing . . .

"Bring tissues," she warned. And then, because tears of her own were threatening, "Damn it, Jake, I miss you. You'd better be home for my party on Saturday."

"I'll be there," he promised. "I've got Tom's rugby shirt but what can I bring the girls?"

"I'll ask them but, honestly, the only thing Sophie wants right now is the phone her daddy promised he'd give her for Christmas."

"That must have been some time ago."

"She wanted one for her birthday, but I said she was too young." She swallowed. "She was, but if I'm honest I was being petty. I didn't want Howard being the birthday hero when he'd just abandoned his children for a new family."

"That's understandable, Abs. Don't beat yourself up about it."

"I don't have to. Sophie is doing a pretty good job all by herself."

"And I'm the one acting like a spoiled kid when she's missing her dad."

"It's hard for all of them," she said, not rising to that. "But Tom got us through the Christmas tree farm, bless him."

"I should be there. Maybe not the Christmas tree farm, but to support you."

"You're where you're needed, Jake. This isn't your problem."

"And if I want it to be?" He didn't give her a chance to answer. "I'll give the phone problem some thought, and when I get back you can tell me what's really bothering you."

* * *

Abby dropped Sophie and Cara off at school and was heading for her office, blocking out Christmas tunes on the local radio as she mentally ran through the list of what she needed to order from Penny for the party on Saturday.

The traffic was backed up and she was stationary when the news came on.

". . . launched into the death of Mr Gregory Tatton, sixty-three . . ."

Hearing Tatton's name, Abby jolted out of her mental calculation of the number of mince pies she'd need and turned up the volume.

". . . found at his home in Maybridge on Monday morning. Detective Chief Inspector Iain Glover, who is heading up the inquiry, has asked anyone who was in the vicinity of Kingfisher Lane on Saturday evening to get in touch. In other news . . ."

Abby stopped listening.

DI Glover?

If a detective of his rank was involved, the results of the post-mortem had to suggest Tatton's death was due to something more sinister than overindulgence.

She became aware of a cacophony of horns sounding behind her and, raising a hand in apology, she moved on just as her phone began to ring.

It would be Dee or maybe Megan, but even if she hadn't been driving, she was in no hurry to talk to anyone.

Cal was already working when she arrived at her office, servicing a rotavator.

"My calendar tells me that tomorrow is your last day at college for this term," she said. "How's it going?"

"Good. They treat you like adults, not like kids."

Abby smiled, delighted that she'd taken him on and that he was doing so well. "I'm glad to hear it."

"I thought I might see if there are any spaces on the evening class in mechanics. It would be good to get a qualification."

"Good idea. If you can get a place let me know about the fees."

"I didn't expect—"

"I know, but the business will benefit. Coffee?"

"Thanks, Abby."

She made him a mug of coffee, then ran through what he had in his diary for the rest of the week. "I don't know if they've covered it yet in your course, Cal, but some common plants that you'll find in most gardens are toxic and shouldn't be touched with bare hands. There are some that shouldn't even be sniffed, although I doubt you'll come across those. There's a book on the subject in the studio. Take it home with you and make sure you know what they are."

"Oh, right."

Then she told him the news about the show garden.

"Wow. That's brilliant!"

"It's going to be hard work. Eric will be bossing up the build, but I want you closely involved in preparing the plants."

She left Cal beaming, and aware that she'd been putting off the moment when she'd have to confront the fact that Gregory Tatton had almost certainly been murdered, she returned to her studio.

The light was now flashing on her answering machine. There were calls from her clients, excited for her, and Gary Jackson from the *Maybridge Observer*, effusive in his congratulations, keen to arrange a time for an interview and photograph.

She was sorely tempted to suggest he used the same one he'd taken from the Earthly Designs website when she'd uncovered the bones of a long-dead baby in the Lodge garden. When he'd gone to town dragging up every Finch family tragedy in a story filled with innuendo. A story that had led to the death of her husband.

But cooperation with the media was part of the deal so, much as it galled her, she called him back to set up a time.

After that she turned to her mobile and checked her voicemails. Again, congratulations from friends, except for the last one, which was Dee Newcombe.

"Abby, when you have a moment, the DI would like a word. Will you call in at the station as soon as it's convenient?"

How to kill the moment.

CHAPTER TWENTY-ONE

"I'm sorry to call you in, Abby," DI Iain Glover said, inviting her to sit down. "I just wanted to go through what you told DC Newcombe about the chocolates. At the seniors' Christmas lunch."

They had been on first-name terms at her husband's funeral so, taking her cue from him, she said, "I heard the news this morning, Iain, so I'm guessing it wasn't his heart."

"There was nothing wrong with his heart. It was ricin that killed him."

Abby felt her stomach drop.

"I'm trying to find out how it was administered," Iain continued, checking the notes in the file in front of him. "I understand you took some seed heads to the parish hall on Wednesday." He looked up. "Is that right?"

She remembered her conversation with Fiona and Lisa about the plant's toxicity. Presumably one of them had mentioned it.

"I did," she said, hoping her voice sounded less tense than she felt. "I had removed all the seeds and spray-painted them. They were no danger to anyone."

Iain made a note.

"How well did you know Gregory Tatton?" he asked.

"I knew him by sight," she said, determined not to be caught out, "but I had never spoken to him until last Wednesday. Penny Henderson passed on a message, via Trish Porter, that he wanted some mistletoe. I took it along with some other plant material. Holly, ivy and some flowers and seed heads that I'd sprayed gold." She swallowed. "The seed heads were from the castor oil plant. *Ricinus communis*," she added. "That's the plant that produces ricin."

"And where did they come from?"

"The garden at Linton Lodge. All parts of the plant are poisonous, but as I said, I'd removed the seeds and, having painted them, they were perfectly safe to handle. I was planning to use them in the garland I make every year for my mantelpiece." She hadn't done it yet and it was unlikely that she'd use that particular plant ever again. "I have some at my studio if you'd like to see them."

"You grow poisonous plants in the garden of Linton Lodge?" he asked.

"I didn't plant them. These have self-set over the years, but there are poisonous plants in most gardens. You'll find them listed on the internet," she added.

"And are the ricin seeds readily available?"

"The seeds or small plants are available to buy from any good online nursery."

"You say you removed all the seeds from the ones you took to the parish hall. One couldn't have been missed?" he suggested. "Possibly fallen onto a plate?"

"No." Except they had been used in the table decorations . . .

"That couldn't have happened?" he persisted when he sensed her hesitation.

"No. Absolutely not." She'd just told him that she'd been planning to use them in her own home, for heaven's sake. "I was very careful."

"How big are the seeds?" he asked. "What do they look like?"

"They're cream in colour, flecked with brown and the size of a small bean. I have the ones I removed in my seed store if you want to see them."

"I'll have someone go back to your studio with you to pick them up. And the sprayed heads."

Before she could double-check them. He was evidently going for an accidental poisoning. One for which she was going to be held responsible. He might say this was not a formal interview, but it was beginning to feel like one.

"Tell me about Saturday," he said. "Why were you at the parish hall?"

"Fiona Keane, the vicar's wife, asked if I could spare an hour to help set things up for the seniors' lunch."

"Do you normally help out?"

"No, but they were short-handed and I went along to set up the tables."

"What did that entail? Were you alone?"

"The tables had been put in place and the cloths laid. I started with the central table decoration—"

"Describe them."

"They were arrangements made with the holly, ivy and the gold seed heads."

"Who made them?"

A few days ago, she would have suggested that he ask Gregory Tatton, because she was sure he would have delegated that task to one of his favourites.

Iain looked up from his notepad, eyebrows raised in question.

"I've no idea."

"What next?"

"I laid out the cutlery, cruets, glasses, side plates, napkins, crackers and place names—"

"So you knew where everyone was sitting?"

"Yes."

"Go on."

"The caterers followed me with bottles of wine and water, butter, and plates containing the cold first courses. I had just about finished when Mr Tatton approached me with the chocolates and asked me to put one at each place setting."

"The boxes were unopened?"

"One had been opened and two chocolates were missing. When I commented, Mr Tatton admitted that he'd eaten them. There were a few left over when I'd finished and, as I told Dee — DC Newcombe — I put them on the table by the grotto where Mr Tatton, as Father Christmas, would be sitting to hand out gifts after lunch."

"And the boxes? What happened to them?"

"I've no idea," Abby said, beginning to resent the lengthy inquisition. She'd done nothing wrong. "I left them in a pile on the grotto chair and someone whisked them away while I was piling up the leftovers. I assume they were put in the recycling."

"And you didn't stay for the lunch?"

"It's been a tough few days, but despite appearances, I'm not yet qualified to become a member of the seniors' lunch club."

Iain was supposed to smile. He didn't.

"And you didn't speak to Mr Tatton again?"

"He was at the door greeting people as they arrived. I left through the kitchen and went home."

"But he called you later that evening." He checked his notebook. "He apparently expected you to wait for a gift?"

"He mentioned that he had something in his sack for all the helpers," she explained, "but he can't have expected me to stay for three hours in order to collect it."

"No, and yet he seems to have been very eager to give it to you."

"What he really wanted was to talk to me about Earthly Designs giving his garden a fresh look."

"Had it been arranged?"

"He was deaf to anything he didn't want to hear, so I went to River View on Friday morning in order to take measurements and photographs. I didn't have time to discuss plans with him then and we didn't go inside the house."

"We?"

"Eric Braithwaite came with me. He's employed by Finch Developments and has done some work for Earthly Designs." Iain's face gave nothing away but Abby felt the need to justify his presence. "I needed someone to hold the other end of the tape measure."

He made a note then said, "Thanks for coming in, Abby. I'll get someone to go with you to pick up the plant material."

CHAPTER TWENTY-TWO

The painted seed heads were safe to handle and Abby put a couple of those into a bag. Then she put on a pair of thin latex gloves and shook a few of the ricin seeds into a small plastic container and, with a thick black Sharpie, wrote *POISONOUS — DO NOT TOUCH WITH BARE HANDS* on the lid.

The PC looked at her. "Is that for real?"

"It's for real," she confirmed, peeling off the gloves and handing him the bag.

She waited until he'd gone and then — because she was afraid, if she sat down, that she'd weep with rage and frustration at what Tatton was putting her through — drove down to the vicarage.

Fiona opened the door. "Oh, Abby, come in. I suppose you've heard the latest news about Gregory? On top of Edward's death . . ."

"It's shocking," she agreed. Shocking that someone felt so desperate that they had been driven to such lengths. Desperate or angry . . .

And, because of those wretched seed heads, she was involved.

If it was proved that Tatton had somehow ingested the ricin at the Christmas lunch, it wouldn't matter that she swore there were no seeds left in her seed heads, there was no way of proving it and she would be found responsible.

Involved right up to her armpits.

But she'd promised Dee the table plan, which was an excuse to visit the vicarage, where Fiona could, hopefully, update her on the gossip.

"I've talked to the police," Abby explained. "They seem concerned about the chocolates that were donated anonymously and want to know exactly how many I put on the tables on Saturday. Do you still have the table plan?"

"No, but it'll be on the computer. I can print you off a copy."

"Perfect. I don't suppose you saw who delivered them?" Abby asked, following her into the office.

"The chocolates?"

"Gregory told me he found them at the entrance to the Parish hall."

"There was no name?"

"He assumed it was the new chocolate boutique drumming up business," Abby told her, "but they'd have wanted everyone to know where they came from."

"Well, yes, but they can't suspect the chocolates. Everyone had them. Nigel had two . . ."

"Two?" Abby asked. "Did someone pass theirs on to him?" If people were doing that it would mess with any calculations.

"No, there were some on the table by the grotto and Nigel helped himself to one. Gregory told him not to be greedy and swept the rest of them into his sack," Fiona told her. "I suppose, since he did all the organising, he thought he was entitled."

"Yes . . ." *Entitled* described Gregory Tatton very well. "I understand that Sandra Monkford found him on Monday morning. Did she really take him a croissant every morning?"

"Silly woman . . ." Fiona rolled her eyes. "The truth is that he was good-looking and active and a lot of these widows are lonely, but after he'd abandoned Maisie and went to Venice without her, you'd have thought they'd have been a little more cautious. Maisie's daughter realised what was going on there and took her out of harm's way."

"Yes. Thank you for her address. Going on?" Abby prompted.

Fiona, realising perhaps that she was being indiscreet, said, "Sorry, I'm rattling on here. You want the table plan."

Abby wanted to know what Maisie's daughter had said, but Fiona had turned to switch on the computer and a few minutes later the page was printed out.

"There were a couple of no-shows," she said, looking at the list. "Diana Higgins called at the last minute to say that she had a dental emergency, although she did pop in on her way home to wish everyone a happy Christmas and pick up her present from Gregory. She's one of his fans and wouldn't have passed up the opportunity to take advantage of the mistletoe."

"It's an 'ambush'," Abby said. "The collective noun for widows." And then she wished she hadn't.

The women might appear to be making all the running, but she had the strongest feeling that at least some of them were caught in an ambush of Tatton's making.

"Isn't Diana the woman who runs the seniors' Zumba class?" Abby asked.

"A real live wire. She runs along the towpath every morning," Fiona said. "Just being in the same room as her exhausts me."

She looked exhausted now, Abby thought. It couldn't be a lot of fun being a vicar's wife in a big busy parish like St Bart's. Not just a wife, but an unpaid personal assistant, always expected to have a kind word and a smile however you were feeling.

"Did you ever find the defibrillator?" Abby asked, unconvinced by Tatton's assertion that it had been rowdy youths.

"Is it missing?" Fiona put a hand to her head as if it was hurting. "Is that everything, Abby? Only, I've got to make mince pies for the Mother's Union Christmas tea and there's a pile of surplices that need ironing. Why their parents can't do it . . . Except, of course, we'd never be sure to get them back starched and ironed. People don't seem to iron anymore."

"I thought the Mother's Union and Friends of St Bart's pitched in to lighten the load."

"They take care of the church, but Nigel doesn't like to take advantage."

A consideration he didn't extend to his wife, Abby guessed.

"I'm sorry to be a nuisance, but before I go, can you give me an address for Edward's family? I wanted to send a card and I imagine they've been in touch about the funeral?"

"The funeral . . ."

Fiona paused.

"Fiona?"

"Sorry, there's just so much . . . The funeral, yes. The coroner's given the family a temporary death certificate so they can make the arrangements and Nigel went out of his way to fit it in before Christmas. It'll be next Tuesday at ten o'clock."

She wrote the address down on a notepad, tore off the sheet and gave it to her.

"Christopher, Edward's son, has been living with his father since he moved back to Maybridge. He and Stephanie came after the morning service on Sunday to arrange the funeral, but she's not local. You'll have to get her address from her brother. Thankfully the choir will all be at school, or it would mean another round of surplices to launder."

"You're clearly rushed off your feet. Why don't I see if I can get you some help?"

Abby didn't wait but took out her phone and called Pam. She answered on the first ring.

"Abby, have you heard about Gregory?" she said in a panic. "He left a message on my voicemail asking if I'd seen you, but I sent him a text saying I hadn't seen anyone because I was so sick. It's why I didn't go to the lunch because he would have known I was lying, but now I can't stop shaking. Can I come to your house?"

"I'm not there, Pam, and Lucy's at school, but I rang because Fiona, Mrs Keane, is desperate for some help and I wondered if you felt up to coming over and giving her a hand with some ironing?"

"At the vicarage?"

"Yes."

"Now?"

"She'd be really grateful."

"Okay," she said, sounding much brighter. "And Gregory won't know because he's dead. I'll just get my coat—"

"Pam, wait!"

"What?"

"I was just going to say that if you haven't got anything else planned, you're welcome to come to us for Christmas Day." She cut short a rush of thanks and turned to Fiona. "She's on her way."

"That's such a kind thought," Fiona said. "And your invitation for Pam to spend Christmas with you."

"She used to work for Howard's aunt and she spent a lot of time with Lucy when she was doing a social science project. That's how I know she likes ironing. She needed to do something with her hands while she was talking about her time in St Catherine's and it seemed to soothe her."

"Yes, well, I imagine they used the women they kept locked up as skivvies under the pretext of training them for domestic service. Punishing them for wanting to be loved. So wicked . . ." She shook her head. "Obviously I'd be grateful for her help, but I've just realised that she was the other no-show on Saturday. A stomach bug?"

"It was a diplomatic illness," Abby assured her. "Gregory Tatton had asked her out to lunch and she stood him up. No doubt she lost her nerve at the prospect of seeing him."

She suspected quite a few people would be relieved that he was dead.

And one of them had murdered him.

CHAPTER TWENTY-THREE

Abby bought a condolence card at Linda Bradley's shop and wrote it there. Edward's home wasn't far out of her way, so she could drop it in the letterbox.

He'd lived in a small artisan cottage that fronted the street and, as Abby arrived the front door opened to reveal a woman she recognised.

"Stephanie . . ."

It took Stephanie March a moment to make the connection before she exclaimed, "Abby Lawrence! I haven't seen you since high school."

"I was bringing a card. I didn't realise that Christopher was back in Maybridge or I'd have got in touch."

"It was just a few months ago. His marriage broke up and when a job came up here, well, it seemed a good idea for one of us to be close to Dad. I'm in Cheltenham. I was going to call you this evening, to thank you. The police told us what you did."

"I'm sorry I wasn't successful."

"Don't, Abby . . ." Stephanie put out a hand to reassure her. "His heart was a mess. They'd fitted a pacemaker but it seems likely that the shock stopped it. At least it was quick. The cancer was cruel."

Abby nodded. The paramedic had suggested he'd been dead before he hit the floor. At least he didn't suffer.

"Come on in. I've got to get back to work, but Chris would want to thank you himself." She stepped back to let Abby in and called, "Chris, you've got a visitor." Then, "Will I see you at the funeral? It's on Tuesday at ten."

"I'll be there."

"I don't suppose . . ." Stephanie hesitated. "You knew him when he was a teacher. I don't suppose you'd consider giving a reading?"

"I'd be honoured to. Let me know if there's something special you think he'd have liked."

"I will. Give Chris your number and I'll be in touch."

Stephanie gave a wave and Abby was left standing in the narrow hall until Christopher March appeared. He looked so like his dad that for a moment Abby struggled to speak. "Chris . . . I brought a card. I'm so sorry about what happened."

He smiled. "Abby Lawrence, or should I say local gardening celebrity Abby Finch?"

"I don't think a garden at the Maybridge Show makes me a celebrity," she replied.

"Don't undersell yourself. Next stop, Chelsea. Come on through. I'll put the kettle on."

Abby followed him into the kitchen. "I didn't realise you were back in Maybridge. Stephanie told me that your marriage has broken up. I'm sorry to hear that."

"It wasn't a big drama. To be honest I'm not sure what it was . . ." He looked a little lost, she thought. "I heard what happened to Howard. How are you coping?"

"It's not easy. We'd already split up, but we'd been married a long time so there's a lot of history. And it's tough on the children. They were angry with him for leaving us and then he was killed."

"How many have you got?"

"Three. Seventeen, fifteen in January and ten. What about you?"

"Two boys. William is twelve, Edward is nine. Claire is bringing them up for the funeral. It's all very civilised."

"That does help when there are children," she said. "Stephanie asked if I'd give a reading on Tuesday. Is that okay with you?"

He smiled. "Absolutely. Dad would have liked to have someone he'd taught there. He really missed teaching when . . . Well, you know. Tea or coffee?"

"Tea would be great." Abby hadn't intended to stay, but he looked as if he could do with some company. "Have the police talked to you about what happened?" she asked, easing herself onto a stool.

"Only that there was a fault with the wiring on the tree lights. It seems to have stopped his pacemaker." He dropped teabags into two mugs. "They told us that you tried CPR."

She nodded.

"I can't understand why he was up there in the first place. He had always been nervous of heights."

"I remember, but Gregory Tatton wanted to talk to me about his garden and he asked your father to take over the final fixings."

"Tatton? The man who was found dead on Monday?"

"Yes."

"That's weird. I've been going through Dad's papers and I found a note from him suggesting lunch at the Queen's Head. He said he'd discovered something that might interest Dad and they should have a chat."

"An expensive chat," Abby suggested, her heart picking up a beat at this evidence of contact. "Did he go, do you know?"

"Well, yes. There were several entries for meals there on a credit card statement I found. Actually they were the only entries. Dad must have applied for a new card. Probably some cashback deal."

"Probably," she said. "Were they all with Gregory Tatton? The lunches?"

"Dad never mentioned them, but the entries were every couple of weeks. You know, it's odd . . ."

She waited.

"I noticed that a couple of them were on days when he had hospital appointments. I know he kept them because I took time off work to go with him."

"And yet they were charged to his new credit card? That is odd."

Chris frowned. "I need to go through all his statements more thoroughly. It's possible his card has been cloned. Or stolen. It wasn't in his wallet. I need to get in touch with the bank and cancel it."

Abby doubted that there was any rush to cancel the card. She doubted there would be any more meals at the Queen's Head. Or anywhere else for that matter.

* * *

Abby didn't go back to her studio. Instead she drove to the Queen's Head hoping that the maitre d', who she'd been at school with, would be on duty.

She was in luck.

"Darren! Just the man I wanted to see!" Lunch was just about over and they exchanged pleasantries, catching up on news, then Abby explained why she was there.

"A cloned credit card?" Darren repeated, looking worried. "When was this?"

"Over the last few months."

"As I said, I haven't seen Mr March here for a while, but Mr Tatton has been coming for lunch every other Friday for several months. He's always with a lady."

"Oh?" That was unexpected. "Anyone you know? Can you give me her name?"

"Abby, you know I can't . . ."

"It's important, Darren, or I wouldn't ask. And if the card has been stolen . . . ?" She left him to imagine the repercussions.

He thought for a moment, then clearly realising he'd already said too much to stop now, sighed. "Okay, but you didn't hear it from me. She's not local. Her name is Barbra White. Very smart, tall, slim, short dark hair. Cashmere coat, designer dress, handmade shoes. Oh, and always a velvet beret. She leaves her coat in the cloakroom, but doesn't take off her hat."

"Could she be wearing a wig?"

"If she is, it's a very good one."

"Anything else?"

"Glasses."

"Really?" She sounded the kind of woman who'd wear contacts. Unless, of course, she wanted to disguise her appearance.

"Navy-blue kitten frames and slightly tinted lenses. And pearl earrings. They make a very handsome couple."

Clearly Darren hadn't heard the news.

"Made," she said, and broke it to him.

"He's dead? But they've a booking for Friday!"

"Mrs White hasn't phoned to cancel?"

"No, but then . . ." He gave an awkward little shrug. "I got the impression that it's an assignation," he said.

"An assignation," Abby repeated, struggling to keep a straight face.

"She wears a lot of money on her ring finger."

"She could be a widow."

"She could be," he said, doubtfully, "but you get a feeling for the out-of-hours encounters, if you know what I mean. There's a sexual frisson that you don't get with married couples."

"I see. Well, since she hasn't phoned to cancel, she may not have heard the news."

"You mean she's going to turn up here expecting to have a lovely lunch and I'm going to have to break the news?" he asked, clearly horrified.

"You don't have contact details?"

"No, but she uses the car park, so her car reg will be in the book. Can you find her from that?"

CHAPTER TWENTY-FOUR

Abby's evening was taken over by a last-minute request for a costume for Sophie's Christmas end-of-term school play.

Cara's mum, Emma, who did the evening school run, came in to deliver the news. "You've got off lightly," she said, handing over a sketch of a star. "Cara's a sheep."

"It's all a bit last minute, isn't it?"

"A gap in communication between the director and the school secretary. The WhatsApp gossip is that they haven't been on speaking terms this year."

Miss Marple doesn't have these problems, Abby thought as she sought inspiration for Sophie's costume. *She has a housemaid who lives over the garage. Or is it the stables?*

She'd just be grateful for someone to come in for a few hours a week. Maybe she should employ Pam.

In the end, an old sheet was sacrificed for the costume, along with an insert of plastic foam to give it its shape. With the addition of some tinsel stapled around the edges, and Lucy's contribution of a set of tiny battery-powered fairy lights that were draped around her dressing table mirror, it got a grudging acceptance from the star herself.

It was however, a useful excuse to duck out of a Zoom call with Jake.

She sent him a text to explain that she was in costume panic stations and then, at his request, sent him a photograph of the final result with her love and was in bed by the time she remembered that she hadn't sent Dee the details of the table layout.

* * *

"I'm so sorry I didn't get back to you yesterday," Abby said when she phoned Dee the following morning. "Life got in the way."

"But you have the number now?" Dee asked, unusually abrupt.

"Um, yes." Tatton's death was causing a lot of extra stress, Abby guessed. She should have made more of an effort to get back to Dee yesterday. Abby took a breath. "There were ten chocolates in each box and forty place settings. Pam Lewis and Diana Higgins missed lunch, but Diana arrived after the meal and might have eaten her chocolate. Gregory Tatton had eaten two and I piled the rest on the table by the grotto."

"So that would be eight chocolates."

"I didn't count, but that would seem right. I've got the list of who sat at which table, although it won't show you what chair they were in. Would you like me to send it to you?"

"If you would. Meanwhile I can check your numbers against what was found at Tatton's house and the wrappers in the recycling bin at the hall."

"Some people may have taken theirs home to pass on to a grandchild. Not everyone likes chocolate," Abby said. She was puzzled — surely who ate which chocolate wasn't that urgent. It couldn't have been in one of them or anyone could have eaten it. "And there are bound to have been some people at the lunch who weren't supposed to eat sweets at all."

"We have thought of that and we'll be checking everyone who was present."

Abby felt taken aback by Dee's chilly response.

"Is there anything else you can think of that might be useful?" Dee asked.

"No . . . Yes . . . Fiona Keane mentioned that her husband took one of the chocolates from the table by the grotto."

"The vicar?"

"Yes. That was when Mr Tatton swept the rest of the chocolates into his sack, presumably before anyone else got the same idea."

"Greedy," Dee suggested, a touch less formal.

Encouraged, Abby asked, "Can I ask if you're any nearer to finding out what happened to Edward? I understand that the coroner has only issued a temporary death certificate."

"How do you know that?" Dee asked, sharply.

Feeling on the back foot, Abby said, "Mrs Keane mentioned it when I asked about the funeral."

"Oh, I see. Well, that's perfectly normal until he's ascertained the exact cause of death."

"Is there any doubt?" Abby asked.

"Only the coroner can answer that."

"Yes, sorry, it's just that I was talking to Christopher and Stephanie March this morning. I knew them at school. They've asked me to give a reading at the funeral." Which reminded her to check if her grey coat needed cleaning. And she'd need a hat . . . "It's on Tuesday morning."

"Someone will be there to represent the force," Dee said and cut the call.

Abby was not imagining it. Dee was being very cool indeed.

Did that mean they'd found Tatton's file on the Finch family? He would have kept a copy of the photograph of Jean and almost certainly made detailed notes of any suspicions. Anything that he could use to jerk her strings and make her jump to his command.

She took a photograph of the table plans, attached it to a two-word email, *As promised*, and sent it to Dee.

Then, in an effort to find out more about the elegant Mrs White, she checked the registration number Darren had given of the Mercedes she drove and asked her search engine, *How do I find out who owns a car?*

A list of websites immediately appeared. Abby selected one that looked reputable and clicked on the link. With just the number plate, you could check whether a car had been stolen, or was a cut-and-shut put together from a couple of traffic write-offs — useful if you were buying second-hand.

It showed her every detail of the Mercedes, when it was registered, its engine number and its MOT history. It gave her everything but the name of the owner.

She had to pay a fee for *that* bit of information.

"No luck," she told Megan, later. "The Mercedes is registered to a car hire company."

"It's hired? That's interesting."

"No, it's not, it's annoying," Abby said, cross that she'd spent good money for nothing. "They'll go all data protection on me if I ask for the driver's name and address."

"True, but if she's renting a luxury car for the occasion, it's possible that Barbra White is the one hoping to catch herself a well-heeled man."

"Surely it's more likely that she's had a shunt in her own car and it's an insurance replacement while hers is in dock."

"In my considerable experience," Meg replied, "insurance companies provide something rather more basic than a high-end Mercedes to bridge the transport gap."

Abby pushed back her hair and caught a glimpse of herself in the mirror. It was a mess. It needed cutting and she hadn't had a touch-up since Howard's funeral. And the *Observer* photographer was coming on Wednesday. She scribbled another reminder beneath the one about the dry cleaners and forced herself to concentrate.

"Do you really think Tatton could have been taken in by a con woman who'd spotted him as a mark?"

"If that's her game she'll have been smart enough to let him think he was the one making the running. He did pretty well out of it with a couple of wealthy widows," Meg pointed out, "and women appear to be attracted to him, so

I doubt he'd think twice if one of them started flirting with him. Expensively dressed, driving a luxury car, he must have thought his luck was in."

"And what about her?" Abby asked.

"She'll have spotted him somewhere, and if she's a grifter, he'd look like a catch," Megan suggested. "Kingfisher Drive is prime real estate and I've done a bit of digging in the electoral rolls. I found a possible match for Elaine Tatton living under the name of Devonshire in Longbourne. The occupier's name changed to Eaton around the time that Elaine and Tatton married. I couldn't find a sale so she may have let it."

"She was divorced. It could have been a rental," Abby pointed out.

"That's true. I'll keep digging. But even if he didn't inherit property, he'll have had a good pension from his job in local government, plus whatever life insurance he collected on his wives."

"Actually, that's a thought," Megan said. "Who benefits now he's dead? Isn't that what they do in a suspicious death, follow the money?"

"Maybe we should ask one of those women who cleaned and ironed and cooked for him. They must have gone through his drawers when he wasn't looking," Abby suggested.

"If I were him, I'd keep my drawers locked and my keys in my pocket, but presumably someone passed a duster round and watered his plants when he was away. Didn't you say he was on a cruise with his second wife when she died? They're prime hunting grounds for men in search of a rich widow. And vice versa. Maybe that's where he met Mrs White."

"His first wife, Flora, was a widow. At least everyone assumes she was his first wife," Abby said. "I didn't get any-where looking for him on the internet, which is unusual. I wonder if he changed his name? How could we find out?"

"Have you talked to your solicitor yet? Freddie Jennings will know. Ask him"

"I will. And forget about cruising. Tatton was in Venice earlier this year. Barbra White could have met him there."

"Unencumbered by Maisie and not having had to spend a penny on his flight or hotel, generous entertaining would be an investment if he spotted a likely prospect," Megan agreed. "One he would need to keep warm when he got home. Which is maybe when he started using Edward's credit card to pay for their lunches."

"But why would he go to all that effort? I know the Queen's Head is pricey, but he can't be hard up."

"He'd do it because he could," Megan replied. "It's a game. Unless . . ."

"Unless what?"

"I suppose he could have lost money in dodgy investments. We need more information. You were going to give me the contact details of that woman who delivered croissants and cleaned for him."

"Sandra Monkford! Yes . . . hold on, Penny gave me her number."

"Perfect. I'll give her a call and ask her in for a chat about a job," she said, "and it wouldn't be out of the way to ask Dee if Tatton had any family. Obviously, as a prospective client, you'd want to send a condolence card."

"I doubt she'd fall for that," Abby said. "She's gone very cool and police officerish on me. I don't want her suspecting that we're poking around."

"Fair enough. Back to his lunch companion: has she called the restaurant to confirm the booking?"

"Not so far."

"But his death was on the local news."

"Darren doesn't think she's local and if, as he suspects, she's married, she wouldn't meet openly in a restaurant if there was any danger of being spotted by someone who knew her."

"And Tatton doesn't appear to have anyone rushing to put a death notice in *The Times*," Megan pointed out. "The police haven't even confirmed that it's murder. They're still toying with idea that one of your poisonous beans might have fallen in his gravy."

"Thanks for reminding me," Abby said.

"A reminder that it's important to get to the bottom of this."

"Yes, but I also need to get to the dry cleaners and go on bended knees to my hairdresser for an emergency appointment."

"You're expecting Jake home?" Meg asked.

"No, he's still locked in negotiations with a potential Italian business partner, but the *Observer* want a photograph for their piece about the show garden."

"In the meantime, what are we going to do about Mrs White?"

"Should we do anything? Whether she was a potential victim or had an agenda of her own, Tatton is dead. It's over."

"Possibly. But someone wanted him dead and she's an unknown, Abby. She could be connected to someone from his past who's targeted him in order to get inside his house. She could have done something lethal to his precious star. Or laced a capsule with ricin that he'd take when she was far away and gone. Is your smitten maitre d' going to call you if she contacts the restaurant for any reason?"

"Darren isn't smitten. He's happily married to a man he met at university. But yes. My payback for him giving me all that information is to be there on Friday and break the sad news."

"Hopefully you'll be able to figure out what's going on from her reaction . . . Oh, wait . . . It's not her real name." And she let out a hoot of laughter.

"What?" Abby demanded.

"Mrs White? Elegant, sophisticated . . ."

"Oh, great," Abby said, catching on. "Mrs White in the Queen's Head with the steak knife . . ."

CHAPTER TWENTY-FIVE

Abby dropped off her coat for an express dry clean, went into High Spirits to pay her bill, and spent the rest of the afternoon with her long-suffering hairdresser, who, having raised her eyebrows, took pity on her, squeezing her in between her other appointments.

All attempts to find a hat suitable for a funeral, both new and in the charity shops, proved fruitless.

"No one sells proper hats these days," she complained to Penny, when she called in that evening with the final list of food she needed for the party. "They're all bits of feather on a hairband. Totally unsuitable for a funeral."

"I did have a black one somewhere, but I left it behind when I moved here. I wasn't going to wear black for my sister."

"No . . ." Molly was at peace and happy to be joining her beloved Gordon. "Howard insisted I wore one when we buried his Aunt Ruth but, desperately short of cash, I was lucky enough to find one in a charity shop."

She had looked like a frump beside Izzy Hamilton.

Howard had chosen that day to present her to the world as his new partner, the perfect political wife-in-waiting, her red hair coiled and glowing against a sharp, wide-brimmed hat and wearing a black jersey dress that left no one in any doubt that she was pregnant.

Abby had made her excuses immediately after the toast. The post-funeral gathering had nothing to do with remembering his aunt, it had been about political networking. And once home, Abby had cut the shapeless charity hat into tiny little pieces and put it in her garden incinerator.

She imagined she could still catch the acrid scent of burning man-made fabric whenever she used it.

"Maybe Edward's family won't want black," Penny said. "People don't go in for that much these days."

"That's true. I'll check." Then, as Penny was running through the list she'd given her, "Has anyone said anything to you about Gregory Tatton's death?"

"What?" Penny looked up. "Oh, that. We've all had a visit from the police asking what we'd done with our chocolates, which seemed a bit strange. Do they think he was poisoned?"

"I don't know what they think. Dee is being very tight-lipped, although she did ask me about the chocolates too. Tatton gave them to me to put on the table."

"Did he buy them? He didn't say anything. It isn't like him."

"To have bought them or to not tell everyone about it?" Abby asked.

Penny thought about it. "Both."

"He told me that he found them on the table in the entrance of the hall that morning. An anonymous donation."

"Really? Why wouldn't they have come in? There were people there from early on. I dropped in first thing to help move the tables and chairs before I went to have my hair done."

"I've no idea." But it was a good question.

"I suppose we should be grateful they weren't left by some weirdo who'd decided the old were a burden to be got rid of," Penny said.

"That's a grim thought." But accepting something from an unknown donor didn't seem that sensible now Penny had put the idea into her head.

"Are you feeding the five thousand?" Penny looked up from the list Abby had given her.

"Is it too much for you? I could manage the sausage rolls—"

"No, I've got it. What time do you want to pick it up? Or if he can use your van, Cal could deliver."

"That would be perfect. Around four o'clock? If he's not doing anything else. I'd have thought Saturday would be a chance for his band to rehearse."

Penny rolled her eyes. "They'll have to do without him on Saturday. He'll be helping me."

* * *

Abby arrived home to a note pushed through the door to let her know that her High Spirits order had been left with her neighbour.

She went across to thank June and Beattie for taking it in and promised to send Tom over later to pick it up.

"You look very glamorous, Abby!" Beattie said. "Is Jake coming home today?"

"No, but he's sent a text to say he'll be back by Saturday. This is for the *Observer* photographer."

"Oh? Oh," she said, catching on, "because of your garden. Congratulations."

"Thank you. Have you heard that Edward's funeral is on Tuesday?"

"Yes, there was a message on the seniors' WhatsApp. Do you want to come in for a cup of tea?" she invited. "I heard the police think Gregory was poisoned."

"Oh? Is that more WhatsApp gossip?"

"Well, they've been asking about the chocolate, although how it could have been in one of those, I don't know. We all had some."

"Even those of us who shouldn't," June said, coming up behind her.

"Did everyone eat theirs?"

"The police asked that too. Some people kept them to pass on to grandchildren. They were so pretty. Some just handed them on to other people. Are you coming in?"

Tempting as it was to stay and listen to their gossip, she doubted they knew more than her and, making her excuses, she went home to call the chocolate boutique.

"Le Petit Chocolat . . . How may I help you?"

"It's Abby Finch, from Earthly Designs. I was helping out at the seniors' lunch on Saturday and they were given several boxes of your Christmas cracker chocolates. There was no note. We wondered if you had left them."

"The police have already asked us that, and no, they weren't from us."

"Has anyone bought a large quantity of boxes from you?"

"Again, the police asked that, but at this time of year we get a lot of multiple buys for gifts, especially for staff," the woman said, clearly irritated. Well, any rumour that their chocolates had been the cause of Tatton's death at the height of their busiest season was not going to go down well. "And a lot of people buy online."

"Of course. I'm sorry to have bothered you. Thanks for your help."

That had been a waste of time, and when she'd told Jake that she was rushed off her feet in the weeks before Christmas she hadn't been kidding. Ever since Penny had asked for the mistletoe, her time had been taken up with the ensuing drama.

If there had been no mistletoe this year, she wouldn't have been at the parish hall. She wouldn't have met Gregory Tatton and had him creeping into her life with the threat of blackmail.

And Edward wouldn't have died, because it would have been Tatton on the ladder fixing the lights.

Now her head was filled with suspicion, and questions to which there were no answers.

Were his wives' deaths really accidents?

Tatton's story was that Flora had been going to stay with a friend when she died, but could she have been leaving him? Angry? Afraid? Not giving her full attention to the road . . .

And poor Elaine, who everyone swore never touched alcohol, stumbling drunkenly down ancient stone steps. Was she really a secret drinker or had he been topping up her orange juice with vodka?

Her sister thought so.

Megan was going to try and find her, but she was busy too.

And who was Barbra White?

Was she being lined up as the third Mrs Tatton? A potential victim? Or did she have her own plans to ease him away from his money?

Or could she be planning revenge for someone she loved?

And what about all those people who were blackmailed into making Tatton's life so comfortable? Could one of them have had enough and decided to give him a shock and, in the process, killed Edward?

Or could Tatton have overreached himself and approached the wrong person? Someone who wasn't going to sit back and take it.

Someone like her.

CHAPTER TWENTY-SIX

That night, unable to sleep, Abby went downstairs and forced herself to make a list of what had to be done before Christmas. Not just the gifts still to buy, the problem of Sophie's phone and the rest of the food she needed for the party.

She still had a business to run and it wasn't all about cutting grass and planting borders. There were outside taps to be lagged against freezing, the less able would need help lifting the winter vegetables that she'd planted and Cal would have to make sure that paths and decks weren't slippery.

And she was behind with the hardwood cuttings.

The fruit bushes had been done and tucked up in their trenches, and the viburnums and jasmine. But she still needed honeysuckle, *Philadelphus*, *Cornus*. And willow and hazel. She was determined to make the most of the Linton Lodge garden before the house was sold.

She'd blitz them tomorrow after the *Observer* photographer had been.

Bugger . . . What was she going to wear?

Her phoned buzzed with a text.

Jake.

Sorry, it was a late one. I'll call you tomorrow.

She texted back. *Have you been out partying with some gorgeous Italian?*

Actually, I have.

Not what she wanted to hear . . .

There was a brief pause before a video of an extremely good-looking Italian male, older than Jake, with a touch of silver at his temples, raising a glass to her, arrived on her WhatsApp. *"Buona notte, signora! Sogni d'oro!"*

An extremely good-looking and well-wined Italian.

Our agreement was finally signed today and we've been celebrating. Nico is good company and he knows some great restaurants, but I wouldn't want to share a bed with him. Why are you still awake? Jake texted.

I'm making lists. Congratulations on the signing. I imagine you'll be spending a lot of your time in Italy now.

You could come with me. Say the word and we could start with our honeymoon.

Sogni d'oro, Jake.

I'd sleep better if . . . Then again, maybe not. I'll be home on Friday. Sweet dreams. xxx

She smiled briefly, then sighed. She missed him, but he was an added complication to an already complicated life.

She added *prune acers* to her list. She'd taught Cal the technique, so their clients' trees were safely done. It was her own garden that was becoming sadly neglected and she was running out of time for a job that should be done before Christmas.

"Sod it . . ."

She put on a coat and her boots, grabbed a torch and pair of secateurs that hung by the back door and went outside.

Abby had been working for a little over half an hour when she heard a window open.

"Mum . . ." Lucy hissed. "What are you doing?"

She didn't look up. "I'm just catching up with some pruning."

"It's the middle of the night!"

"I'm nearly done. Since you're awake is there any chance of a cup of tea?"

When she came in five minutes later, she kicked off her boots, replaced the torch and secateurs on their hooks, washed her hands, climbed on the stool beside her daughter and reached for the steaming mug that was waiting for her.

She sniffed. "Camomile?"

"It'll help you sleep."

"Oh, right . . . So why are you awake?"

"Exams. Uni. Stuff going around in my head."

Hands clamped around the mug for warmth, Abby said, "You know you can talk to me about anything that's bothering you?"

"I know."

"It may be hard to believe but I was your age once. You won't shock me."

"God, Mum . . . Why do adults always think it's about sex?"

"Well, is it?"

"No. I was thinking that I might go somewhere more local for my degree."

"Oh?" She didn't have to ask if this was about Cal. It was obvious. "I thought you couldn't wait to get to Goldsmiths."

Lucy slumped over the mug she was holding. "I might not get the grades."

"Three Bs? You'll ace it."

"I could switch to Bath. They have a really good marketing degree course."

"It's a great university, but if your heart is set on an arts career, London is the place to be."

"You want me to leave home? Get me away from Cal?"

It was a challenge and of course she dreaded the moment when her sweet, vulnerable little girl left the safety of home for London, but Abby, who'd had her own career choice cut short by her mother's failing health, didn't flinch.

"Cal is a bright young man. He's enjoying working with me for the moment, but he's ambitious and he's going to want more than I can offer. There's no reason he shouldn't go to university himself."

Lucy looked startled. It clearly hadn't occurred to her that he might be the one to move on.

"What I don't want," Abby said, "is for you to be looking back ten years from now with regret at the opportunities you've missed."

"Because that's what happened to you?" Lucy asked,

"It didn't happen to me," Abby said. "I had a choice and I put my mother first. I don't regret that."

"No. Sorry." Lucy looked at her. "If you needed me, I'd stay too."

Abby found herself on the brink of tears. "Fortunately, I don't."

"And you've got Jake."

Who would be spending time in Italy and who knows where else as his business expanded. While she was fixed in Maybridge, with school-age children and a business of her own.

"Maybe I should take a gap year," Lucy said. "Get a job or travel for a bit while I make up my mind."

On the outside Abby was acting as if this was perfectly normal. Kids took gap years and went off by themselves in their thousands every year.

Inside she was panicking . . .

London was less than a hundred miles away. But backpacking across Europe or the Far East . . .

"Work experience is always useful," she said, carefully, "and if you're not sure, then a gap year is sensible. But travel isn't cheap. If that's your plan, you're going to have to get a job like your friend, Hannah."

Lucy gave her a sideways glance, but she was grinning. "Bet you wish it was sex now . . ."

"Not entirely," Abby admitted, but looked at her mug. "Although I'm not sure that camomile tea is going to do it."

"Sorry."

"Don't be sorry. You're growing up, Lucy. I can handle it," she said with a lot more conviction than she was feeling. "Probably."

"So why can't you sleep?"

Unwilling to discuss murder, she said, "Actually, I think the midnight gardening might have done the job and we both have to be up early."

* * *

"That's a serious make-up job for double-digging," Emma said, when Abby, with a grumpy Sophie on board, stopped to pick up Cara for the morning leg of the school run.

"No one double digs these days," she replied. "We layer on loads of good compost and leave the hard work to the worms. The make-up is for the *Observer*'s photographer, but I'm hoping he's familiar with Photoshop Glow."

"Is this about the garden you're designing for the Maybridge Show?"

Abby nodded. "Gary Jackson is coming to the studio to interview me this morning. I can't say I'm looking forward to it, but publicity is part of the deal," she said. "The plan is to smile, offer him my finest coffee and biscuits and keep my fingers tightly crossed that his headline doesn't include the words 'murder victim's wife', not that I'm optimistic since this gives him the perfect excuse to revisit the Finch family history."

"Maybe you should revert to your maiden name."

"That would mean having a different name to the children."

She climbed back into the car as, undeterred, Emma leaned forward and whispered, "Or you could do Jake a favour and change it to Sullivan."

"Same problem," she whispered back. "With added emotional upheaval."

"So he's asked?"

"Not in so many words. Although he did mention a honeymoon in Italy."

"And you're hesitating? Get a grip, girl . . ." She stood back and raised her voice. "Be good, Cara. And don't forget to bring home your gym clothes."

"It's gym day?" Abby asked, horrified.

"Don't get your knickers in a twist," Sophie muttered from the back seat. "I remembered even if you couldn't be bothered. What do you care anyway?"

Cara gasped, but Abby gritted her teeth. "We'll talk about that tonight."

CHAPTER TWENTY-SEVEN

"I'm losing it, Meg. My mind is so full of other stuff I'm neglecting my kids."

"You're a great mum, Abby. Sophie will be at high school next September and any girl old enough to tell her mother not to get her knickers in a twist is old enough to take responsibility for her own stuff."

"She's my baby . . ."

"Really? She sounds like a stroppy ten-year-old who's giving you a hard time," Meg told her. "You let her get away with it this morning, but you'd better sit her down this evening and tell her that if it happens again there will be consequences. If you don't, she'll be out of control before you know it."

About to demand what the hell she knew about raising a child, Abby bit her tongue. Megan might not have any children of her own, but she was right. Sophie was suffering, and because of it she'd let her get away with behaviour that she would never have taken from the other two.

"I hear you," she said. "And I also hear Gary Jackson arriving. I've got to go."

"Abby, wait . . . I know you've good reason to dislike Gary, but you've got a business to run, so smile for camera and sell it."

"Two pep talks in one day?"

"You're welcome."

Megan was right. Abby didn't wait in her studio but slipped her padded waistcoat over the thick wool shirt and corduroy jeans that she had decided looked "smart gardener" and went out to meet Gary, offering her hand and smiling so hard that her cheeks creaked.

"Good morning, Gary. Good to see you."

"Mrs Finch . . ." he said, looking a touch startled at the unexpectedly warm welcome.

"Abby, please," she invited, dialling down the smile a touch.

"Abby . . ."

"You're on your own. I thought you were bringing a photographer with you?"

"He slipped and hurt his back, so I'm doing both jobs today," he said, reaching into the back of his car for a camera bag. "Don't worry, I've done it before."

"Oh, right. Well, would you like a tour of the garden first? Then I'll make coffee and we can chat."

He readily agreed to a quick tour of the garden, which, still sparkling from a heavy frost, was looking particularly good this morning.

"Well, this looks amazing. The last time I saw it . . ." He stopped.

"That would be when you took photographs of the garden after I found the bones of a long-dead baby," she finished for him.

She congratulated herself on not saying "sneaked in and took photographs". He knew what he'd done.

"Yes." He shrugged, admitting it, but not apologising. "It's my job."

"I understand," she said, "but today isn't about the past, it's about the future. About Maybridge and the show."

There was the briefest pause, then he nodded his agreement. "Absolutely. This is a good story." Then, looking around, "As I said, you've done an amazing job of restoring this garden. It's a real credit to you."

"I had a team of skilled people from Finch Developments to restore the buildings and do all the technical stuff. And before you ask, I paid the going rate for the job," she added.

"Do you want me to mention that?" Gary asked.

"What? No!" Then she realised that he was kidding. "Sorry. People assume . . ."

"Relax, Abby. Tell me about your garden."

"Yes . . ." She took a breath and once she'd launched into her favourite subject, she relaxed while Gary, prompting her with the occasional question, took photographs.

Inside, he took more photographs of her sitting at her drawing board on which her design was pinned.

"Are we allowed to give a few details of your design, or will it be kept under wraps until it's unveiled at the show?" he asked.

"We had to submit our designs to the committee, so now the entries have been chosen, they're no longer secret."

Abby made coffee and offered biscuits as she outlined her idea.

"Well, I can't wait to see it," he said, once he had all he needed. "And I can share some exciting news that will be in the paper this weekend. Daisy Dashwood is going to be broadcasting her television programme from the show."

"Daisy . . . ?" Genuinely thrilled, she said, "That's amazing news. I'm a huge fan of *The Potting Shed*."

"I'm afraid, since she's the home-grown celebrity, she'll get the front page, but you'll have a nice splash on page three," he said.

"She's the star," Abby agreed, then, cheekily, "Just make sure the Earthly Designs name is in the photograph you print."

He laughed. "Why don't you grab a fork or hoe and I'll take a photograph of you standing in front of your impressive gates," he said.

It couldn't have been going better but then, as he was putting the camera away in its case, he said, "You were at the parish hall when Edward March fell, weren't you? I heard you tried to revive him."

"Gary . . ." she warned.

"It's okay. I'm not . . ." He lifted his shoulders in an awkward shrug. "It's not for the paper but I thought you'd want to know that the police are taking a closer look at the tree lights. They suspect they've been tampered with."

"I . . ." She swallowed, unable to speak.

"I'm sorry. I didn't mean to upset you."

"No. Thank you for telling me. It's just that I was at school with his children." Always on her guard with the press, she instinctively chose not to say that Edward had taught her, although if he put the dates together he could work that out for himself. "They'll be devastated."

As Gary left, she returned the hoe to the tool store, grabbed her favourite pair of secateurs and, imagining that the shrubs were whoever had killed Edward, she cut until her fingers hurt.

* * *

Abby was heeling the last of the cuttings into the prepared trenches when Cal arrived on his motorbike.

"Wow, you've been busy." Then seeing her face, "Are you okay, Abby?"

Her hands were sore and her back ached but she straightened and managed a smile. "It's nothing a hot bath won't fix. What have you been up to?"

"Lagging taps?" he reminded her. "Checking that paths and decking are clean so no one slips. Lifting vegetables."

"All done?"

"All done," he assured her. "I was going to help you with this."

"You can do it next time," she said, easing her back. "I think we should both take the afternoon off. Why don't you give Lucy a treat and pick her up from school?"

"On my bike?" he asked, nervously.

"I don't imagine it will be the first time. You did buy a second helmet the moment you passed your test." She

161

raised an eyebrow and, bless him, he looked really guilty. "Of course, you could take the van now you've passed that test too—" *first time and so cocky with it* — "but everyone will think it's her mother."

"I'm really careful on the bike," he said.

"I know you are." The thought of her beautiful girl on the back of a motorbike made her feel queasy, but she'd rather it was out in the open. "It's everyone else you have to watch out for." She dismissed him with a backhand wave, as the phone began to ring. "Go, I'll lock up."

She had six rings before it went to the answering machine. She made it on the fifth. An unknown number.

"Earthly Designs."

"Mrs Finch?" A woman's voice. Not anyone she recognised.

"This is Abby Finch. How can I help you?"

"It's Heather James. You emailed me about my mother. Maisie Goodyear."

"Oh . . . Yes . . ." She lowered herself onto her chair. "Thank you for getting back to me. How is your mother now?"

"Physically recovered. I can't say the same about her state of mind. I don't think she cares about the money, it's the fact that it was all a lie. That Tatton was just using her . . ."

"I'm so sorry."

"We were completely oblivious," Mrs James told her. "She seemed so happy. It was only when she was here recovering that I realised she had paid the whole cost of the Venice trip. That's when we looked more closely at her bank statements . . ."

"There was more?" She wasn't going to drop Ryan in it by mentioning the wine bill.

"A lot more. I suppose I should be grateful for that dodgy prawn or who knows how long it would have gone on. The bastard actually sent flowers and a card saying that he'd see her when he got back from Venice."

"Did he try to see her?"

"Yes, but we told him she wasn't well enough for visitors and he must have realised the game was up when we put her house on the market, because he hasn't been in touch since."

"Did you tell the reverend, Nigel Keane, what he'd been up to?"

"Yes. I told him that he needed to watch out in case he did the same thing to some other poor woman. Is that what's happened? You've just inherited that big estate and your husband's company, haven't you? I read about his death in the papers. I'm sorry for your loss."

"Thank you."

"Anyway, that's the reason I called. To warn you. Tatton may not have done anything that's actually illegal but he's a leech. It wasn't just the Venice trip. Mum paid for it because he promised to repay her when some undoubtedly mythical investment matured, and since she thought he was going to marry her . . ."

"It had got that far?" Abby asked.

"Oh, yes. Mum had loaned him the money to have a new kitchen and bathroom installed."

"Surely he paid that back."

"Our solicitor wrote asking for him to return the money since it was loaned, but he insisted it was a gift and of course there was no paperwork."

And in the meantime he'd come up with a plan to bank Maisie's money and get it done for free by Finch Developments . . .

"We discussed taking it to court," Mrs James continued, "but there was no way I could put Mum through the stress of that."

"I understand, but her bank will have details of the transfer. I'm not a lawyer, but it might be possible to claim it from his estate," Abby suggested.

"His estate?"

"Mr Tatton died last Saturday."

There was a sharp intake of breath. "Painfully, I hope."

"The police suspect that he may have been poisoned."

"By some other poor woman he'd scammed out of her savings, no doubt."

"It may have been accidental," Abby said. "They're still investigating. Did your mother ever mention if he had any family?"

"No, and you'll understand that we don't want to grill her, but his second wife had a sister. It seems that she wrote to my mother warning her about him. She believed that he'd caused her sister's death. Of course, we're only hearing all this now."

"What did your mother do?" Abby asked. "When she received the letter."

"She showed it to him." She sighed. "Of course Tatton convinced her that the woman just couldn't accept that her sister was an alcoholic."

"Does she still have it. The letter?"

"No, Tatton tore it up and threw it on the fire."

Of course he did. He couldn't risk anyone else seeing it.

"I don't suppose your mother noticed her address? I'd really like to talk to her — the sister," she added, to be clear.

"Mum could only remember that it was a business letterhead and the address ended in 'ham'."

"So perhaps Melksham, Chippenham, Corsham," Abby prompted.

"I'm sorry I can't be more helpful."

"No, thank you for calling me back and being so frank. If your mother should think of anything else . . ."

"I'll let you know. I just hope that whoever put rat poison in his tea gets away with it."

And with that she hung up.

"Whew . . ." Abby let out a long breath. There was anger to spare and plenty of motive there. That parting shot was heartfelt.

Or purposefully used to disguise her guilt?

There was no way of knowing without solid evidence and, gathering herself, Abby put *Yvonne Thompson, Wiltshire, Somerset* into her search engine.

It came up with a long list, most of which only matched part of her search terms. Some had different spellings, but the newspaper might have got that wrong.

She finally narrowed it down to half a dozen possibles and then began to work her way through the list.

The first two had moved on. The third turned out to be dead, which resulted in a long conversation with her husband who, assuming that she was one of his wife's friends who hadn't heard the news, launched into an emotional description of her end.

Abby listened, adding only the odd "Oh, dear . . ." and "I'm so sorry", allowing him to unburden himself.

Thankfully, the next call, to a hairdressing salon in Keynsham, produced a positive response.

"Yvonne? Were you a client?"

"No. I was hoping to talk to her about her sister."

"Poor Elaine . . . Yes . . . That was so sad. They hadn't talked for years and she felt so guilty about not being there for her. She had a bit of a bee in her bonnet about the husband. Thought he was responsible for her death. Did you know her?"

"Elaine? I'm afraid not, but I wondered if Yvonne had heard that Elaine's husband, Gregory Tatton, has died. It was on the local news but I'm not sure if you get that . . ." Then, belatedly picking up on the "were", she said, "But I gather she's not at the salon now."

"That's right. She sold it to me six months ago and moved to Longbourne."

"Longbourne?" That was where Elaine lived before she married Tatton.

"It's on the river," the woman told her. "She showed me pictures of her cottage. Thatched. Very chocolate box."

"It is a pretty village," Abby said. "I used to work there."

"Oh, right. Well, hold on and I'll give you her number and you can tell her the good news."

Abby sat for a moment, wondering what she was going to say to Yvonne. Then, as it occurred to her that the woman she'd spoken to might have had second thoughts about passing on the number and called Yvonne to warn her, she wasted no more time in making the call.

It went straight to voicemail.

"I'm sorry I can't take your call right now. Leave your number and provided you're not trying to sell me something I'll get back to you."

Abby decided against leaving her name and hung up.

The phone instantly rang, making Abby jump, but Christopher March's name popped up.

"Chris . . ."

"You sound breathless. Have I caught you at a bad time?"

"No. No . . . How are you?"

"Good, thanks. Stephanie asked me to call and let you know that she'd like you to read a poem called 'As We Look Back' by Clare Jones. It's online."

"Okay, I'll look for it. Can I ask you about the dress code for Tuesday? Or is that above your pay grade?"

He laughed. "You've got me. Stephanie has decreed anything but black."

Abby had been joking, sort of, but wasn't entirely surprised it was Stephanie who made the decisions. "And what has she decreed about flowers?"

"Charitable donations. The undertaker has all the details."

"Okay, but can I organise something seasonal to decorate the church?"

"That's a kind offer, but I wouldn't know what to do with it."

"The flower arrangers will be decorating the church for Christmas anyway. Would you like me to ask them to put something together?"

"Well then, yes, that would be very kind. Maybe I could take you out to lunch one day? To thank you. Are you free this week?"

"I'm afraid not, but I'm having some people for drinks on Saturday. Just a thank-you to people who have supported me since Howard died. I know you've only recently returned to Maybridge, and if you feel up to socialising, it would be a chance to meet a few people."

"Well, yes . . . Thank you."

"Oldfield Cottage, Mill Lane. From about seven until nine. There will be food."

"I'll be there."

"Great." She hesitated, then went for it. "Have you heard any more about your father's death?"

"Someone rang from the coroner's office this morning to update me on the situation. Apparently, they're still awaiting the results on the lights from forensics before they can issue a death certificate. I assume it must be something to do with health and safety at the hall. What made you ask?"

"It's just that I know the vicar is worried that if there's an inquest, he'll be held responsible."

"If he's worried about a claim for compensation, I know that Dad wouldn't have wanted that."

She made some non-committal sound, repeated that she hoped to see him on Saturday and disconnected.

Edward March might not have wanted his family to put in a compensation claim, but Stephanie was clearly the one making the decisions, and the possibility of a considerable payout would always be a temptation.

She called the head of the church flower arranging group, who'd already been given free rein to take whatever she needed from the Lodge garden for the church and asked if someone could make a special arrangement for Edward.

"There's wintersweet, jasmine and plenty of Christmas roses," Abby said. "There's no one to see them, so take what you need."

Then, resisting the call of a hot bath, she did a quick run around the supermarket before driving along the river to Jake's boathouse.

It was cold and, apart from a couple of visits to make sure all was well, it had been shut up for the best part of three weeks and there was a damp, musty smell.

She opened it up to air it, stocked the fridge with essentials and removed the layers of dust. It was heated by a wood-burning stove which wouldn't be safe to leave unattended, but she'd brought along an oil-filled radiator that was her standby for power cuts.

The houseboat had been fine in the summer, fun even, but why he'd insisted on staying there when Megan had found him at least three perfectly good houses with the desired river frontage and a reasonable garden, she couldn't imagine.

The bedding and mattress felt decidedly damp and she put the heater as close to the bed as was safe before gathering the bedding to put through the wash to get rid of the smell.

That done, she braced herself to explain to her youngest that feeling sad and angry was no excuse for rudeness.

There were going to be tears before bedtime and she had a feeling that they wouldn't all be Sophie's.

CHAPTER TWENTY-EIGHT

Normally Emma would just drop off Sophie after school, but that afternoon, she came to the door alone.

"I've left Sophie in the car. We've had a few tears. She's nervous about facing you after this morning."

"That's understandable . . . Thanks, Em. I'll come and get her."

Her baby's forlorn and tear-stained face was heart-wrenching, but she took her hand and stood and waved while Emma drove off with Cara. "Shall we have a cup of tea and a little chat about what happened this morning?"

Sophie shuddered in the aftermath of tears but nodded, her repeated "sorry" coming through stuttering bursts of misery.

"Okay . . . I've got it," Abby said, struggling to hang onto her own tears as she gave her a hug. Then, because she couldn't put it off, "I know that you're sad about Daddy and angry. That's natural. We're all sad, so it's not fair or kind to take out your feelings on the rest of us. Do you understand?"

She swallowed, nodded.

"I need to hear you say it, Sophie."

"I understand."

"You can come to any of us when you need a hug, or to talk about Daddy, or we can just sit and think about him together."

She nodded again.

"Good girl. Now it's my turn." She apologised for forgetting that it was gym day and congratulated her on handling it herself.

"Lucy reminded me," Sophie admitted. "She said you were really busy and she found my gym kit for me."

"That was good of her but you're growing up, Sophie. You'll need to remember a lot more things when you're at high school next year and I think it would be a good idea to start practising now. Let's make a date for the holidays to design and print a wall planner."

Sophie brightened a little. "Like the ones Lucy and Tom have?"

"Absolutely. You can put in all the things you have to remember, and you can check it every night and get everything ready for the morning. Now, I've had a really busy day and I'm going to have some toast. Can I tempt you?"

"I could make it," Sophie offered.

"Great. All we have to decide is what we're going to have on it. Marmite, jam, peanut butter . . ."

"Urgh! Peanut butter sticks to your mouth. It's totally gross . . ."

Abby grinned.

"Oh, you were kidding."

They were both laughing at one of the kittens swinging on a swag of tinsel when Tom and Lucy arrived home, with Cal tagging along.

Leaving them to decimate a loaf of bread, Abby went to look up the poem that Stephanie had requested.

It didn't have the grandeur or beauty of Rossetti or Shakespeare, but it was heartfelt and spoke to a fractured relationship.

Chris hadn't mentioned his mother. Abby wondered if she'd be at the funeral. To support her children if nothing else.

Saddened, she gave Lucy her credit card and carte blanche to order a take-out supper for everyone, bagging the hot comfort of a chicken jalfrezi for herself, then went for the long overdue soak in a hot bath.

* * *

The intention had been to put everything out of her mind, forget about the women who'd died in dreadful accidents, the women who'd believed a mendacious and manipulative man.

But Abby's brain refused to slow down and succumb to the relaxing scent of the lavender bath bomb.

It wasn't just the emotional turmoil that refused to let up. She had to finish the online delivery coming on Saturday with stuff for the buffet.

She kept running everything through her head, worrying about what she might have forgotten, and in the end gave up, hauled herself out of the bath and, determined to get an early night, put on her PJs and her dressing gown before going downstairs to check what she had in stock. Most of it was there, but she added sour cream for the blinis before calling Megan to update her on her conversation with Maisie's daughter.

"Wow. That's a motive right there."

"I agree," Abby said. "It's a lot of money, but would you kill someone over it?"

"I wasn't thinking so much about the money but the emotional betrayal. How would you feel if someone had treated your mother that way?" Megan asked.

Abby didn't have to use her imagination. She only had to think of her own mother, widowed so young, standing on an airfield as her beloved husband was carried from the plane in a flag-draped coffin. Stiff, holding back her tears through the funeral until she'd got home and broken down. She had never fully recovered. Dying long before her time . . .

You couldn't fight back against war, but if a man had done that to her mother, she would have felt murderous.

And she had an entire garden from which to pick her weapon.

"Abby?" Megan prompted.

"Sorry. Yes. It's what he's done to her mother that's upset Heather James more than anything. The cynical betrayal." She repeated Heather's hope that his death had been painful and her parting shot about the rat poison. "She made no attempt to hide the fact that she was glad he was dead."

"Revenge is a powerful motive. Just because she didn't disguise her anger, we shouldn't discount her. The chocolate boutique is a chain. I wonder if they've got one where she lives?"

"I've no idea. I only had an email address. I did call the shop to ask if they'd donated the chocolates — they hadn't — or if someone had come in and bought multiple boxes. The police had already been there asking the same questions."

"The police can check the card receipts. We don't have that luxury. What we need to concentrate on is how could someone have got the poisoned one to Tatton? You're sure it couldn't have been in the boxes you put out?"

"No, that was completely random. There must have been another box," Abby said, "but there wasn't one at Tatton's house. Just empty wrappers."

"If the poisoner was at the lunch, they could have left the chocolates — it would explain why there was no name with them — and had a poisoned one with them and passed it to him."

"Still risky. He might have taken it into his head to give it to one of his helpers. A reward . . ."

"Don't!" Abby shuddered. "I can see him handing one to some poor woman with that mendacious smile."

"You said he swept chocolates from the table by the grotto into his sack. Maybe the poisoner took the chance to add theirs to his sack when they were collecting their gift."

"That sounds more likely. Sandra Monkford was at the lunch," Abby said. "Have you talked to her yet?"

"Yes. I called her and said I'd heard that she'd lost an employer and wondered if she was looking for a few hours. She leapt at the chance, so I invited her in for a chat this afternoon."

"She's looking for paid work?"

"It's the very best kind," Megan pointed out.

"True, so why was she wasting her time cleaning up for Tatton for sweet nothing?"

"I can tell you that."

"Oh?"

"When she arrived at my office she was clearly very nervous, explaining that she hadn't actually been employed as a cleaner. She'd just helped out a friend because he had a heart problem. He'd died, she told me, and she didn't know what she'd do with herself."

"All that dicky-ticker stuff was a lie," Abby told her. "Tatton as good as admitted it to me, and Iain Glover confirmed that there was nothing wrong with his heart."

"There's a surprise. Not."

"Did they all go along with it because it gave them a legitimate reason to be helping him?"

"Apart from their eagerness to be the third Mrs Tatton?" Megan asked.

"Not all of them were women."

"Point taken. Anyway, I explained to Sandra that our high-end rentals are offered cleaning and gardening contracts and I'm always looking for good people, and then I asked for her employment history. I explained it didn't matter what she did, I just needed to be able to check that she hadn't been in prison. She twitched a bit at that, but wrote down a list of employers and dates."

"Did it tally?" Abby asked.

"Very straightforward. Retail until her son was born. She was a stay-at-home mum until he went to pre-school, and after that there was a long list of part-time jobs in retail and offices. Then she was warden in a complex for retirees."

"Did she say why she left that job?"

Megan sighed. "Damn fool rules meant they had to retire her when she hit sixty. I phoned to check for a reference and they were devastated to let her go. Anyway that was when she moved to Maybridge to live with her son and daughter-in-law."

"Why would she do that when her daughter-in-law clearly doesn't want her there?"

"That's where it gets interesting," Meg told her. "When I explained to Sandra that we'd have to do a DBS check, she immediately said she couldn't take the job."

"Oh . . . ?"

"I suggested she tell me what was worrying her and maybe we could work around it, and she sort of crumpled."

"Oh, good grief. That must have been awkward."

"Abby, in my business you see it all — death, divorce, tears and tantrums . . . I applied the customary tea, tissues and patience and out it all came. Sandra is not a widow. Mr Monkford is very much alive and serving a lengthy stretch for fraud. He was apparently using company funds to feed an online gambling habit."

Abby let out a little huff of breath. "Oh . . ."

"Sandra didn't have a clue until he was arrested. He was in debt up to the eyebrows, maxed out credit cards and her home had been mortgaged to the last penny. She lost everything."

"Poor woman."

"In every sense of the word," Megan agreed. "When she was forcibly retired from the warden post her son, very grudgingly, took her in, but she had to swear to keep quiet about his jailbird father."

Hence the sour-faced daughter-in-law.

"If that's the dirty secret that Tatton discovered," Abby said, "it's no wonder she was desperate enough to clean and feed him expensive croissants. Her home depended on it. But how on earth did he find out?"

"How hard could it have been?" Megan said. "A new woman joins the seniors and the first thing he's going to do is check her out to see if she's worth cultivating. The case must have been in the papers, and for someone used to digging around, I don't imagine it took him long to find out the truth. I imagine he invited her for coffee at the Buttery, casually drops enough of a hint to let her know that he knows all about her, so that when he asks her to do something for him—"

"Like, 'I really enjoy the croissants they make here. If someone were to bring me one every morning . . .'"

"Precisely. It pretty much confirms our suspicions about the bastard. I can't give the poor woman a home of her own, but I've always got empty flats and houses that need a thorough clean before they can be put on the market. I've given her a couple of those. Once the DBS comes back clean, I'll give her as many hours as she wants."

"Fingers firmly crossed for both of you. And unless she's a superb actress, we can cross her off the suspect list."

"Who else is on it now?"

"Good question, let's write it down." Abby grabbed a notebook and pen.

"Have you got that woman who works in the bookshop café?" Megan asked.

"Trish Porter," Abby confirmed. "What could she have done to get in his little black book?"

"It doesn't have to be anything very terrible. Just something they're ashamed of," Meg pointed out.

"She's on the list, although frankly she doesn't seem to have enough 'go' about her to turn to murder."

"The worm can turn. And didn't you mention a man who cut his grass until he had a stroke? I imagine he has a family who might have realised what was going on."

"Yes . . ." Abby tried to remember the name. "Paul something. Paul Jefferson. But that's pushing it a bit."

"They might have blamed Tatton for his stroke. Did he survive? Maybe he kept a diary, the detective's friend."

"Even if he did," Abby protested, "he must have done something that Tatton found out about, and his family aren't going to tell us that. But there is another man. David Hogg."

"The painter and decorator? He used to do work on our rentals."

"Well, Ryan at High Spirits told me that he painted Tatton's kitchen after a fire. When he sent in his bill, Tatton said he thought he was doing it as a favour."

"That would certainly make him angry. Angry enough to kill?" Megan asked. "It wouldn't have been more than a few hundred pounds."

"Unlikely, but while he was doing the job, he could have let someone in quite innocently," Abby said, getting quite excited by the idea. "One of his helpers who said they were delivering something or had come to do a job."

"I still think Heather James is a strong contender."

"I really hope not, but she's on the list," Abby said, adding her. "And Beattie mentioned a woman who does his shopping. Linda . . ." She thought for a minute. "Linda Bradley. And someone called Wendy."

"We need to find out more about these people. Find out what they did before they retired."

"Beattie and June probably know everything about them, but if I get too inquisitive they'll begin to suspect something. June will, anyway."

"You could tell them I'm looking for cleaners, which is always true. Ask if they think any of women who fussed around Tatton might like a few hours."

"Okay, but not tonight. I've had a bath, I'm in my PJs and — oh sugar, that's the doorbell. It'll be the food . . . Can someone answer that!" she called.

There was no response. After a moment there was a second, rather more emphatic peel on the bell. "Hang on, Meg, I'm just getting the door . . ."

"Abby? Are you okay?"

"I'll see you tomorrow, Meg," she said, as Jake took the phone from her, and then she didn't say anything for quite some time.

CHAPTER TWENTY-NINE

"Oh, hi Jake . . . I thought it was the food." Tom was standing in the doorway grinning. "Mum wasn't expecting you until tomorrow."

"Which is why I was able to take her by surprise." Jake released her and picked up a handful of glossy carriers he'd dropped in the hall. "Your rugby shirt," he said, handing one to Tom as Abby shut the front door and led the way through to the kitchen.

"Thanks, Jake. How much do I owe you?"

"Nothing."

"Oh, but—"

"Open it and you'll see."

Tom took the package from the carrier and ripped it open. And then, as he held up a muddy, slightly stinky shirt, he did. "Oh . . . But this is . . ."

"Nico, my new Italian business partner knows the father of Italian fly-half Paolo Garbisi. The shirt goes with box seats at the next England–Italy international at Twickenham, where you'll get a chance to thank him in person."

Tom for once was speechless. "This is . . . well . . . it's . . . I don't know what to say."

"Always the best response to a gift. And I haven't forgotten the girls. Sophie, Lucy . . ." Sophie's eyes lit up as he handed the second carrier to her.

"What is it?"

"Sophie — where are your manners?"

"Sorry. Thank you, Jake."

"Have you eaten?" Abby asked, while the girls took more care with their beautifully tissue-wrapped gifts. "I left the children to order take-out, so you'll be saving us from eating cold pizza for breakfast."

"I like cold pizza," Tom said, "but there's also chicken, and Mum ordered curry."

Jake grinned. "It's good to be home."

"If I'd known—"

He raised an eyebrow. "You'd have baked a cake?"

"I'd have gone back to the houseboat and lit a fire for you."

He just looked at her and said, "No need. I'm already blazing . . ."

There were squeals of delight from both girls as they unfurled long, silk chiffon scarves. Sophisticated shades of aqua for Lucy, subtle pinks for Sophie.

Lucy immediately draped hers around her neck. "Thank you so much, Jake. I love it."

"Thank you, Jake," Sophie echoed, copying her sister. "I love it too."

"You're welcome. Do you want to pass the other bag to your mother, Sophie?"

"You've been very generous, Jake, but the request was for sun."

"There wasn't any," he said, "so shoot me."

The name on the bag Sophie handed her, Borsalino, seemed familiar but she couldn't think why. The contents, bulkier than a scarf, were swathed in a cloud of tissue paper. Searching, her hands touched something silky soft, then she felt the brim . . .

"How did you know I wanted a hat?" But even as the words left her mouth she knew. He hadn't bought her a hat because she needed one for the funeral. This was the sleuth hat Megan suggested she ask Jake to bring from Rome . . . She shook her head. "Megan."

"She said you wouldn't ask."

"She was right . . ." But as she took out the fedora, the rich, deep red of Rosa *Grande Dame*, with a slightly darker silk band, she let out a little sigh of pure pleasure. "Oh my God, it's beautiful."

"Put it on," Lucy urged.

Abby set it on her head. "What do you think?"

Jake reached out and tilted it slightly before turning her so that she could see her reflection in the bi-fold doors — skin shining from her bath, PJs, faded dressing gown. She looked at the hat.

"I think I'm in love," she said, and unwilling to kiss him in front of the children, touched his arm. "Thank you."

"And once again, the perfect response."

"It will look better when I'm dressed," she said, without thinking.

He said nothing. He didn't have to. A sideways look, an almost imperceptible twitch of his lips, had her self-consciously tightening the belt of her dressing down. "I was planning on an early night."

"Abby, Abby, Abby . . ." he murmured. "I ate on the train, so Tom can have pizza for breakfast, but I wouldn't say no to a decent cup of tea."

Lucy and Tom both leapt to do it. Tom was first to the kettle, Lucy got the mugs down and added the teabags. Sophie, trailing her scarf, took the milk from the fridge.

Such rare cooperation . . .

"I'm sorry to spoil the mood," Abby said, "but the houseboat felt really damp when I went there today."

"No surprise there."

"No, really. I had to bring your bedding home and put it through the washing machine to get rid of the musty smell. I took an oil-filled radiator which I hope will have dried out the mattress . . ." Afraid that she was blushing, she said, "You really need to move into somewhere sensible."

"I've always thought sensible was overrated," he said, with a look that invited her to be anything but.

"You should stay here tonight," Tom said, with just a hint of a smirk. "The sofa in the den is a pull-out."

"Thank you, Tom, but I called in a neighbourly favour when I touched down and the stove has been lit. I only called in to give you your gifts."

"Leggy Laura lit your fire?" Abby asked.

He grinned. "Heaven forbid. I would never ask her to risk those long nails. Not now she's got a muscular Scandinavian at her beck and call."

"So useful," she replied, curling her own nails, kept short for practicality, into the palms of her hands.

Tea consumed, Abby went to collect his bedding from the airing cupboard. He was waiting for her at the bottom of the stairs. "Your quilt isn't quite dry, but I have a spare you can borrow . . ."

Taking advantage of the fact that she had her arms full, Jake gathered her in and held her. "Will I see you tomorrow? Lunch at the Pike and Heron?"

Followed by an afternoon checking that the bed was thoroughly aired . . . "I wish," she said, "but I have a meeting."

"You didn't keep the day clear when you were expecting me home? Should I be worried?"

"Don't be ridiculous. Something unexpected came up."

"Dinner, then?"

"I'll be cleaning and prepping for the party."

"I could help," he pointed out.

"Tempting as that is, you'd be a distraction."

"I do hope so. Okay, what time do you want me on Saturday? I'm available for furniture shifting and general dogsbodying whenever you want me."

"The children will help with the dogsbodying and I'll need time to get ready. You can arrive at ten minutes past seven. Not a minute before."

"That's very specific . . . Oh, I get it."

"You do?"

"You want people to see me arrive."

"Jake . . ."

"You don't want these people, some of whom you don't know that well, thinking that you've moved in your lover barely six months after your husband was killed."

She swallowed. "Please, Jake . . ."

"Even though he'd already deserted you for another woman who was pregnant with his child."

Then, cupping her cheek in his hand, he looked at her for a moment before taking the bedding from her arms and walking out to his car. He threw it on the back seat, climbed behind the wheel and, without another word, backed carefully out of the drive.

Abby, not sure if she was angry with him or with herself, watched until his lights disappeared down the lane, then stood gulping in deep breaths of the frosty air until the scooter arrived with their food.

CHAPTER THIRTY

Friday was always busier in the town and the bar of the Queen's Head was packed with business people meeting for lunch.

Abby, informed by Darren that Mrs White hadn't phoned to check on the booking, was sitting at a table in the reception area where she could see people arriving.

Would she turn up?

If she had left a poison time-bomb for Tatton, surely she'd be keeping an eye on the local news, wanting to know if it had gone off?

She hadn't called the Queen's Head to confirm the booking but had she tried calling Tatton? Or were phone calls off limits since they'd leave a record for a suspicious husband to find? Or suspicious police officers.

Whatever the truth, Megan was right. There was something off about this.

The thought evaporated as at ten minutes to one, Mrs White stepped through the impressive double doors.

Darren had described her perfectly. She was tall, slender, elegant in her cashmere coat with a pale-blue velvet beret worn at a saucy angle atop her dark curls.

She stopped at the desk to leave the details of her car, at which point Darren, who'd been watching for her arrival, approached her.

"Mrs White . . ."

"Darren . . ." She smiled. "Am I the first to arrive?"

"Yes . . . At least . . . Would you mind stepping into the office for a moment?" Abby saw him glance across at her and she rose to her feet. "Mrs Finch would like a word."

Barbra White turned to look at her, an assessing glance that took in every detail of her appearance. Then, with a smile she said, "Great hat."

"Thank you," Abby said.

Barbra White looked back to Darren. "What's this about?"

He stood back and indicated his office. With a sigh, she went in, and Abby followed her. "I have to get back to the restaurant," Darren said, "but Cindy's on the desk and she'll get anything you want."

Mrs White turned to Abby. "What is this?" she repeated.

Abby indicated one of the two comfortable chairs that Darren had placed for them to use. "You might want to sit down, Mrs White."

Barbra looked at the glasses, brandy, water and box of tissues on the table. "This doesn't look good."

"No," Abby said. "I'm very sorry to have to tell you that Mr Tatton, Gregory, died on Saturday."

Barbra White sank into the nearest chair, looking genuinely shocked. Abby poured some water into a glass and offered it to her.

"I'll take the brandy," she said.

"It's up to you but I thought, since you're driving . . ."

"Drat." She took a breath. "Who exactly are you? A friend, a relation? He never mentioned a daughter."

Not "how did he die . . . ?"

"I'm just an acquaintance. Mr Tatton wanted me to do some work on his garden."

"Oh, yes, he was talking about that the last time we met. He said he knew a talented local garden designer who'd offered to do it for him if she could use the photographs to promote her new business."

183

So, that's how he did it. A subtle suggestion that he knew your dirty little secret and then the offer of a face-saving way of explaining why you were working for nothing.

"I hadn't got beyond measuring up."

"Even so, I don't understand why his gardener would come to tell me that he was dead."

"I'm not sure anyone else knew about your lunches."

"I hope not. I'm in the middle of a divorce, and if my husband found out . . ." She let that hang.

"You're not local?"

She shook her head. "Oxford. I met Gregory in Venice. Charles and I went there for our honeymoon and I wanted to recapture a time when I was happy. Recapture myself, maybe."

"I understand. I've been through it. Although with three children, Venice wasn't an option. Not that we had a honeymoon. I was pregnant at the time . . ."

Abby stopped, unable to believe she'd said that. She was here to get information, not pour out her own life story, but Mrs White's face had softened into a sympathetic smile.

"Look, I've driven from Oxford, I'm starving and I don't want to eat on my own. The table is booked. Will you join me, Mrs Finch?"

Abby, for whom breakfast was a distant memory, thought that was a very good idea. "I'll check that the table is still available. And please, call me Abby."

"Darren said you might want to stay," Cindy said, taking their coats and showing them to a quiet spot in the corner of the restaurant.

"And if you've got a room, I'll stay the night," Mrs White added.

"I'll check."

Mrs White took her time over the menu, chose a wine that Abby knew from her rare visits to the restaurant would be eye-wateringly expensive.

That done, she sat back and said, "Men, generally, keep their brains in their trousers. My husband is besotted with a girl the same age as his daughter. He was an attractive man when I married him. He still is to me, but the reality is that he's put on weight and is losing his hair. I hoped that, if I didn't make a fuss, he'd get it out of his system, see how ridiculous it was. When I realised that wasn't going to happen . . ."

"You took yourself off to Venice and met Gregory Tatton?" Abby guessed.

"We were staying at the same hotel. I was alone, he was alone . . ."

Here came the bit where Mrs White might lose her appetite. "I hate to break it to you, Mrs White—"

"Barbra. My mother named me after Barbra Streisand but actually I prefer Barb."

"I hate to break it to you, Barb, but Mr Tatton was alone because the woman who had paid for the trip, who thought he was going to propose to her while they were there, had been taken ill with food poisoning."

"What?" She was definitely shocked. "He was going to marry her?"

"She certainly thought so."

"He broke it off because of our fling?"

"No. While her daughter was looking after her, she discovered that her mother had not only paid for the Venice trip for both of them but had loaned Mr Tatton a substantial sum of money to make improvements to the house. When asked for its return, he claimed it had been a gift."

"He hasn't asked me for money," Barb said, instantly on the defensive.

"I imagine it was a little too soon for that. He may not have told you, but both his previous wives were comfortably well-off. A widow and a divorcee."

"Both? What happened to them?"

"One died in a car accident, one in a fall. I don't know how you'll come out of your divorce, Barb, but it's possible he was setting you up for number three."

"Christ . . ."

The sommelier had arrived with the wine and, having removed the cork, offered Barb a taste. "Just pour it," she said, downing it the minute he'd filled her glass.

He glanced, expressionless, at Abby, who nodded. He filled her glass then refilled Barb's before making a dignified retreat.

Wine consumed and ready to face the worst, Barb said, "And now Gregory is dead. What happened?"

"He appears to have been poisoned. It's possible it was accidental, but the police are talking to everyone who knew him."

"God, no! If my husband finds out . . ."

Abby noted that she was more worried about that than concerned about Tatton.

"Who are you!"

Startled, Abby looked up at a man approaching their table. A touch overweight, thinning hair . . .

"Speak of the devil," murmured Barb. "Abby, may I introduce my husband, Charles White."

"Abby Finch, Earthly Designs, Mr White. How d'you do?" Abby offered her hand, but stayed seated. He ignored it. "Barb and I have been having meetings to discuss her garden makeover for a while," she said, hoping against hope that Barb didn't live in a high-rise apartment.

"What?" He looked confused.

Barb was quick on the uptake. "You know how I hate all those ghastly rhododendrons, Charles. One flash of colour in the spring and then that bank of boring, boring green for the rest of the year."

"So heavy, so dark," Abby agreed. "And nothing for the wildlife."

"Wildlife?" he repeated.

"Abby's going to remove them for me," Barb explained, now clearly enjoying herself.

"Absolutely. We're going for something much more eco-friendly," Abby said, fishing out her phone and finding the design for a wildlife garden she'd be creating in the new year. "Like this," she explained, holding her phone up so that he could see.

He stared at it for a moment then, appalled, said, "Those are weeds!"

"The term *weed* is so dated," Abby said with a pitying sigh. "These plants are vital for the sustainability of the planet. You need ragwort for the cinnabar moths and nettles for red admiral, peacock and small tortoiseshell butterflies—"

"Nettles!"

Abby offered him her card. "I'm designing a garden for the Maybridge Show next year. Do come along, Mr White, and you'll see that we've moved a long way from the striped lawn and perennial border."

Ignoring her proffered card, he said, "I'm warning you, Barb, accept my offer on the house or you'll be sorry. And you," he said, turning on Abby, "I don't care who you are or what you're designing. Touch one blade of grass in my garden and you'll be hearing from my solicitors."

With that he turned and stormed out.

Neither of them spoke until he had left the restaurant, then Barb said, "Weeds!" They both burst out laughing.

CHAPTER THIRTY-ONE

Two hours later, a touch light-headed from a couple of glasses of a very fine red wine, Abby fell into the chair in front of Megan's desk.

"Well?" she demanded. "What happened?"

Abby shook her head, which was not her best idea. "You won't believe it."

"Probably not," Megan said, eyeing her thoughtfully, "but try me."

"We were sitting there, talking about Tatton, when Barb's husband turned up."

"Barb? I'd ask, somewhat astonished, if you had lunch with her, but from your wine-flushed cheeks I think that's fairly obvious. Was it good?"

"Steak, beautiful baby vegetables, triple-cooked chips and a bottle of Châteauneuf-du-Pape followed by sticky toffee pudding. I'm not going to eat for a week."

"Maybe a coffee," Meg suggested, getting up and putting her machine through its paces. "Tell me about the husband."

"Five ten, slight paunch, thinning hair. Mr White has decided that it's time for a younger Mrs White, and yes, it is her real name. They're in the settlement stage of a divorce and he turned up hoping to find her *in flagrante*."

"Unlikely in the dining room of the Queen's Head, I'd have thought. If that's what he wanted he should have waited for them to leave and followed them back to River View."

"Maybe he wanted to confirm his suspicions before he hung around for a couple of hours. When he saw she was with me, I suspect that he was so unmanned that he forgot himself."

Megan laughed. "That's hilarious."

"I blame the hat."

"It is very striking," Meg said, putting a cup of black coffee in front of Abby. "I love the colour . . ."

"Anyway, he charged up to us and demanded to know who I was, so I told him. *Abby Finch, Earthly Designs, how d'you do?* I even offered my hand. He didn't take it, but it held him for long enough for me to gather my wits."

"Very wit-reducing, Châteauneuf-du-Pape, taken at lunchtime."

"Fortunately, I'd only had a couple of mouthfuls at that point. Anyway, I went with the garden theme and explained that Barb and I had been meeting to discuss a redesign."

"I hope she was quick on the uptake."

"Oh, brilliant, despite being way ahead of me with the wine. It wouldn't surprise me if the garden has been a bit of an issue." Abby realised that she was slipping down in the chair and straightened herself. "I showed him the design I've created for a wildlife friendly garden that's on my spring schedule. He stormed off."

"Well done on seeing him off but what do you think? Is she a potential victim or on the prowl for a wealthy replacement?"

"Oh, definitely the first. As we suspected, they met in Venice when she was at a low ebb about the divorce," Abby continued. "Tatton was good-looking, charming and she was up for some fun — which she was happy to pay for. They had a very good time — I got way too much information about that — and they've been meeting for lunch, followed by fun and frolics in Kingfisher Drive, every couple of weeks since."

"So you're writing off the 'woman with a grudge, hell-bent on murder' theory?"

"She seemed really shocked when I told her about Maisie and his wives, although there was a moment when I wondered if she could be Yvonne Thompson, the sister of his second wife, Elaine. They sound very much alike."

"You've spoken to her? When? How?" Megan demanded.

"Maisie's daughter helped. It turns out that Yvonne was a hairdresser. It took a while, but I managed to track down her salon, but she's retired and living in Longbourne."

"That's where Elaine had a property."

"Maybe it was a family home," Abby said. "Anyway, I called the number I was given but I got her answering machine."

"Oh . . . But Tatton would have known Yvonne."

"Apparently not. The woman who gave me her number told me that Elaine and Yvonne hadn't spoken in years. She blamed herself for not being there for her sister. I assume that's why she wrote to Elaine. She wanted to warn her."

"That makes sense. Did you manage to get to the bottom of the hire car?"

"After Mr White's arrival, Barb never stopped talking. It seems that, with Barb's help, her soon-to-be ex built up a very large car hire business from scratch. Not just self-drive, but chauffeur-driven limousines, and a fleet of vans on permanent rental to the local authority. He put her on the board in the early days for tax reasons and she's still there."

"So the Merc is a business perk?"

"For now. He's desperate to get her out of the marital home and off the board, but she's holding out until he makes it worth her while. It's going to cost him serious money, something I suspect she'd told Tatton. I'd say she's had a very lucky escape."

"It sounds like it. Are you going to tell Dee about her?"

"No . . ."

"She's been in his house, Abby."

"From what she told me — again far too much information — I didn't get the impression she had time to fiddle with the fitting on the star while she was there. And the chocolates didn't turn up until Saturday."

"As far as we know. She could have sent them to Tatton as a donation for the lunch. With a little side order for himself."

"He'd certainly have pretended he'd bought them himself. Oh, and that's another thing. The last time she was there, he told her that he knew a designer who was going to give his garden a makeover in return for photographs to promote her new business."

Meg raised her eyebrows, shocked but not surprised.

"I really shouldn't drink at lunchtime," Abby said. "I don't suppose you have something for a headache?"

Megan provided painkillers and water without comment. "I take it Jake's home?"

"Yes, how did you . . . ? Oh, the sleuthing hat . . . Which I absolutely love, by the way. Thank you for suggesting it."

"To be honest, it was a way of getting his attention," Megan admitted. "He'd been ignoring my appeals to make an offer on a house he saw before he went to Italy."

"And?"

Megan shook her head. "No joy."

"He needs to find somewhere soon. The houseboat is really not good at this time of year."

"He's already found somewhere, Abs. It's just that the occupier is being stubborn about inviting him to move in."

"What?"

Megan gave her a quizzical look.

"Oh. You mean me. He understands."

"Does he? Really?"

"Of course he does." Then, with a shake of her head, "Maybe not. He offered to help before the party and I totally messed up."

"You turned down help?"

"It's a lot worse than that. I didn't just turn down his help, I asked him to come late. It didn't take him ten seconds to realise that I didn't want people thinking that he'd moved in and that's what he said to me. 'I get it.' And not in a good way."

"That would explain why Jake called me this morning and offered to pick me up at seven if I needed a lift. Not just arriving late but, extra thoughtfully, with another woman."

"Extra thoughtfully?"

On the contrary, it felt like he was underlining that 'I get it'. Underlining it, bolding it, putting it in italics.

"I hope you turned him down."

"And miss out on another chance to bend his ear about that house?" Megan said. "Not a chance. But maybe you need to think about your future. The children won't be around for long. It's none of my business—"

"If only!"

"—but maybe it's time to stop putting yourself at the back of the emotional needs queue." And having got that off her chest, Megan held up a hand. "Lecture over."

"Getting back to the subject of murder," Abby said, "despite the hat, we're no further forward in finding out who killed Edward and Tatton."

"I'm not so sure. Barb White may be innocent of murder, but you can't have an afternoon of fun and frolics without leaving traces. Whoever was doing his laundry might have noticed a trace of lipstick, if nothing else, on the sheets."

"Linda someone," she said, trying not to think of the sheets. "Beattie did tell me her name. It'll come to me."

"The relationship might be abusive," Megan said, ignoring her, "but she'll have been persuaded that the more she gives the safer she'll be."

"So, it's back to the ladies who lunch," Abby said. "More specifically, the ladies who lunch and service Tatton's every need."

"Don't forget Yvonne Thompson. Do you have an address?"

"No. Just the phone number."

"Longbourne . . ." She frowned and shook her head. "It's not a big place. You concentrate on June and Beattie and leave Yvonne to me."

"It won't be this evening, Meg. I've got cooking and party prep."

"Why would you cook when all the best supermarkets will deliver a ready-made buffet?"

"It's not the same."

"No, it's a lot less work," she pointed out.

"Well, yes, but you're ordering from pictures. It all looks gorgeous and probably is, but experience has taught me that it's always smaller than you expect. But I bought a cooked ham, and Penny is doing pretty much anything that involves a hot oven."

"Well, that's something. Did you bring your car into town?"

She shook her head, then really wished she'd kept her head still. Red wine at lunchtime . . . Such a mistake.

"Parking is nightmare at this time of year, so I walked."

"In that case, bearing in mind your fragile state, I'm going to take pity on you and drive you home."

CHAPTER THIRTY-TWO

Jake and Megan arrived late. Very late. "Don't blame, Jake," Megan said quickly. "Jake arrived on the dot but I diverted him to drive by a house that's just come on the market."

"At night?" Abby said, less than thrilled with either of them. "How did that go?"

"The hedge was a lot higher than I remembered so we couldn't see much. Oh, there's Dee. I'll just go and say hello." She made her escape, leaving her alone with Jake.

"I'm sorry," she said.

"It's okay, I—"

"Don't! Please don't say you get it. The bar is in the kitchen. If you're driving, there's non-alcoholic beer and gin . . ."

"I came in a taxi. I didn't think you'd want my car left outside all night."

So, still not forgiven. "You thought right," Abby told him.

"If it helps, the house Megan wanted to show me put at least twenty pounds on the taxi fare."

"Was it worth it?"

"No, but then, as Megan is very well aware, the house I want is not for sale."

She was saved from a response by the arrival of Chris March, bearing a large poinsettia and a box of chocolates. Through the transparent lid, Abby could see ten red mini crackers . . .

"Chris, how kind," she said, accepting a kiss on the cheek. "I'll go and put this somewhere safe. Jake, you remember Christopher March? Will you find him a drink? Cal is in charge of the bar."

"You left an eighteen-year-old in charge of the bar?" Jake asked.

"It's legal and he doesn't drink anything stronger than cola. And when the man assigned arrives late, you take whatever you can get."

"Can I help?" Chris offered, hovering.

Jake raised an eyebrow at her.

"No need. The man may be late but he's arrived, and I'm sure, if you follow him, he'll get you something to drink."

Chris glanced from her to Jake, reading the subtext and, with an almost imperceptible shrug said, "You've done well for yourself, Jake, but I confess I was surprised when Stephanie told me you'd moved your company to Maybridge. She's in your line of business . . . Cyber security."

"Why wouldn't I move here? It's where we all grew up. And since the town is on an expansion drive, I got a very good deal on premises in the business park." And, having driven home the point, he said, "Is Stephanie coming this evening?"

"No, she's living in Cheltenham—"

"She's a spook?"

"I believe the job title is cyber consultant, but she'll be here on Tuesday for the funeral so you can ask her yourself."

"I will. I'm always looking for good people and I pay a lot more than the civil service." Then, all the macho postering dealt with, "I was sorry to hear about your father."

"Thanks . . ." More people were arriving and they moved towards the kitchen. "We all assumed it was a stupid accident, but I was telling Abby that the police are taking a closer look at the lights."

"Are they?" Jake glanced back at her, looking thoughtful. She pretended not to notice, greeting the new arrivals and, having shown them through to the kitchen, looking for a vacant spot for the plant.

Dee, who to Abby's relief had arrived earlier with Paul, her partner — she'd wondered if, in view of her involvement with Tatton, the constabulary would stay away — was grazing the buffet and, when she saw the chocolates in her hand, raised an eyebrow.

"Will you be eating those?"

Abby pulled a face. "Did you ever find out who donated the ones left at the parish hall?"

"Not yet."

"I imagine the only reason he didn't claim to have donated them himself was fear that someone might have seen who left them."

"Whatever happened to not speaking ill of the dead?" Dee asked. "Is there anything you want to tell me?"

Abby shrugged. "He was hassling me to do some work in his garden." Now she had the excuse he'd thought up, it was safe to admit that. Drop a hint . . . "He thought I'd accept photographs for promotion in lieu of payment."

"Really? What planet was he on?"

"Maybe all those women who were so keen to look after him gave him an inflated idea of his value. Chocolate?" Abby held out the box she was holding.

"I'll pass, thanks." But Dee, too, was looking thoughtful.

More people had arrived. She caught sight of Fiona Keane sitting alone on the kitchen sofa, looking like death. Before she could go to her, Penny handed her a cup of something hot and then Nina Jennings — the wife of Freddie Jennings, Abby's solicitor — joined her.

The police constables Harry and Elvis arrived with their partners, and delighted as she was to see them, she excused herself to look for Jake, but he had disappeared. Chris was talking to Megan, so she and Cal sorted out drinks and encouraged everyone to help themselves to food.

"We've been careful to avoid nuts and sesame, and it's vegetarian and vegan at that end. It's all labelled, but if you're not sure about anything, Penny and Lucy can help."

The invitation had been from seven until nine so that parents could bring their children. Kids had their own food and drink station in the den, and Abby took a moment to check that they were all happy hanging out or playing video games.

The kitchen was crowded, the noise levels rising. Megan was still talking to Chris, June had cornered DI Iain Glover and, as she returned to the living room, she realized that Izzy Hamilton had arrived and was in close conversation with Jake.

"Izzy, I'm so glad you could come. You didn't bring May?"

"She's in the car with my mother. We're going to dinner at my godmother's, but since we were passing, I thought I'd pop in with gifts for the children. From May," she added. "I've left them in the hall."

"That's kind of you. I'm nowhere near that organised. I'll be doing my Santa drop later in the week. When are you going to your mother's?"

"Not until Christmas Eve . . . Is Sophie about?"

"In the den — it's through here. Sophie? Izzy wants a word."

"Not just a word . . ." Izzy said, folding herself down to Sophie's level and taking a box from her bag as Sophie reluctantly picked herself up off the sofa and slouched over to them. "This is for you, Sophie."

Sophie gave her a hard look, then opened the box. "It's a phone," she said and looked up at her mother, clearly not sure if this was going to go down well.

"I know that your daddy was going to buy you one," Izzy said, "but he's not here so I thought you might like his. I've cleared off all his business stuff, but it's his voice when you leave a message. You can hear it whenever you like." Izzy stood up. "I hope that's all right, Abby?"

"Izzy . . ." For a moment she was lost for words. "It's perfect, Izzy. Thank you."

"Well, it was in a drawer . . ." Izzy sniffed. "I have to go."

"Sophie?" Abby prompted.

Sophie was staring at the woman who was so nearly her stepmother in disbelief.

"Thank you, Izzy," she said, ultra polite. And then flung her arms around her. "Thank you, thank you, thank you."

Abby and Izzy exchanged a look, both blinking back a tear but for different reasons.

"Do you want to come and see May?" Izzy asked. "She's asleep . . ."

"I won't disturb her," Abby said, leading the way down the path.

Izzy's mother lowered the window. "Abby . . ."

"Lady Hamilton."

"Thank you for the offer of holly, but I have plenty of berries this year." Her eyebrows raised. "You seem to have quite a party tonight. I hope you have tolerant neighbours."

"Most of them are inside. It's a thank-you for all the people who were there for us after Howard was killed. I've just come to take a peek at my goddaughter," she said, as Izzy walked around to the driver's seat.

Mary Louise, known as May, was tucked up in her car seat in the care of her nanny, and as she looked in, Abby caught her breath.

"She's just like . . . her mother. Beautiful." Abby stepped back. "Thank you so much, Izzy. I really appreciate what you did and I hope you all have a wonderful Christmas."

Jake was waiting for her at the door. "What just happened?" he asked.

"Nothing . . ."

"I saw your face."

She sighed. "You think there's nothing else that can catch you out."

"What?"

"Izzy's baby is the image of Lucy at that age. I shouldn't be surprised. They're sisters." Then, as a tear trickled down her cheek, "And she gave Howard's phone to Sophie. Oh, hell."

She brushed the tear away with her hand and then, as Jake opened his arms, she leaned against him, grateful for his warmth, his strength.

"I'm sorry," she said. "I'm soaking your shirt."

"I'm happy it's mine you chose."

"What does that mean?"

"I saw the way Chris March was looking at you. Flowers *and* chocolates?"

"It wasn't flowers, Jake, it was a plant. They don't count."

"Don't they?"

"Especially not poinsettias. I dropped off a condolence card and Stephanie asked me to give a reading at Edward's funeral." She took the handkerchief he offered her. "Is that what that macho face-off was about when he arrived?"

"Not just the horrible plant, but chocolate," he said. "And that hopeful puppy-dog look?"

"Idiot." But he was right. "I invited him because I felt sorry for him. Starting over after a marriage break-up." She'd have gone out for a thank-you lunch with him without a second thought. "Megan seems to have taken him under her wing."

"He's not her type," Jake said. "Too soft."

"Maybe she needs a little softness in her life."

"We're leaving, Abby." She turned as Reverend Keane helped a weeping Fiona out of the door.

"Oh my goodness. Fiona?" She looked at Nigel. "What happened?"

"She hasn't been sleeping and it's been hectic for the last couple of weeks, but making a spectacle of herself over someone she barely knows . . ." He looked absolutely furious.

"It's shock," Abby said. "Let me drive you home."

"You can't leave your party and the fresh air will do Fiona good."

"Really? Fiona, are you sure?"

"I want to walk," she whispered.

Abby, concerned, remembering how upset Fiona had been before the lunch and in the bookshop, watched Nigel hurry her down the lane, taking the shortcut into town along the path by the mill.

She shivered.

"You're cold," Jake said. "We should go in before people start talking."

"You think they're not talking?" she asked. "You have an army of devoted followers urging me to grab you before you lose interest." Before he could say anything, she held up a finger. "Not. One. Word." And then, when he had been silent for all of three seconds, she kissed him.

CHAPTER THIRTY-THREE

The more formal guests and those with children left at around nine.

Lucy and Cal had already gone to a gig where his group were playing and Sophie, after a sugar rush, fell asleep on the den sofa clutching her phone and Jake carried her up to bed.

Tom, having filled a plate from the buffet, retired to his room. By ten only close friends and those with no one to go home to remained.

Chris offered Megan a lift but she said, "That's very kind, but I'm staying over tonight to help put Abby's home back together."

"That's what friends are for," he said, "but in that case I won't wait for a taxi, I'll walk. I'll see you again, I hope." He turned to Abby. "Abby, thank you for inviting me. I'll see you on Tuesday."

Jake came with her as she found coats and they saw him and the last of the stragglers on their way.

"Not interested?" she asked Megan, when they returned to the kitchen.

"He hasn't given up hope of getting his wife back."

"He told you that?"

"He didn't have to. He's still wearing his wedding ring."

"So?"

Meg turned as Jake, hands full of glasses, headed for the dishwasher. "What did you do with your wedding ring after your divorce, Jake?"

He glanced from one to the other. "Is it important?"

"It's a cultural question," Meg explained.

He shrugged. "I took it off when I signed the papers, went into one of those places that buy gold and gave the money to a kid's charity. Do either of you want coffee?"

"No, thanks. It's been a long day," Megan said, looking at her phone, "and my taxi has arrived. I'm going to leave you two sweet things to do the washing-up while I go home and fall into bed."

Abby walked her to the cab and gave her a hug. "Text me when you get home."

"Will do."

"The question is," Jake asked as she returned to the kitchen, "whose home? Whose bed?"

"What?"

"Megan isn't interested in Chris because she has some-one else."

"Oh?" Well, she'd suspected as much. "Did she tell you that on your long meandering journey here this evening?"

"No, but I have eyes in my head."

"But . . . Are you saying it was someone here tonight? I didn't see her with anyone."

"They were doing a very good job of avoiding one another but I caught a moment when their eyes made contact. I've seen a less intense lightning strike . . ."

"But I don't understand . . . Please tell me he's not married. Was he here with his wife?"

"Not with his wife. With his colleagues?" he offered.

She scrambled to think and then it came to her. "No!" Her hand flew to her mouth. "Iain Glover?"

"I'm interested why they chose to be quite so discreet," Jake said. "It's not as if they don't know each other. They met when he was investigating Howard's death."

"The thing is," she said, "there's been a suspicious death and my fingerprints were on the wrappers of the chocolate the police think may have contained the poison that killed him."

"Abby . . . I knew there was something. Why didn't you tell me?"

"It's okay. There was a good reason for them being there and the constabulary wouldn't have turned out for me tonight if I was a suspect. But my best mate dating the SIO might conceivably be considered a conflict of interest."

CHAPTER THIRTY-FOUR

Megan popped her head around the back door the following morning. "Great party last night. How did the washing-up go?"

"All done. The glasses are packed in their boxes ready to be collected," Abby said, ignoring the innuendo. "And in twenty minutes I'm going down to St Bart's."

"Church? The washing-up was that good?"

"Please!"

She and Jake hadn't been about to start something they couldn't finish. Instead Jake had called a taxi, and since it was Saturday and there was a half-hour wait, they'd sat together on the sofa, Jake's arm around her, while she'd told him about the second death and explained how her fingerprints came to be on the chocolate wrappers.

Fortunately, his taxi had arrived before he could start asking the questions she could see piling up behind those intelligent brown eyes.

She wouldn't be able to put off telling him the whole sorry story for long, but he'd got tickets for a rugby international and he and Tom were off to Cardiff for the day, so for the moment she'd been let off the hook. "Actually, I'm glad you dropped in. I was going to ask if you saw what upset Fiona Keane last night."

"Poor woman. She just seemed to crumple."

"I saw Penny give her a hot drink. I should have checked on her."

"She wasn't on her own. Chris March was with her. If he hadn't caught her, she'd have been on the floor."

"She was with Chris? Did you hear what they were talking about?"

"Just snatches." Megan sipped her coffee as she thought about it. "I imagine she'd been offering Chris her condolences because he was talking about his dad. How he hadn't seen him for years after his parents split up and was just starting to build a relationship with him."

"Fiona was very upset about Edward when I saw her the other day in the bookshop and her husband forbade her to buy a book for a cousin she's lost touch with."

"Was Edward a friend of the Keanes?" Megan asked.

Abby shook her head. "Nigel was furious that she'd made a scene over someone she barely knew." And yet her reaction to Edward's death when they'd been standing in front of the Christmas tree on Saturday had seemed so personal.

No . . . More than personal. She'd been angry. Fiona had passed it off as worry about Nigel, fear that he'd be blamed, and it had been obvious that she wasn't sleeping.

She'd been wearing more make-up than usual last night, but it hadn't been enough to disguise the signs of exhaustion.

"To be honest I'm quite going off the Reverend Keane and, as a caring hostess, I'm making it my business this morning to ensure that Fiona is okay."

"You're that concerned about her?"

"When I offered to drive them home last night, Nigel point-blank refused, saying that the walk would do her good. Frankly, I wasn't sure she'd make it and would have insisted, but Fiona quickly agreed that she wanted to walk and there was nothing I could do."

"Is that why you're going to church? Wouldn't it be easier to call her?"

"I could, but . . ."

"But?"

"I don't think she'd be able to say anything on the phone, and if I call at the vicarage Nigel will be there."

"Abby . . ."

"I'm not going to the service but they have coffee and biscuits in the parish hall afterwards. I won't be able to talk to her there, but I might be able to persuade her to meet me somewhere safe."

"Abby, be careful—"

"And I want to find out where the Father Christmas outfit was hanging before Tatton transformed himself."

"You think someone might have slipped the poisoned chocolate into the pocket?" Megan asked.

"I don't see how else it could have been done."

"But Tatton would have known he didn't put it there," Megan pointed out. "Wouldn't that make him suspicious?"

Abby thought about it. "Okay. How about someone whispering in his ear that she had a little something for him while he was giving her a gift from the sack. A slightly tipsy kiss under the mistletoe, a suggestive fumble in his pocket . . ."

"You really have been thinking about it."

"Yes . . ." And there was one thought that refused to go away. Which brought her right back to Megan. "Did you get home all right last night?"

"Yes, thanks. Tucked up cosy and warm twenty minutes after leaving you."

"That's what I thought. And no doubt why you forgot to text me."

"Did I? Sorry, I was so tired . . . But there was something that crossed my mind as I was falling asleep. What prompted Chris March to tell you about Tatton meeting his father in the Queen's Head?"

Abby doubted that thought passed through Megan's head until she wanted to change the subject, but she let her get away with it. For now.

"I thought I'd told you that when I mentioned Tatton's name. Chris remembered a note he'd found from him inviting his father to lunch at the Queen's Head to talk about something of mutual interest. Clearly to set up a blackmail scam."

"Yes, but how did Tatton pay for his lunches with Barbra using Edward's credit card?"

"There was a statement for a card with only payments to the Queen's Head. We'll never know for sure, but I assume Edward applied for a new one which would have a low credit limit and gave it to Tatton to use." She checked the clock. "I have to go."

"And I'll take a drive out to Longbourne for a nose around. I can pick up some Christmas gifts in the garden centre while I'm there."

"Good plan. You never know who you'll bump into having a ginger latte in their coffee shop."

"Maybe even Yvonne Thompson," Megan agreed. "I'll let you know what I find out."

* * *

Having left Lucy scrolling through social media for vegetarian lunch recipes, with a plea that it wasn't entirely plant-based, Abby picked up a tin of biscuits from Mrs Shah in the corner shop and arrived at the parish hall ten minutes before the service ended.

The side door was unlocked, the urn had been switched on but the kitchen was empty, so she left the tin of biscuits and took the chance to look around.

Trish found her in the cloakroom.

"Oh, it's you, Abby. I thought I heard someone. Were you looking for something?"

"Just trying to find a spare hanger for my coat," Abby said quickly, then spotting an overflowing box of Nativity costumes. "Sophie's going up to Maybridge High in September. This is my last year for Nativity plays. Not that I'll miss the costumes. I had a last-minute demand for a star this year, which reminds me: I was wondering where Mr Tatton's

Father Christmas costume came from. A friend wants to hire one," she added, long beyond mental finger-crossing.

"It was his own," Trish said. "He was Santa for all the parties."

"Oh, I didn't realise that."

"He won't need it again, but the police have it."

Abby doubted that her imaginary friend would want to use the one that Tatton had died in, but she said, "I don't remember seeing it in the cloakroom."

Trish gave her an old-fashioned look. "He didn't leave it where everyone could see it. It would destroy the illusion."

Abby grinned. "The seniors believe in Father Christmas?"

"We all need a little magic in our lives," Trish replied disapprovingly. "He left it in the storeroom with his sack."

Trish, Abby realised, was looking and sounding a lot more confident today. She was standing taller, no longer that cowed woman apologising for not having made a cake.

And not looking totally convinced by her reason for being in the cloakroom — understandable, since she was still wearing her coat. And Abby remembered Megan urging her to be careful.

She'd been talking about the vicar, but there was a reason that Trish was on their suspect list.

Her life was going to be a lot better without Tatton. She had motive and the opportunity. And if she'd killed once . . .

CHAPTER THIRTY-FIVE

"Did you find the biscuits?" Abby asked, by way of a diversion.

"I wondered where they came from. Thank you. We were down to ginger nuts and they're a bit hard on the teeth for some people. Do you know Diana Higgins?" Trish said, as she led the way back to the kitchen and introduced her to a slender woman laying out the cups and saucers.

"The Zumba lady? I've seen you at charity events, I think."

"I bought some plants from your stall at the summer fete."

"I remember. *Salvia?*" Abby said. "Hot Lips. You took three. I hope they thrived."

"They were glorious right up to the frost," Diana assured her. "Can I get you a cup of coffee, Abby? Or tea?"

"Coffee, thank you. Just a splash of milk." It was quickly made and, hearing the congregation crossing from the church, she took the cup. "I'll get out of your way."

Fiona spotted her right away and came across. "Abby . . . I'm so sorry about last night."

"No need to apologise. How are you now?" Stupid question. There were hollows in her face, dark circles beneath her eyes betraying a lack of sleep. She instinctively took her hand and it was shaking. "Sit down and I'll get you a cup of tea."

"I can't. I have to—"

"Sit," Abby insisted. "Stay there and I'll be right back."

Fiona looked as if she was about to argue but then sub-sided wearily into the chair. Satisfied, Abby crossed to the serving hatch. "Excuse me," she said, easing past a man who looked as if he was going to object to her queue jumping. "Mrs Keane is a bit shaky. She needs a cup of tea."

"She looks as if she should be home in bed," he said. "Trish, a cup of tea for Mrs Keane. Plenty of sugar."

"Is she okay?" Trish asked softly, as she poured the tea. "I thought she was going to pass out in church."

"I'll walk her home when she's had this." Then with a smile for the man who let her queue jump, she turned and saw Nigel Keane glaring at his wife.

"Fiona, what are doing? People need—"

"Fiona seems unwell, Nigel, but don't worry," Abby said quickly, "I've got this. A cup of tea and then I'll walk her back to the vicarage."

"Oh, Abby. Yes . . . thank you." He was instantly all smiles. "I blame Christopher March upsetting her last night . . . I told her to stay in bed this morning, but she would insist on coming . . ."

"I imagine she didn't want to let you down." Abby returned his smile despite her certainty that he was lying through his teeth. "Especially after the shock of what hap-pened to Edward." She leaned in, hand on his arm. "Such a shock for all of us . . . ?" she murmured.

"Yes, well, if you'll see her home that would be very helpful," he said, taking advantage of the fact that someone wanted a word, to turn away.

Abby took a breath and then returned to Fiona and gave her the tea. "Drink this and then we'll get out of here."

"Why are you here, Abby?" she asked, clearly nervous.

"I was worried about you. Nigel shouldn't have made you walk home last night."

"He was furious with me for making a spectacle of myself."

Remembering that little scene, Abby looked across to where Nigel was talking and laughing with a group of parishioners. Well-liked, kind she would have said, but last night he'd appeared to punish his wife for her overreaction to Edward's death.

A man she barely knew, he'd said.

"You were there when Edward fell, Fiona. Talking about him to Christopher must have brought it all back—"

"No . . ." The teacup rattled in the saucer. "No . . . I'd gone back to the vicarage for something . . . I was on my way back when I saw the lights go out, heard the commotion, and then the lights came on and I saw . . ."

"It must have been a dreadful shock," Abby said gently, "when you loved him so much."

And with that Fiona seemed to relax. She took a mouthful of tea, then set the cup down on the table beside her. "Let's go. Now," she urged.

"You want to go back to the vicarage?"

"No, not there. Somewhere quiet."

Abby's first thought had been to suggest they go to the park and walk along by the lake. But Fiona was looking fragile. She'd have taken her home, but the children were there.

On a Sunday the riverside car park would be busy and so, on an impulse Abby drove up to the walled garden at Linton Lodge and opened the gates. Once inside, she closed and bolted them.

Fiona had climbed out of the car.

"This is lovely, Abby."

Sensing that Fiona needed a little time, she said, "Come and see."

They walked, mostly in silence. Fiona watched the birds swooping down to the feeders and a squirrel galloping along the newly restored roof of the buildings.

Finally, Fiona paused at a bench that caught the low winter sun and sat down. "Love isn't bad, is it?" she asked.

"You loved Edward," Abby replied, avoiding a direct answer.

"He was in a bad way after his career crashed and he lost everything he cared about — his home, his family, his career. His children were grown up by then but their mother was so bitter, so humiliated, that they refused to see him."

"You knew him?"

"His wife was a churchgoer. He occasionally accompanied her until the divorce. She moved away then. I was working as a counsellor back then, just a couple of afternoons a week, and when I saw him in the town, I encouraged him to come along and talk."

"And you fell in love."

"We were both unhappy. Nigel's congregation think he's wonderful but they don't live with him. He was a curate when I met him. So sweet, so thoughtful. He said I would be the perfect wife for a vicar — and I was, Abby," Fiona insisted. "But he began to resent the fact that the parishioners turned to me for help rather than him and he began to squeeze me out of things."

Abby said nothing.

"He always had a good reason," Fiona insisted. "The Mother's Union was taking too much of my time. I was helping with the Brownies, but he needed me that evening. I used to sing in the choir . . ."

Abby had to swallow hard as a picture of control began to emerge. Tears were not going to help.

"I wanted children," Fiona went on, "but it never happened, and when I finally went to the doctor he told me to talk to my husband. When I asked Nigel what he meant, he admitted to having had a vasectomy. He told me that he loved me too much to put me through such pain, loved me too much to share me . . ." Fiona's voice caught on a sob. "I wanted to believe him, Abby."

"That's not love, Fiona. That's a man who sees you as a possession."

"After that, he started to control everything I did, everyone I saw . . ."

"And yet you were working as a counsellor?"

"We were at a church function and I mentioned to the dean that I'd trained as a counsellor. When he asked Nigel if he could spare me for a couple of afternoons a week he couldn't refuse. But he accused me of going behind his back, flirting with the dean. On those days he would find endless jobs for me, my car would never start so I had to walk, but it was worth it to get away for a few hours."

"And you met Edward."

"He was broken and so was I. It wasn't about the sex, although that had a sweetness that was new to me. We were soulmates."

"How did Nigel find out?"

"I stopped the counselling and instead spent those precious afternoons with Edward. Maybe Nigel saw the change in me and he told the dean he couldn't spare me . . ."

"Who was surprised because you'd stopped."

"Once he knew that he started following me, and of course we were meeting at Edward's house."

"I'm so sorry."

"Nigel had been the chair of the school governors when Edward was suspended and he said that I was just another of his dirty little hole-in-the-wall affairs, but it wasn't like that, Abby. Edward's marriage was a sham, his children were away at university and when comfort was offered . . ."

"He paid a high price."

"And then Nigel confronted him, promising him a repeat performance. Shame for him, shame for me . . . It brought on a heart attack that nearly killed him, and his children, realising they were about to lose him, rushed to his side. We had planned to go away, live in France, but he had his children back in his life and I could see what that meant to him."

"So you told him that you'd changed your mind."

"Don't credit me with an enormous sacrifice, Abby. Edward wasn't well enough to go to another country and start a new life. And you can imagine the headlines if we'd stayed in England. The redtops love a vicar's wife in a sex romp . . ."

"Would you have cared?"

"No, but his children would have been faced with a second scandal and I couldn't put them through that. I accepted that it was all a pipedream and promised Nigel that I wouldn't see him again."

"But he was a member of the seniors' lunch club," Abby said, confused.

"That was a recent thing." Fiona sighed. "Edward knew he didn't have long left. His heart was being kept going by a pacemaker, but they had found a cancer . . ."

"Yes, I'd heard."

"He'd stopped coming to church for obvious reasons, but one day, a few months ago, I found a note in my coat pocket after I'd been serving teas at the after-service social. He wanted to be close to me, in the same room, just once a week, he said."

Fiona looked up at the clear blue sky, silent for a moment, lost in a love that had endured despite everything. Then, coming back to present, "That first day, I thought Nigel would warn him off, or stop me from going to the lunches, but he simply reminded me what would happen if I spoke to him. He must have seen my confusion because he said that seeing him would be a reminder of how I'd sinned and not speaking to him was my penance to God."

Fiona was so still, speaking so softly that a tame robin that had perched on the arm of the bench cocked his head on one side as if to listen closer.

Abby reached out and took Fiona's hand. "God," she said, "had nothing to do with it."

"No. I could see that it gave him pleasure to see us in the same room, knowing that he was controlling us both."

Abby didn't know Nigel Keane that well but he'd been a presence in her life for years. He'd been kind when her own mother had died and had buried Penny's sister, Molly, with a beautiful service.

Until yesterday, she would have said he had a good Christian soul.

To discover that he had such a dark, sadistic streak of cruelty running through him, to realise how little you could know someone, sent ice running through her veins.

"I don't have a close acquaintance with God, Fiona, but I believe you've done more than enough penance for one lifetime. Walk away."

"I can't do that, Abby."

"Nigel can't stop you," she said, although she knew how hard it was to leave the safety of everything you knew. "I know someone who will talk to you, help you."

"You don't understand," Fiona said. "When I saw Edward, saw that he was dying, I couldn't stay away."

"You were seeing each other? Did Nigel find out?"

"He didn't say anything, but I saw a sermon he was writing. He'd taken as his text the whore of Babylon . . . *And the woman was arrayed in purple and scarlet colour, and decked with gold and precious stones and pearls, having a golden cup in her hand full of abominations and filthiness of her fornication . . .*"

"Fiona," she warned, not wanting to hear any more, but it was too late to wish she'd never started this. To wish she'd stayed at home this morning sending out the Christmas e-card that Lucy had designed, making lunch, exchanging texts with Jake, nagging the children about homework. Normal, ordinary things. "Please think long and hard before you say any more."

"That's the problem, Abby, I can't stop thinking about it. About Edward. About—"

Before Fiona could finish, Abby's phone began to ring, sending the robin whirring up into an espaliered peach tree.

She took it from her pocket and glanced at the screen, hoping that it was one of the children wanting to know where she was.

But it was Nigel.

Afraid that if she didn't answer he'd go to her house, she stood up, took a steadying breath. Managing a surprised query, she said, "Nigel?"

Fiona started nervously, made a move as if to stand, but Abby put a reassuring hand on her shoulder, keeping her where she was.

"Abby . . . I thought you were taking Fiona back to the vicarage, but she's not here," he said, not quite able to disguise his irritation.

Breathe . . . She could do this . . .

"Fiona decided she needed some fresh air and decided to go for a walk. I'd have gone with her, but the children were waiting for me," she told him, without the slightest qualm about lying to him.

"Did she say where she was going? Only she hasn't taken her phone."

"I'm sorry, Nigel, she didn't say. The park?" she suggested. "Or it's such a lovely day, she might have decided to walk along the river. I'm about to take the children out for lunch," she added, in case he didn't believe her and went to the house to check.

There was silence as he absorbed the possibility of what a desperately unhappy woman heading for the river might have in mind. Then he said, "Yes, that's probably where she is. I'm sorry to have bothered you, Abby. I've no doubt she'll be home soon."

She was not the only one shading the truth, she thought as, without waiting for her assurance, he cut the call, no doubt already on his way to the river.

If a vicar's wife sex scandal was meat and drink to the tabloids, a vicar's wife's suicide would come a close second as they dug around for a reason.

CHAPTER THIRTY-SIX

"Nigel will be looking for me," Fiona said, standing up and looking around as if for a means of escape.

"Even if it occurs to him to come here, he won't be able to get in," Abby said, anxious to reassure her. "What we both need is tea and carbs," she said. "Then we'll decide what to do."

She unlocked the studio, turned on the heater but not the lights, put on the kettle and took down the tin with what was left of Penny's shortbread. Then she texted Lucy to tell her that she'd been held up and they should get on with lunch.

Fiona sank into the visitor's chair.

"Nigel wasn't the only person who knew that you and Edward were seeing one another again, was he? If it helps," Abby continued when Fiona didn't answer, "I know that Gregory Tatton preyed on the vulnerable, both men and women."

Fiona nodded. "Clearly Nigel had his suspicions and was no doubt following me, but I was beyond caring by then. How Tatton found out . . ." She shook her head.

Abby thought about what Jake had said the night before. How he'd seen the unspoken exchanges between Megan and Iain Glover. The lightning strike . . .

"He watched people, Fiona. All it takes is one unguarded look . . . I know he was blackmailing Edward."

"The credit card. Just a few lunches, he said. Worth every penny, Edward said. But I'd seen the way Tatton manipulated people, got him to do things for him, and I knew he wouldn't be able to resist coming for me."

Abby poured the coffee, took milk from the fridge, offered sugar and the biscuit tin. But it wasn't going to go away, and finally she sat down and asked the question.

"What did Gregory Tatton want from you, Fiona?"

"A pound from the collection plate."

"What!"

"He came up to me in the church hall after the service a couple of weeks ago, wanting a word. He was the last person I wanted to talk to, but I put on my vicar's wife smile and that's when he told me, right there, surrounded by people talking, laughing, oblivious, that he wanted me to give him a pound from the collection plate."

Abby frowned. "I don't understand . . . ?"

Fiona nodded. "I thought I must have misheard him. It gets noisy in there and I said, 'I beg your pardon, Mr Tatton?' and he repeated it. 'Every week, Fiona,' he said. 'I want to see you take a pound from the collection plate and put it in your pocket. You can give it to me after the service, when you bring me a cup of coffee and two chocolate biscuits.'"

That was an escalation, Abby thought. There was no gain in it for him, just the power it gave him over a woman who had never done a thing to hurt him. She felt sick.

"I pretended not to understand but then he said, 'It's for Edward.'" She looked up. "That was when I knew I had to kill Nigel."

CHAPTER THIRTY-SEVEN

"Nigel?" Abby repeated. "The shock was meant for Nigel, not Tatton?"

"Well, yes," Fiona said, as if it was obvious. "Nigel was the problem. Without him, Tatton was powerless."

Despite having already guessed what was coming, if not the intended victim, Fiona's confession dropped like a stone in Abby's heart.

She didn't know her that well, but the thought of her caught between two vile men appalled her and she didn't want to know the rest, but she was in too far now.

"Are you saying that you fixed the star, Fiona?"

She frowned. "No, not the star. I fixed the lights," she said as if it was obvious. Calm now, quite still as she made her confession, relieved to get it off her chest. And Abby knew that she had to remain calm too.

"How, Fiona? How did you know what to do?"

"It was easy. My grandfather was an electrician and I loved being with him in his workshop. He taught me how to wire a plug when I was six years old, and by the time I was ten, I was helping him wire an extension he and my dad had built on our house. I wanted to be an electrician, but my mother said she wasn't having her daughter working on construction sites with a load of men."

"Times have changed."

"Have they?" Fiona shook her head. Clearly not for her. "I saw somebody fix the wiring on one of those police dramas recently. One of those where half a dozen people get killed in bizarre ways before the policeman finally works it out. I sat there watching it and realised that I knew how to do that."

"But it had to be the star," Abby said, confused. "The electricity wouldn't have been switched on until the star was fitted, and Gregory always did that."

"Nigel had other plans for this year. He never supported Tatton's annual performance with the star, although I don't suppose that was the sole reason. The man had a way of stepping in to take charge of things that Nigel considered his responsibility."

"Like the seniors' Christmas lunch?" Abby suggested. "I don't imagine he liked that,"

"That was the last straw and Nigel made up his mind that this year he was going to put the star in place himself, but then the Bishop called him at the crucial moment. He wouldn't have come down for anyone else."

Abby swallowed. "Fiona, you shouldn't be telling me this."

But Fiona was on a roll, determined to unburden herself.

"But you'd already guessed, hadn't you? That was why you were there this morning. Waiting for me."

"No . . . Well, maybe . . ."

It had been a gradual understanding that something was wrong, Abby realised. That moment in the bookshop when Fiona had talked about how difficult it was to lose someone you cared for. Nigel's determination that she shouldn't get in touch with her cousin. And then her grief before the lunch and at the party.

Maybe even before that. Fiona had seemed a bit tetchy when she was decorating the grotto, complaining about the fuss over the lights.

Clearly she'd been on edge, waiting for her husband to fix the star. And now, thinking about the scene, she realised that when Nigel Keane came down the stepladder, he'd taken something from his pocket. Like Edward, he must have slipped the star into his pocket intending to put it in place before Tatton had a chance to do it himself. When he took the call, he must have put the star back.

"You guessed at the party, didn't you?" Fiona said. "Chris was talking about his father, his regret at how much time he'd missed. How he'd wanted to spend those last few months with him . . ." Her eyes were swimming with tears. "The guilt overcame me, Abby, and I just fell apart."

"Nigel was so unkind to you, insisting that you were making a fool of yourself over someone you barely knew . . . But if that were true, then neither reaction made sense, and afterwards, when I thought about it, I realised that you must have been very close to Edward."

Which explained not only Fiona's distress, but Nigel's anger.

And once that idea had got into her head, Tatton's hold over Edward made sense and the suspicion, if not the victim, no matter how unwelcome, had followed.

"I wanted to watch Nigel fall," Fiona said. "See his expression when he realised what I'd done, but at the last minute, when I knew what was coming, I couldn't face it . . ."

"So you went to fetch the throw."

That was something else that had been niggling at the back of Abby's mind. The missing throw. It had just been an excuse to get away.

"If I hadn't been so cowardly, if I'd had the stomach to stay and see it through," Fiona said, "I would have seen what was happening and I could have stopped it."

There was nothing Abby could say that would change that. It was something Fiona would have to live with.

"Was it you who took the defibrillator, Fiona?" Abby asked.

She nodded. "It's hidden in the storeroom."

"It wouldn't have made any difference," Abby said quickly, taking her hand. "I'm so sorry that you've faced this on your own. Was there no one you could talk to?"

Fiona sighed. "Nigel's congregation adore him," she said. "Who would believe me?"

Abby knew she was right. Nigel Keane was one of those ideal vicars, the kind that went with the picture postcard villages. Everything perfect on the surface, but underneath . . .

"It's ironic," Fiona said, "that it's what I used to do. Listen to people like Edward, like me, talking through their problems, telling me the things they couldn't tell anyone else." She shook her head. "I've helped get women into the safety of a refuge," she said, "but when it was me, I felt as if I was cut off from the world. Until Edward came back."

"I know how hard it is," Abby said.

"Hard, but it's time." She took a breath, got to her feet. "If you'll be kind enough to drive me to the police station, Abby, I need to tell them that I killed Edward March. That I killed the man I loved. Once I've done that no one and nothing can hurt me."

"I'll do that for you, Fiona, but you can't go alone. I'm going to call my solicitor, Freddie Jennings. Do you know him?"

She nodded. "Yes. His wife was very kind to me on Saturday."

"Talk to him, tell him everything that you've told me, and he will look after you."

"I've no money."

"Let's worry about that later. Stay in the warm, drink your tea. I won't be long."

Abby went outside to make the call.

"I'm sorry to disturb another Sunday, Freddie, but Fiona Keane has just told me that she caused the accident that killed Edward March."

"How?" he asked, going straight to the point. And she told him everything. Including the way that Tatton had tried to manipulate her into working for him.

"Dear God," he said. "Why didn't you . . . ? Not now. We can talk about it later. Where is she now?"

"We're in my studio in the walled garden. She wants to go to the police station but I'm concerned about Nigel Keane. If they contact him, he'll turn up with a lawyer in tow who'll do his best to shut her up and get her bail, at which point she'll be returned to the control of her husband. Fiona has to be protected from him."

"I agree. Stay there. I've got this."

* * *

"I've got news," Megan said, when she called in on her way home from Longbourne later that day.

"So have I," Abby said, heavily. "It was Fiona Keane who tampered with the tree lights."

Megan opened her mouth, closed it again, then said, "Fiona Keane was trying to kill Tatton?"

"No, Meg. She was trying to kill her husband."

"What?" She shook her head. "Run that by me again."

"It's a long story."

It had felt like hours, but when Freddie had said he'd "got this" he hadn't been exaggerating. He'd arrived within twenty minutes and once he'd talked to Fiona, she'd given him the name of her sole remaining family member, the cousin the book had been for. Then he'd contacted both police and victim support.

At this moment, Fiona was being driven to a secure facility for abused women by someone from a victim support charity. Abby hadn't been told where and knew that it was safer that way.

"Is anyone going to tell Nigel Keane?" Megan asked, when Abby had told her everything.

"I'll leave that to the police."

"Very wise. So," Megan asked, full of questions now she was over the shock, "what about the poisoned chocolates? Did she kill Tatton, too? After what he did to her . . ."

223

"No," Abby said, shaking her head. "She denied that, and once she'd realised what she'd done . . . Well, you saw what happened on Saturday at the party."

"What will happen to her? Do you know?"

Abby sighed. "Fiona planned to kill her husband so she'll be charged with something. What exactly will be down to the prosecutor, but she's going to plead guilty and Freddie said that the defence will probably go for the balance of her mind being disturbed."

"Mental cruelty and blackmail. That's enough to disturb anyone," Megan said. Will Iain— the police want to talk to you?"

"Oh, yes," Abby said, grimly. "Interview number three. Did I tell you that they found Tatton's file on the Finch family?" She shook her head, waved a hand, not wanting to talk about it. "You had news. Do you want to come through to the kitchen? There's plenty of ham and salad left from last night." Abby raised an eyebrow. "Unless of course you have something more interesting to do?"

"Only my accounts," Meg replied. "And I can't remember the last time I ate. Let's go."

The kitchen was empty.

"Where are the children?" Megan asked as Abby started to pass things from the fridge.

"Jake's taken Tom to a rugby match and they'll probably stop for man food. I just hope he remembers that tomorrow is a school day. Lucy and Cal are watching the latest Marvel movie in the den with Sophie and they've already had a left-over feast. We won't be interrupted," Abby told her. "So, did you find Yvonne Thompson?"

"It was surprisingly easy," Megan said. "Oh, there's potato salad . . ."

"Wine?"

"I'd better stick with water." Megan took a carving knife from the knife block and began to attack the ham, while Abby put out the salad, but it didn't stop her talking. "The woman behind the counter at the village shop said she couldn't give out addresses to just anyone who asked — fair enough, I wouldn't either — but someone recognised me and followed me out of the shop wanting to know if Yvonne was putting her cottage on the market because if she was, her mother would be interested."

"How lucky can you get?" Abby asked, peering into a bowl and discarding it.

"Longbourne is a small place," Megan reminded her. "I told her that I'd been asked to value Yvonne's cottage but the details were on my phone, which had died on me. Not just lucky, but quick-thinking."

"And did she point you in the right direction?"

"She did. Not before asking if I had time to look at her place as well, which is why I was so long."

"Cushy . . ."

Megan smiled. "It's a lovely family house. Large garden, river frontage, dock, five bedrooms . . . Perfect for a growing family," she said, innocently. "It needs updating but that wouldn't be a problem. You're in the business."

"I love this house. I have it exactly the way I want it and I am not moving," Abby said. "What I want to know is, did you find Yvonne Thompson?"

CHAPTER THIRTY-EIGHT

"Yvonne Thompson lives in Bramble Cottage and when I, very casually, walked by she was in the garden sweeping up leaves."

"Giving you the perfect excuse to stop and admire her thatched roof?"

Megan grinned. "It would have been rude not to," she said, "but how did you know it was thatched?"

"Bramble Cottage is just down the road from the garden centre where I used to work," Abby informed her. "It was once photographed for the lid of a biscuit tin."

"Oh, right. Well, anyway, when she saw me, she came over to chat," Megan, clearly proud of her detective work, explained. "I told her who I was, and said I was on my way to value a property in the village but I had a buyer desperate for a thatched cottage in the area and that if she ever thought of selling . . ."

"And?"

"And she really opened up, telling me that she'd only recently moved in. She told me the cottage had belonged to her sister who'd died tragically in Turkey. That's where Yvonne has been, by the way, following the journey that Elaine took in the last two weeks of her life. Athens, Mycenae, a cruise around the islands, then Troy, Ephesus and finally to the spot where Elaine died."

"That suggests she regrets their estrangement, especially since Elaine left her the cottage, although it's taken her a while to get around to moving in."

"Maybe she didn't have the time until now," Meg said. "Didn't you say she'd recently retired?"

"Yes, although . . ."

"Although what?" Megan asked.

"I was told that the reason Yvonne got so worked up about Elaine's death was because she'd been cut out of her sister's will."

"Chinese whispers?" Megan suggested. "People gossip about wills and usually get the wrong end of the stick."

"So presumably Bramble Cottage is the property Elaine owned when she married Tatton," Abby said, adding a couple of cheese puffs to her plate. It had been a long and difficult day.

"Oh, I got chapter and verse," Megan told her. "It wasn't a family home. Elaine lived there with her first husband until he went off with some dancer. It seems that when Elaine married Tatton she let the place to a family friend. Yvonne hadn't been able to take possession until that person moved into a care home."

"You two did have a lovely chat," Abby said.

"Oh, by this time, she'd invited me in to look around. People can't resist finding out how much their home is worth and she just kept talking. I heard all about how she'd fallen out with her sister over a man   not Tatton," Megan added quickly, before Abby could ask. "I'll have a bit of that brie . . ."

Abby passed the brie and added some tabbouleh that Lucy had made to her own plate.

"It seems that Yvonne had been engaged to an actor, but when he met Elaine . . ." Megan made a dramatic boom gesture.

"Ouch."

"Ouch indeed, but it seems that Elaine had managed to see a solicitor before she went on that trip to view the ancient ruins, which is when she transferred ownership of the cottage to her sister. By the time Yvonne found out, her sister was dead."

"They didn't get a chance to make up?" Abby said, saddened for them. "That's tragic."

Megan nodded. "I did the 'gosh, how dreadful, how did it happen' thing, and she told me about Elaine's fall. That was when I frowned and asked if her sister was Elaine Tatton. I told her that I remembered reading about her accident in the paper. Such a tragedy. Then, after a suitable pause, I asked if she knew that Gregory Tatton had died recently."

"Oh, nice segue, Ms West."

"Thank you, Ms Finch," she said, responding with a little bow. "She did seem really shocked. She'd only got back from her trip yesterday so she hadn't heard," Meg said, then laughed. "When I told Yvonne that the police suspected poison you won't believe what she said."

"Try me."

"She said she'd better check her machine for messages since there would undoubtedly be one from the police wanting to know if she had an alibi."

"You're kidding?" Abby said, shocked. "She just came out with that?"

"Of course I laughed, as if she was joking, which is when she admitted that she'd made quite a fuss when her sister died, haranguing the police, accusing Tatton of all sorts. She admitted to making a complete fool of herself. But then she laughed too, saying that she had to be in the clear since she was wandering around ancient ruins at the time."

"I suppose that rules her out," Abby said.

"If she was in Turkey last week, she couldn't have left the chocolates," Megan agreed, "but I suppose she could have got someone else to do it for her. I wonder how long ago the chocolate boutique started selling those Christmas crackers?"

Abby thought about it for a moment, then shook her head. "No. We've already established that the poison couldn't have been in the chocolates left at the hall. If it was in a chocolate it had to be from another box, which suggests the anonymous delivery was to cause confusion and cover up the delivery of the one with the poison.

Something else occurred to her. "Didn't the police think it suspicious that Elaine had been putting her assets out of Tatton's reach just before she died?"

"That's what aroused Yvonne's suspicions, but when he was questioned, Tatton told the police that he'd encouraged Elaine to do it. He was concerned about her 'dizzy spells'," Megan said, doing the quote thing with her fingers. "He wanted her to heal the family bond with her sister in case there was something seriously wrong."

"And they accepted that?"

"Why wouldn't they? There was no evidence of foul play and there were a dozen witnesses not only to the fact that Tatton was nowhere near Elaine at the time, but that she had seemed a little unsteady after lunch."

"So he got away with it. At least until someone slipped him that poison," Abby said. "But while she's off the suspect list, I'm back on it. Means, motive and opportunity . . ."

CHAPTER THIRTY-NINE

"Mrs Finch . . ." Detective Inspector Iain Glover was making it clear that they were back on formal terms this morning. And no doubt wishing he'd had an urgent callout on Saturday night that would have prevented him from coming to her party. "Please take a seat."

The DI took a seat opposite her, another officer at his side, opened his notebook and uncapped his pen.

"No Mr Jennings this morning?" Iain asked.

"It didn't occur to me that I'd need a solicitor," Abby said, confused at the formality. "I was told this was to take my statement about what happened yesterday with Mrs Keane."

"I'm afraid that will have to wait. Some facts have come to light regarding the death of Gregory Tatton. We will be requiring a DNA swab."

Startled, Abby said, "Why?"

"At this point it's just for elimination purposes. I'm sure you have no objection?"

"Are you going to arrest me if I decline?" she demanded.

"Why would you do that?"

"No reason," she said, quickly, "but I don't understand . . . You have my fingerprints. DC Newcombe knows how they got there."

"I have read your previous statement. However, forensic evidence has shown that Mr Tatton may have had company before he died, and in view of evidence we've now found on his computer, I need to ask you where you were in the afternoon and evening on the day of the seniors' lunch."

"Is that when you think he died?" She didn't ask what he'd found on Tatton's computer. She already knew.

"Your whereabouts, Mrs Finch?"

"Gregory Tatton didn't walk home in that Father Christmas costume," she persisted. "Who drove him home?"

Iain Glover sighed. "The way this works, Abby, is that I ask the questions and you answer them."

Abby considered calling a halt and asking for Freddie to be present. But she hadn't set as much as a foot in Tatton's house, so whatever physical evidence they'd found, it hadn't come from her.

"Saturday afternoon," she said. "Okay. Well, as I have already told DC Newcombe, I helped lay out the tables for the seniors' lunch. I left as people were beginning to arrive just after twelve and drove home. The children were out—"

"Where were they?"

"Lucy had taken Sophie to her dance class, then she went to the bookshop to pick up a book she'd ordered, met some friends and later she called to let me know that she and Cal were at his grandmother's — Penny Henderson," she added. "You met her at my party on Saturday."

"And Sophie?" he asked, heavily.

"She went home from dance class with her friend Cara. Her mother dropped her back just before tea. Around sixish. I'm not sure of the exact time."

"Cara's mother will be able to confirm that?"

"Yes." Abby took out her phone, called up Emma's details and showed it to the officer taking notes. "After that I spent the afternoon catching up on my cleaning and then prepared supper."

"Did you see or speak to anyone else?"

231

"I had texts from several people," she said, "and a call from Emma, to let me know what time she'd drop Sophie home. Although I suppose I could have been anywhere."

"No." Iain took the phone from her and scrolled through it. "We can position your phone from the masts."

"Well, that won't take long. It's going to show that it was in Mill Lane all afternoon and evening," Abby told him.

He looked up. "Who is Heather James?" he asked. "And why did you want her address?" He tilted his head to one side, waiting for her answer.

"Shouldn't you ask my permission before reading my texts?"

"I could get a warrant."

"Oh, for heaven's sake. Heather's mother, Maisie Goodyear, thought Tatton was going to marry her. He'd relieved her of a considerable amount of money before her family discovered what was happening and moved her out of his reach."

The room was silent for a moment, then the Iain said, "I get the impression that quite a few people would have been glad to see Mr Tatton dead."

Abby was fairly sure that Freddie wouldn't have wanted her to respond to such a leading question and said nothing.

Iain looked down at the folder in front of him. "Following a statement that Fiona Keane made to her solicitor, we now know what he did to Edward March and attempted to do to her," he agreed. "And there is evidence to suggest that he might have put other people under pressure."

"Too damn right. The man was a monster."

So much for keeping her mouth shut.

"I take it from your response that he had approached you?" He looked at her long and hard for a moment but she didn't respond. "He had a file on the Finch family."

"Whatever it contained would be nothing but specu-lation based on the article in the *Observer* when I discovered those remains. Nothing that you don't already know."

"DC Newcombe said that she saw him at your studio recently."

Thanks, Dee.

"It was a week ago last Thursday. He wanted me to take a look at his garden. I believe I told her that when I gave my statement after Edward's death."

"It was a straightforward business request?"

"I treated it as such and went with Eric Braithwaite to take some measurements and photographs of his garden in order to make some suggestions. I later discovered that he was telling people I'd offered to do it in return for publicity photos."

"And would you have done that?"

"I run a business, Iain. I work hard, I do a good job and I have any number of clients who are happy for me to use photographs of their gardens for publicity. If you don't believe me, check my website."

Iain nodded and stood up. "I think we'll leave it there. Once the DC has taken a swab, you can go."

Abby felt the air leave her in a rush as, faint with relief, she asked, "What about Fiona Keane? I thought I was here to go through what happened yesterday."

"We have the statement she made to her solicitor but she's not well enough to be interviewed at the moment. If we need more from you, we'll be in touch."

Abby sat in her car, her head on the steering wheel, trying to wipe out the indignity of having a DNA swab taken to eliminate her from traces found on Tatton.

Traces.

She shuddered, mentally watching this week follow the previous one down the drain. How on earth she was going to get through the run-up to Christmas with the cloud of Tatton's death hanging over her? The suspicion that she was somehow involved.

And not just her.

The police had been through his computer. There must have been more than a file on the Finch family. Who else was being asked for a DNA sample?

A young constable tapped on her window. "Are you all right, ma'am?" he asked, and when she looked up she saw Iain Glover watching her from his window.

Two days ago he'd been in her home, eating her food, ignoring Megan . . .

Megan. She groaned.

"Ma'am?"

"I'm fine," she lied, started the car and backed out of the spot with no plan in her head other than to be anywhere but the police station. "Fine, fine, fine, abso-bloody-lutely fine . . ."

The next few minutes were a blank. She had no memory of driving to Linton Lodge, or the dim, oak-panelled hallway . . .

It was the smoke catching her throat, making her eyes water, the sudden flare of heat sending her back from the surge of flames that were engulfing the portrait of another monster — Howard's grandfather dressed in his mayoral robes and chain of office — which had, for more than half a century, had pride of place in the entrance hall of Linton Lodge.

Her phone began to ring in in her pocket, but she ignored it, watching the flames burn away the robes of office, melting his face.

Abby didn't move until all that was left of the picture was the charred remains of the frame.

She stamped on it, until it was in pieces then, when it was cool enough to pick up, hurled the remains into the bushes to rot and be taken down into the earth and turned into something useful, something good, by worms, insects and microbes.

That done, she sank to the ground and with shaking hands took the phone from her pocket.

One missed call. *Jake* . . .

He'd left a message on her voicemail. "*Have I been stood up?*"

Yesterday, when he'd dropped Tom home, they'd made plans to have lunch on his houseboat. Spend some precious time together.

She checked the time. It was nearly half past one.

She thought about calling him, telling him about Fiona, about her shitty morning at the police station.

Instead she sent a text. *I'm sorry. Life got in the way.*

Jake had returned to his hometown with a thriving business. The last thing he needed was to get involved in yet another murder. She waited for a response, a text if not a phone call, but there was nothing.

It felt like that moment when he'd turned and walked away from her, offended that she didn't want his help at the party. But there was a limit to how much even the most devoted man would take before he accepted that he was always going to come a long way down the list of her priorities.

After her children . . .

And right now after the murder of Gregory Tatton.

The temptation was to switch her phone off so that she wasn't forced to listen to the silence, but mothers couldn't do that. They always had to be ready for a call from school or the rugby club, to deal with any one of a dozen dramas involving their offspring.

Instead, she walked back down the Lodge garden and stood for a moment by the lake, breathing in the sweet scent of the spidery, yellow flowers of a *Hamamelis mollis*, planted by Ruth more than thirty years ago.

Beneath it the tips of snowdrops were already showing, a reminder that the season was turning, the solstice was just days away and this dreadful year would soon be over.

Then she went and sat for a while on a bench in the secluded corner of the garden where she'd dug up the bones of a baby boy and where her husband had died, and thought about Fiona and what would happen to her.

And then she'd thought about who might have been with Gregory Tatton before he died, because until that was settled, there would be no peace.

There was something else. Something niggling at the back of her mind, something she'd heard or seen, but it wouldn't come.

She needed to talk to Beattie and June again . . .

CHAPTER FORTY

"The police asked us that," June said, when Abby asked her who had driven Tatton home from the lunch. "He called a taxi."

"There were quite a few people standing with him while he waited for it," Beattie added.

"Did you notice who exactly?" Abby asked.

"Diana was there. At least I think it was Diana. She wears a red coat. And Sandra . . . Someone else was there too, though I can't say for certain who." Beattie shook her head. "I have to say that he looked utterly ridiculous standing there in his Father Christmas outfit clutching his empty Santa sack . . ."

"Except it wasn't empty," June pointed out. "Far from it."

"No, well, a couple of people hadn't turned up," Beattie said, "so he still had their gifts and he'd had quite a haul of presents."

"And I saw him take some chocolates off the table by the grotto and drop them in too," June added.

"As you say. Quite a haul. Did anyone else give him their chocolate?" Abby asked.

"Probably," June said. "I saw him take one out of his pocket and look at it."

"Did he seem surprised to see it?"

"No, he just smiled."

Abby remembered what she'd said to Megan about someone slipping it into his pocket as an excuse for giving him a feel-up, and felt queasy.

"Did either of you see who got in the taxi with him?"

"It couldn't have been Sandra. I saw her walking down the hill into town and I'm pretty sure Diana was with her."

"That wasn't Diana. Wendy was wearing the red coat and she was with Glenda," June insisted. "I heard her say that she wanted to look around the Christmas Market. David Hogg was there. Gregory was asking him if he'd touch up the paintwork on his windows when he had a moment and I heard him offer Penny a lift."

"Penny goes everywhere on her bike," Abby said.

"She had a flat tyre, but she said she needed to walk off her lunch."

"There was someone else," Beattie said.

June huffed. "Well, it wasn't Sandra or Diana."

"Which taxi firm did he call?" Abby cut in before they fell out.

"Ours came before his," June said, "but he always booked that man in Moffat Street. I can't think why. He only has one car and he always keeps you waiting."

Abby could make a guess why Tatton would use someone less convenient. There were any number of secrets that a taxi driver might want to keep hidden. A drink-driving conviction? A fatal accident? Or could he have been running a taxi without a licence?

And taxi licences, she knew, were issued by the county council.

* * *

Finding the telephone number for Moffat Cars wasn't difficult. It had a very basic website, little more than an email address and a telephone number, offering local runs and promising reasonable fares for local trips and airport runs.

The following morning, after dropping the girls off at school, Abby drove along Moffat Street, parked up and waited, taking a chance that, after the early morning rush when the big taxi firms would be booked for school runs, he'd come home for breakfast, or at least a cup of tea.

Sure enough, just after nine thirty, a taxi drew up and Abby got out of her car.

"Excuse me . . ."

The driver turned to look at her. "Yes?"

"I'm so sorry to bother you but I believe Mr Tatton is a regular customer of yours and you picked him up at St Bart's parish hall the Saturday before last."

"I really can't discuss my customers—"

"No, of course not, but my friend was with him and thinks they may have left something in your car." She didn't know whether it had been a man or woman with Tatton so she opted for something that wasn't gender specific. "It was a favourite scarf. Cashmere."

He looked momentarily taken aback. "A scarf?" Then he smiled. "Scarves, gloves, phones . . . You wouldn't believe the things I find in the back of my taxi. Cashmere, you say?"

"Blue." Since it didn't exist there was no harm in inventing a colour.

"Is your friend that skinny woman he sometimes has with him? She wasn't wearing a scarf when she got in the car but hang on, I'll go and check."

She nodded, surprised that he wouldn't remember picking up a cashmere scarf, but at least she now knew that Tatton had gone home with a woman. Diana was skinny — all that Zumba — but so was Trish. And Penny, but she'd walked home.

Abby waited and, unsurprisingly, he put his head out of the door and said, "No. There was nothing left in the cab. I seem to remember that she had her hands full when she got in, so she could have dropped it in the street."

Abby sighed. "Oh, she will be disappointed. You were her last hope, but thank you for looking."

He grunted and shut the door.

The woman with him had her hands full. So what was she carrying?

Leftovers from the lunch? No doubt Gregory would have wanted anything he could take. It seemed unlikely that it would be food. One of the table decorations? Unopened bottles of wine? Even opened bottles were possible, since the ones on the table had been screw tops. Whoever the woman was, she would have been left to carry it, because Gregory had his sack.

And she would have had her gift from Gregory's sack to carry as well.

The more she thought about it the more questions there were.

Where did she go from here?

* * *

"Penny?" Abby tapped on the back door and put her head around. "Are you busy?"

"I'm just putting together a couple of dozen mince pies for the CID room at the police station. Iain asked for them after tasting mine at the party on Saturday."

"That's great. Let's hope they'll sweeten him up."

Penny turned to look at her. "What's up? You don't look that hot."

"It's been a difficult morning, but June said you had a flat tyre and I wondered if you'd like a lift to the funeral tomorrow."

"No, all fixed," Penny said, pointing at a chair with her rolling pin. "But sit down and catch your breath. I'll put the kettle on and make us both a cup of tea."

"I'll do it. You're up to your elbows in flour." Abby dropped her bag on the armchair normally occupied by Mabel the cat, but presumably she'd been banished in the interests of hygiene.

"Thanks." Penny started cutting circles out of the pastry. "Talking about the funeral, have you heard about poor

Fiona Keane? I saw David Hogg when I did a supermarket dash this morning. You know he's a church warden?"

"No . . ."

"Well, anyway, David told me what happened to Fiona. Shocking news. Presumably that was why she was in such a state at your party."

"It seems likely," Abby agreed, relieved that her part in what happened wasn't making the gossip. She didn't want that getting back to Nigel Keane.

"Nigel's taken compassionate leave. It's a real shame that he won't be there to take Edward's funeral tomorrow," Penny added, sliding the circles into the buttered bun tins. "He knew Edward, and it's not the same when it's a stranger, is it?"

"Edward's friends will be there . . ."

"It'll be Gregory Tatton's next, although he doesn't appear to have anyone pushing to get that over before Christmas."

Abby took down a couple of mugs, dropped in the tea-bags and took the milk from the fridge. "I was at the police station this morning and they believe there was someone with Tatton before he died. Did you see him leaving the lunch?"

"I saw him standing outside, waiting for a taxi," Penny said, spooning in her home-made mincemeat. "He said if I waited he'd give me a lift, but he'd had a few drinks and I didn't want to get in the back of a taxi with him. He wasn't short of company."

"Oh? Can you remember who was with him?"

"David left around the same time I did. Gregory stopped him to ask about some work he wanted done but got short shrift. Wendy was hovering."

"I don't think I know Wendy?" The kettle boiled and Abby filled the mugs. "Would you describe her as skinny?"

Penny looked up. "Okay, are we going to play twenty questions, or do you want to save time and cut to the chase? What exactly do you want to know?"

Abby laughed, she really liked Penny . . .

"As I said, the police now believe that someone was with Tatton before he died, and this morning they took a DNA swab from me."

"Ridiculous," Penny muttered, "but I can see why you'd want to know who got into the taxi with him."

"I spoke to the taxi driver and it was definitely a woman. He said she was skinny and had her hands full. What did they do with the table decorations after the lunch?"

"Each table had a draw," Penny said and, having thought about it, mentioned the winners she could remember.

"So Trish didn't have one?"

"No, she was on my table and it went to that woman who runs the WI. Jane Crawford. Didn't I mention her? She'd made a point of telling us that she'd made all the table decorations."

"Is that Bryan Crawford's mother?"

Howard had caught Councillor Crawford red-handed, using his position on the Planning Committee to line his pockets. Politics being what they were, he'd been allowed to resign to avoid a scandal, but his mother would certainly have done anything to protect his reputation.

As if reading her mind, Penny said, "Her son picked her up."

"What about the gifts from Tatton's sack?" The kettle boiled and Abby filled the mugs. "What were they? Anything big?"

"Books . . ."

"New or second-hand?" Penny glanced at her. "The police have the one with my name on it. It was a second-hand copy of an Agatha Christie."

"Really? All the books I saw looked new, although I suspect most of the gifts came from charity shops or house clearances. There were some pretty individual cups and saucers, small pots, fancy boxes. Nothing of any value, but everyone seemed to enjoy it and the mistletoe got a good workout."

"Oh, please," Abby said, fishing out the teabags and dropping them in the food waste bin.

Penny lifted a damp tea towel and took a second mound of pastry from a bowl. "The only people who left with their hands full would be those who'd won a table decoration," she said. "No, wait . . . I saw Trish with her plastic cake box when she arrived for the lunch."

"Cake box?" Abby swallowed. "Would it have contained a chocolate fudge cake?"

"That's right. The silly cow made one for him every week despite the fact that he treated her like a skivvy. Maybe she hoped it would harden his arteries."

The teaspoon stopped rattling around the mug as Abby froze, milk jug suspended.

Penny glanced at her and straightened. "What? What did I just say?"

"She made him a chocolate fudge cake on that Saturday?"

"Yes, but . . ." Penny caught on quickly. "The chocolate. The police thought the poison was in the chocolate. You don't think . . . ?"

"You said it, Penny. He treated her like a skivvy. The hours she spent on his weekly oblation of chocolate cake, not to mention weeks making that sweater he was wearing the day Edward died."

"But why didn't she just tell him to get lost?" Penny asked, confused. "Despite the fact that she ran around after him with a smile on her face, I never had the impression that she was angling to be the third Mrs Tatton."

Abby hesitated. "If I were to suggest that he seemed to know people's dirty little secrets and used them to apply pressure . . . ?"

"Blackmail?"

"Not for money. For services."

"You know that for a fact?" Abby's silence was answer enough. "Did he try that on you?" Penny asked, attacking the pastry with her rolling pin in a way that would have raised eyebrows on *Bake Off*.

"He implied he knew what went on at Linton Lodge. I suspect a lot of it was guesswork, but the Agatha Christie he planned to give me was called *Crooked House*."

"That's why the bastard was sniffing around Pam. For information."

Abby nodded. "She told him about Ruth arranging for her to live at Spencer Court for the rest of her life."

"And you think he must have had something on Trish?"

"Have you any idea what she did before she worked at the bookshop café, Penny?"

"I've no idea. What are you thinking?" But before Abby could respond, she added, "I suppose the poison could have been in the chocolate frosting. Something that sweet would mask the taste of pretty much anything."

"The police asked me about the chocolates," Abby said, "but they didn't mention a cake."

"She wouldn't have left it there, would she?"

Penny, having cut out smaller circles and topped the mince pies, reached for the pastry brush, coated them with egg wash then slid them into the ancient Aga.

"She would have gone in to make him a cup of tea," she suggested when she'd straightened from the oven and set a timer. "Cut him a slice of the cake and fussed around him until he lost consciousness. How long would that take?"

Abby shook her head. "I don't know."

"She would have cleared up any trace of her presence," Penny said, "maybe used latex gloves to open up the chocolates, leaving the empty wrappers to make it look as if he'd eaten them all."

"And then taken the remains of the cake away with her," Abby finished.

Penny thought for a moment. "There's a risk that someone would have seen her arrive or leave."

Abby shook her head. "It's a quiet cul-de-sac, the kind with high hedges," she said, remembering Tatton's overgrown copper beech hedge. That had been at least two metres and the leaves clung on all through winter. Perfect for a man who valued his privacy. "And Tatton would have expected the taxi to deliver him to the front door."

"But leaving? Surely someone walking away with a big plastic cake box would be seen?"

"Not necessarily . . ." Abby took out her phone and flicked through the photographs Eric had taken of his garden. "See here? There's a gate at the back that leads directly onto the towpath."

"I hope she didn't throw the rest of the cake in the river. I wonder if there were any unexplained duck deaths last week."

"Unlikely. While she could have slipped out of the gate unnoticed, a jogger, or a mother out walking with the buggy, might spot her flinging an entire cake in the water, and they wouldn't forget that. If I were her, I'd have taken it home and flushed it slice by slice down the loo."

"What are you going to do, Abby?"

Ask the audience and fifty/fifty weren't options. "I'm going to phone a friend . . ."

She took out her phone, called up her contacts and tapped the link to Dee Newcombe's mobile phone.

"Abby? Are you okay? I'm really sorry about that session with the DI this morning."

"I have never set foot in Tatton's house, but the DI was just doing his job. Can I ask you a question?"

"You can ask," Dee warned. "I might not be able to answer. What did you want to know?"

"I wondered if forensics found a cake at Gregory Tatton's house?"

"A cake?" Dee repeated, clearly surprised.

"A chocolate fudge cake, to be precise."

"Abby . . ." She was clearly wondering what it was about, but just sighed. "Let me call up the file and check."

Abby looked at Penny. "She's checking."

"No chocolate cake," Dee told her. "Is that good or bad?"

"What about the contents of his stomach?"

"I shouldn't be . . ." There was another pause. "Yes, there was cake, but according to his menu choices at the lunch, he had a chocolate brownie with ice cream for pudding, which was provided by the caterers."

"And that's all they found? Just the brownie? I mean that has the same ingredients as chocolate cake. Could they tell the difference?"

"That's all it says here. Would you like me to ask the pathologist to double-check?" she asked, with the faintest touch of sarcasm.

"It's just a theory," Abby said. "Would they have picked up traces of latex on the chocolate wrappers?"

"Yes," Dee said, with her patience wearing thin. "But the staff in the shop use those."

"Oh, okay."

"I'll ask them to double-check on the cake," Dee said, "but Abby, whatever you're doing, please stop. Fiona Keane was ready to talk, and you did a really good job with her, but whoever killed Gregory Tatton is still out there. If you know something, tell me."

"Find out about the cake and I might have something for you," she said and ended the call before Dee could say more.

CHAPTER FORTY-ONE

Penny raised an eyebrow. "She's making enquiries," Abby said.

"Then you can drink your tea in the knowledge that you've given her something to think about. But Trish . . ." Penny shook her head. "I can't believe it. That woman wouldn't say boo to a goose."

"She seemed to have a bit of a spring in her step when I saw her yesterday."

"Oh? Did you go to the bookshop?"

"No, she was doing the coffees when I called in at the church hall. I wondered where Tatton had left his costume. It occurred to me that someone might have put something in the pocket."

"Oh, right. I gave coffee a miss yesterday. Too much to do."

"I'll drink this and get out of your way. Is there anything you need in town?"

"No." Then, "Abby . . . You will be careful?"

* * *

Abby watched Trish deliver a tray of tea and cakes, smiling in spite of the packed tearoom, checking to make sure the family at the table were happy before turning to look around for any new customers.

As she caught sight of Abby, a moment of panic crossed her face and she glanced from side to side, but there was nowhere to hide.

"More last-minute Christmas shopping, Abby?" Trish said with forced brightness. "I don't think we have a table free—"

"It's okay, I'm not here for the coffee. I just want to know what you did with the cake you made Gregory Tatton on the Saturday he died."

Trish stiffened. "Excuse me?"

"You had a cake with you, you went home in the taxi with him, but the police didn't find a cake. So what did you do with it?"

"What business is it of yours?" The words came out in a fierce whisper.

"My fingerprints were on the chocolate wrappers found at his side, Trish, the police suspect that someone was with him before he died and today I was invited to give a DNA swab. That makes it my business."

For a moment her mouth worked but no sound emerged. "Not here," she finally managed.

"When is your break?" Abby asked.

"Are you kidding? Look at this place . . ." Abby didn't move. Trish put down the tray she was holding, took off her apron and flung it over a vacant chair and called across to another waitress. "I need ten minutes, Beth."

Ignoring Beth's howl of protest, Trish led the way up through the bookshop to a small quiet area and indicated the window seat. "This is the school textbook section," she said. "No one comes here at this time of year."

"The police have Tatton's files," Abby said, getting straight to the point.

All that new bounce went right out of her and Trish seemed to shrivel up like a balloon forgotten after a kid's party.

"I wondered if he'd kept records," she said.

"I imagine he kept everything he found out about all the people he knew. You weren't the only one."

"No. I wondered about Sandra . . . All those damn croissants."

"How is she?" Abby asked.

"Better off?" Trish said, managing a smile. "She told me that she's got a job."

"I know about Sandra. What did he have on you?"

She sighed. "I used to have a wool shop in Ship Street, Abby. It was a really lovely business."

"That was yours? I used to buy wool there for my mother, but I don't remember seeing you there . . ."

"I had staff. It wasn't just a shop, it was a social place. The knit and natter group . . ." She sighed, shook her head. "But what with the business rates and a huge rent increase, it became unsustainable. I had to let the staff go one by one and I lost the lovely group of friends that used to come in every week. There was room at the back where we used to sit and chat while we knitted caps for premature babies, scarves for the homeless, blanket squares for refugees . . ."

"I'm so sorry, Trish. I had no idea."

"I didn't need the things I took. I was just so angry . . ."

"Took?"

"Gregory caught me shoplifting." Abby didn't say anything. "He sat next to me at the seniors' lunch one day and he handed me a photograph. It was in the pharmacy in Bridge Street. He'd taken a photograph of me slipping a packet of painkillers into my pocket. When I looked at it, I nearly passed out."

Abby reached out and took her hand. "If he'd been ready with his phone out to take a photograph, he must have seen you before and followed you. Waiting for his chance."

"I only took little things," Trish insisted, "but it made me feel better. At least, for an hour or two."

"What happened after he gave you the photograph?" Abby asked.

"I froze. I didn't know what he was going to do, but then he started talking about cake and I heard him say to someone, 'Trish makes a wonderful chocolate fudge cake . . .' And he turned and looked at me and said, 'You'd make one for me if I asked you, wouldn't you, Trish?'"

"That was it?"

"He didn't have to say any more. I said, 'Of course, Gregory,' and the next week he said he thought the frosting had been a bit on the thin side and he'd like a little more this week. It was the same with the jumper. He admired the one I'd made for Sandra's grandson, then he looked at me and said he'd seen a man-sized one with snowflakes."

"I'm so sorry, Trish." No point in saying she should have told someone. That was the thing about embarrassing secrets . . . They held you prisoner.

"I hated Gregory Tatton," Trish said, tears in her eyes. "I wish I'd had the courage to kill him, but it wasn't me."

"So, what happened to the cake this Saturday?"

"I gave it to him, but he said he couldn't manage it with everything else so I'd better go with him. He'd been drinking and when we were in the car . . ." Trish had her eyes down, talking barely above a whisper. "He started touching me. He'd never done that before and I brushed his hand away, told him to behave, but he grabbed my wrist, opened his costume, unzipped his trousers and put my hand down on him, rubbing himself against it." She looked up, her eye pleading. "I tried to pull away but he . . ." She shook her head, rubbed her wrist as if to erase the memory. "He said he needed a good seeing to and it was about time I took a turn. When the car stopped he had to let go of me, but the taxi driver had another pick-up waiting so I had no choice but to get out too."

"Did you go inside?"

"He unlocked the door, threw it open and . . . Well, I won't repeat what he said."

"It's okay, Trish, I get it."

"If I'd had a knife in my hand at that moment, I think I might have killed him," she said. "Standing there in that ridiculous outfit, looking so pleased with himself. Thinking that I'd demean myself . . . And I thought, *Whatever people think about me is not going to be as bad as what I'll think of myself if I go inside his house and do what he wants.* So I turned around and walked away. That took him by surprise because by the time he'd straightened himself out to come after me I was too far down the street and he could hardly chase after me in that ridiculous outfit."

"And the cake?"

"I'd left it on the seat of the taxi. The shock, I suppose. Presumably the taxi driver found it and took it home. Me . . . I'm never going to make another chocolate fudge cake as long as I live."

Abby remembered the surprise on the driver's face when she'd said her friend had lost a scarf. He'd thought she was going to ask about the cake, which would have been well beyond eating by then.

"I'm truly sorry you had to go through that, Trish. I imagine it was your DNA they found on him."

"Do you think I should go and make a statement?"

"It would help but I can understand your reluctance. Let's see how it goes. You're not still shoplifting?" she asked.

"No. Instant cure." Trish pulled a face. "I have to get back."

"Of course. Thank you for being so frank." Abby squeezed her hand and let go. It had taken a lot of courage to share that ordeal. "Why don't you restart your knitting group? You could put up a notice in the library. They have a meeting room you could use."

"Yes . . . Maybe I will," she said, and smiled.

Abby waited for her to leave and was about to follow when her phone beeped to let her know she had a text.

No cake. Do you have any more bright ideas to make me unpopular with the pathologist? D.

She texted back. *I'm sorry for wasting everyone's time but I now know what happened to the cake. The poison has to have been in something else. He had a very sweet tooth.*

250

He had been given a lot of chocolate and some of those fancy fruit jellies. They've all been tested.

It only needed one.

Stick to gardening, Abby, and leave the detecting to us.

It was sound advice. But first there was something Megan said about her chat with Yvonne Thompson that she had to check out.

CHAPTER FORTY-TWO

Abby was writing an email when the doorbell rang.

"Can someone get that?" she called.

Tom answered the door. "Hello, Jake!" Abby heard him say. "Sorry about the side gate. Mum said there's been a spate of burglaries."

"Actually, Tom, this is front-door business. Are Lucy and Sophie about?" Abby frowned. Front-door business? What did that mean? Things had been a little tense between them since he got home. Her fault, she'd been so focused on Tatton's death . . .

"We're all in the kitchen, clearing up after supper. Mum's in her office." Abby looked up, expecting him to put his head around the door.

"Mum can wait. It's you three I want to see.

"Oh . . . Okay. Well, you know the way."

Abby quickly signed off on the email, hit send and went to her office door in time to see Jake's back as he followed her son into the kitchen. Curious, she went after them but then hovered, uncertainly, in the hall.

"Hello, Jake," Lucy said from the kitchen. "I'm just about to make Mum a cup of tea. Do you want one? Or coffee?"

"Let's see how this goes, first," Jake said.

"Something's up," Tom said.

"Oh?"

"Tom's right. What's up is this." There was a pause and Abby held her breath. "Lucy, Tom, Sophie, I've come to ask your mother out on a date. Before I do, I want to know if that's okay with you."

Tom laughed. *Well he would*, Abby thought. He'd caught them kissing.

"Why do you need our approval?" Lucy asked. "Oh, because you're serious."

And Sophie said, "Does that mean you're in love with her?"

By this time Abby was behind him, ready to call a halt to the proceedings, but before she could speak, Jake said, "Yes, Sophie. I've loved your mother, been in love with her, for a very long time. Since before she married your dad."

"So why didn't you marry her?"

"Because if I had, she wouldn't have you, Sophie. She wouldn't have had any of you."

Abby's hand went to her mouth. Could there have been a more perfect answer?

Tom had seen her in the doorway and, grinning, said, "It's okay with me."

"Lucy?" Jake prompted.

"Just . . . be kind to her. She deserves someone who'll be kind."

Abby was standing there, tears in her eyes, unable to speak, when Sophie asked, "Will you have a baby with Mummy, like Daddy did with Izzy?"

Jake, clearly aware that she was behind him, reached back a hand. When she took it, he said, "The protocol, Sophie, is that we wait until the third date before we get around to serious questions like that."

Tom smirked.

Lucy spluttered.

Sophie said, "Well, if you do it had better be a girl. Just saying."

"If Mum says yes to the date, I'll babysit," Lucy said quickly. "Minimum hourly rate and I'll need twenty-four hours' notice."

"It's a deal," Jake said. "Thursday? There's a classic movie playing at the cinema that she might like and then I thought supper at Giovanni's. I'll have her home before the clock strikes twelve."

"We break up on Wednesday so you can stay out as long as you like," Lucy assured him. "But it's double time after twelve. I'm saving up for a gap year," she added hopefully.

"Don't I get a say in this?" Abby asked.

Jake finally turned to her, his expression unreadable. "The movie, the Italian or the clock?"

"What's the movie?" she asked, just so that he'd know she wasn't a complete pushover.

"It's a special showing of *Casablanca*. I've never seen it, but I've heard it's very good. And also that it's your favourite movie ever."

He'd been talking to Megan . . .

"You're in for a treat," she told him and saw his expression resolve into a relieved smile. He'd been holding his breath, she realised. But then so had she.

"The idea was to give you one. A night out. Something to dress up for. When was the last time you dressed up?"

"I can tell you that. It was the end-of-year school concert last July," Lucy informed him. "She wore her best black trousers *and* lipstick."

Abby shook her head, but she was laughing.

"Would you care to come into the living room, Jake, so that we can discuss this while the children finish clearing up?"

She didn't wait, but with her hand still in his led him through to the front of the house. He closed the door and leaned against it, pulling her to him. "Am I in trouble?"

"Big time . . ." She swallowed. "Don't you dare give either Lucy or Tom ideas about what's allowable on a third date."

The smile became a grin. "I have just two words to say to that: prom night . . ." And he cut off any argument with a kiss.

"Jake! I'm serious," she said, minutes later.

"So am I, Abby. So am I . . . I know it's not going to be easy. They've been through a lot and so have you. But running away from this isn't going to make it go away."

"I wasn't running from you," she said. "Yesterday, I was at Linton Lodge burning the portrait of Howard Finch Senior."

"Running from the past, then. Did it make you feel better?"

"Not as much as I thought it would."

"Do you want to talk about it?"

Abby shook her head. "Actually, what I'd like to do is to sit on the sofa with you, sipping a glass of that wine you know that warms the soul and lifts the spirits, but since you came empty-handed, I guess we'll have to make do with Lucy's tea."

CHAPTER FORTY-THREE

After Edward's funeral, everyone crossed the road to the White Hart, where Stephanie and Chris had arranged a small wake, but once they'd drunk a toast in his memory and Abby felt able to leave, she turned to Jake.

"Have you got time for a walk by the river?" she asked. "I need to talk to you . . ."

"Let's go."

He took her hand and they slipped away, walking along the riverside path in silence for a while until Jake spotted a secluded bench.

"Here?" he suggested.

Abby nodded, and once they were sitting looking out at the river, she said, "I'm sorry."

He didn't ask what she was sorry about, he just waited.

"You knew something was wrong, but it was all so horrible and you were in Rome negotiating a huge business deal—"

"I would have caught the next flight home if you needed me. I thought you knew that."

"That's why I didn't tell you. It was so nasty. I didn't want you involved . . ."

"Damn it, I am involved—" He stopped, put his arm around her. "I've been involved since the first time you offered me a cheese and pickle sandwich from your lunch-box. The cheese wasn't that tasteless plastic stuff, but the real thing, full of flavour. And the pickle was home-made . . ."

"You remember that?"

"I'll never forget the taste, or the smile you gave me. You had the same sandwiches when we grabbed a stolen lunch-time on the houseboat back in the summer. It took me right back. The taste, your smile . . . It was one of those perfect moments," he said. "But then every moment with you is perfect."

He'd said it to make her feel better, but Abby just wanted to weep, aware that she'd been keeping him at a distance when he was the best thing that had ever happened to her.

Aware that she'd been using the children as an excuse, when she was the one afraid of making a commitment.

He had sensed she was in trouble, but had waited for her to tell him.

It was time for total honesty . . .

"It all began with the mistletoe," she began, and she spilled it all out, leaving out nothing until today, here, sitting with him on this bench.

"I don't understand," he said, when she'd finished. "I don't understand why you didn't tell me."

"You were in Italy," she began, then stopped, realising that she was doing it again. Total honesty, not just with Jake but with herself. "I didn't tell you, because every time I see you I want you more and I'm afraid of that."

"Because?"

"Howard's infidelity must have damaged me more than I realised. I'm not ready to take the risk . . ." And before he could protest, "I don't want you to be hurt either, Jake. I didn't want you rushing home from Italy because I saw how you reacted when Howard threatened me. I didn't want you locked up for assault in time for Christmas."

"That's gives me hope," Jake said. "As for Howard, hitting him was an instinctive reaction and he hit me a lot harder, but this was different. Dealing with Tatton would have needed thought and big legal guns."

"And that's what I did," she said. "I thought. And Megan helped. Tatton was a monster, and after all the things I've found out about him it's a wonder he didn't end up like that man on the Orient Express, with everyone lining up to stick a dagger in him."

"Well, whoever killed him, it's over," he said. "He's no longer able to hurt anyone, so leave it to the police."

"Yes," she said.

"Yes, but . . . ?" he asked, unconvinced.

"Yes, but . . . They still seem to have me on their list of suspects."

"What? That's ridiculous. You had half the Maybridge constabulary at your house on Saturday."

"A slight exaggeration, but I was *Mrs Finch* when I was interviewed again yesterday."

"Abby, Abby . . ." He sighed. "What am I going to do with you?"

She turned to look at him. "Ask me that again on our third date."

His only response was to pull her close and, with her cheek pressed against his shoulder, Abby felt that for the first time in an age, the world was righting itself.

* * *

Abby knew that Jake was right. She should leave everything to the police, but then she received a response to an email she'd sent on Monday. The attachment was a photograph of two pretty young women.

She forwarded it to Megan then phoned her, but the call went straight to voicemail.

"Meg, I've sent you an email and I need to ask you something about your conversation with Yvonne Thompson. Call me when you have a moment."

She tapped the end of her pencil on her notepad.

She'd been making a list of things she needed to do after the holiday.

Buy horticultural fleece to protect the blossom on the peach and apricots.
Remind Cal to check the stakes, ties and supports in the gardens in their care.
Buy ties and stakes . . .

The greenhouses would all need cleaning. Abby, aware that the show garden was going to take up a lot of her time, called Kate Brooks, a keen gardener who'd helped her out in the past when she'd been busy. She asked if she'd be interested in a part-time job and arranged that she start in January.

Restless, she called Jake on an impulse, listened to him inviting her to leave a message. Remembering that he was in London, she said, "It's nothing. I'm about to go and pick up some stuff from the nursery in Longbourne. Meg saw a house there . . ." She stopped. That's what she'd been doing for months. Telling herself that she was doing him a favour by pushing him away. But Jake knew what he wanted. She was the one who'd been running scared. "I just wanted to tell you that I'm looking forward to our date."

She checked on the children. It was the first day of the holidays and they were outside loading a Christmas tree planted out in the garden years ago with lights and food for the birds.

"I'm going to the garden centre to get a few things. Will you three be okay for an hour or so?"

"Are you meeting Jake?" Sophie asked.

"He's in London."

"Will you be back in time for lunch?" Tom asked.

"Probably but you're not helpless. Make yourself something if I'm not back before starvation threatens."

Since it was a business trip, she took the Earthly Designs van and drove to the garden centre where she'd once worked. She picked up the items: an industrial-sized pack of ties, four rolls of fleece and was tempted by a couple of good-looking pots. Then, after standing in the queue for what felt like forever, she drove along the lane and stopped outside Bramble Cottage.

There had been neglect, the paintwork needed a freshen up, but Megan was right about the thatched roof. It was chocolate box perfect.

She'd been sitting there for a couple of minutes, not quite sure how she was going to approach this, when her phone rang.

Jake.

"What are you doing in a garden centre?" he asked. "Shouldn't you be focused on our date? Hairdresser, nails . . ."

"Here's the shocking truth, Jake. Getting a last-minute appointment at the hairdresser the week before Christmas is the equivalent of finding a hoard of Anglo-Saxon gold under my lawn. Freshly washed is as good as it's going to get."

"I love freshly washed hair," he said, "but I hope you're going to give the good black pants a miss and go for a dress. Your legs deserve to be seen and admired."

"I may have to go shopping," she said and then, spotting Yvonne Thompson coming around the side of her cottage, she said, "I've got to go . . ." She dropped her phone in her bag and, before she lost her nerve, opened the van door and climbed out.

"If you want to take a photograph, I charge ten pounds."

Abby stopped, confused. "I'm sorry?"

Yvonne Thompson laughed. "Just kidding. So many people stop to take a photograph for Instagram, especially when the garden is in full bloom, that I thought I might put up a sign."

"I wonder how many people would pay up," Abby asked.

"Not many, but maybe it would stop them parking outside." She tilted her head to one side.

Abby approached the gate, hoping that Megan was right about Yvonne's eagerness to talk. "It must be a nuisance, but I can understand why people stop to take pictures." Her gesture took in the village. "I mean look at it. The green, the cricket pavilion, a pond with a weeping willow and a higgledy-piggledy assortment of pretty cottages. It's the quintessential English village that everyone dreams about."

"I suppose it is," Yvonne said. "Are you in the market for a house here?"

"No, but I have a friend who's been looking for the perfect place for six months, and an estate agent I know, Megan West, mentioned that you might be putting yours on the market."

"I don't remember saying that."

"Maybe I got it wrong. She did mention that she'd looked at one by the river. Or maybe she was just being optimistic. I imagine this cottage would sell in a heartbeat. I can just picture it with the wisteria in flower." She offered her hand. "I'm Abby Finch—"

"I know who you are. The van," Yvonne said. "And your picture was in the paper."

"Oh, yes." Abby had forgotten. "The show garden."

"Yvonne Thompson," she said, taking Abby's hand, "but I'm no gardener. The front has been kept tidy, but the back is a jungle of overgrown shrubs and nettles."

"The butterflies will appreciate them," Abby said, "but if you need a good guide, I can thoroughly recommend Daisy Dashwood's *First Steps in Gardening*. I'm sure they'll have it in the library."

"Thanks, but my main problem at the moment is a houseplant. My neighbour has been taking care of it while I was away, but it looks a bit sick. Maybe you could take a look at it, tell me if it's salvageable," she said, opening the gate. "And then I'll show you around and you can see if the cottage would suit your friend."

"Of course." Abby was hardly able to believe her luck. But then Yvonne knew who she was, and she'd invited Megan in too. Had Yvonne always been so naïve? "What is it?" she asked, and followed her along a short corridor into the kitchen. "The plant."

"I've no idea," Yvonne admitted cheerfully. "Tea?"

Abby accepted gratefully.

"It's a peach *anthurium*," she said, as soon as she saw the wilting plant. Behind her Yvonne put on the kettle, put out two very pretty china mugs and dropped in teabags. "It's not getting enough light here. It likes bright, but indirect light." Abby lifted it and water dripped into the ceramic pot it was standing in. "And your neighbour has been overwatering it. Don't water until the top two inches of the soil feel dry to the touch. They're actually very hard to kill."

"Well, that's good news. It was a moving-in gift from a woman who used to work for me and I live in dread of her dropping in and seeing it."

Abby thought that the chance of anyone dropping in unannounced all the way from Keynsham seemed unlikely but she nodded. "Awkward," she agreed.

"I've never been good with houseplants," Yvonne said, pouring hot water into the mugs. "Milk?"

"Just a splash."

The splash duly added to Abby's mug, the other left black, Yvonne said, "Come and have a look around while the tea gets cool enough to drink."

"Did Megan give you any idea of the market price for the cottage?" Abby asked, as she glanced around the sitting room and the dining room, making an effort to appear genuinely interested in the property. "The dining room is on the small side."

"She anticipated a bidding war if I did decide to sell," Yvonne said, leading the way upstairs. "There are three bedrooms . . . Well, two and a box room."

"It's for a single man. What a lovely space," Abby said, pausing on the half-landing to look down at the garden. It really was overgrown, although there were some fine specimen shrubs among the weeds. "A long garden is so easy to divide up into interesting spaces. And that's a really beautiful *Hamamelis Diane* 'Ruby Glow'. If my friend does make you an offer, I'll be pestering him for cuttings."

"You know the names of all the plants?" Yvonne asked.

"It's all part of the job. That's *Clematis* 'Winter Beauty', over the arch. The flowers are so delicate against that dark green foliage." As she turned to continue up the stairs, her eye was caught by a skeletal clump of *Ricinus communis* with its prickly seed heads. "You should be very careful of that one. Every part of it is poisonous." And then realising that she'd just said something very stupid, she looked up at Yvonne. "But you already know that, don't you?"

CHAPTER FORTY-FOUR

Yvonne smiled. "I already told you, I know nothing about gardening. Is that why you're really here, Abby Finch? Did your friend tell you what a state my garden is in and suggest you might be able to drum up some business?"

"I don't need to cold call for business," Abby said.

"No, I didn't think so. First that estate agent turns up, full of questions about my sister and telling me that Gregory Tatton is dead and now you're here pretending to be interested in my cottage . . ." Her shrug suggested that one of them was stupid and it wasn't her.

Abby realised that she'd been rumbled and there was no point in pretence. "You told Megan that the police would want to interview you. And then you made a point of telling Megan that you were in the clear because you were away when Tatton died. But she didn't tell you when he died, only that it was recent."

She'd gone over in her head what Megan had told her about their conversation and she'd been quite specific.

"You didn't even ask when he'd died."

"I told her that I've been away recently," Yvonne said. "On an extended vacation."

"And she accepted that," Abby said. "You managed to convince her, a woman who takes scepticism to unheard of heights, of your sincerity. But then you weren't just engaged to the actor who switched his affections to your sister, were you? You were on the stage yourself. You and Elaine were the Thompson Sisters."

Yvonne's smile deepened. "Goodness, that was a lifetime ago. I thought everyone had forgotten us."

"Megan is used to getting people to open up to her, tell her things they probably shouldn't. In fact, that's how we met," Abby said. "She thought you were lonely, and desperate to talk, but the way you opened up to a complete stranger, telling her about your sister, how you'd become estranged and your regret . . . It all seemed a little bit too easy to me."

"So you decided to check up on me? Why? What's it to you?"

"Equity were very helpful," Abby told her. The why and what could wait. "They even sent me a publicity photograph of you and Elaine."

"Taken back in the good old days when we thought nothing and no one would ever break us up."

Her sigh was a touch theatrical, Abby decided.

"Elaine was the one with the voice, I just made up the volume, but I put the act together, handled the business. We were never going to be on *Top of the Pops*, but we did very well at end-of-the-pier summer seasons and provincial panto. I've still got a poster . . . Would you like to see?"

She didn't wait for an answer but continued to lead the way upstairs and there they were, in a framed panto poster, on the wall of a small back bedroom. The Thompson Sisters in *Puss in Boots*, wearing tights, thigh-high boots and wearing skimpy costumes that suggested they were the Prince's coachmen.

A response was clearly expected. "Very glamorous," Abby said.

"We were, but solo that wasn't enough. After we broke up, I worked in rep for a while and I had small parts in soaps, hospital dramas. I did a really good dead body . . ."

"That must have been an interesting life," Abby said, in an effort to keep her talking.

"Interesting? I was in cheap digs and endlessly 'resting', while my sister was living here in comfort with the man I loved . . ." Yvonne's voice rose, betraying her resentment. Then, perhaps realising how that sounded, she performed a studied shrug. "It's okay when you're young, but you get to a point where you have to accept that no matter how good you are, you're never going to get the security of a good part in a soap, one of those Greek chorus characters who props up the bar week after week. Shall we go down? The tea will be getting cold."

Abby thought about Yvonne's ready hospitality. She hadn't been fooled for a minute by her casual interest in the cottage, she realised, and it occurred to her that whatever was in that tea, it wouldn't be the cup that cheered.

"But despite your bust up, your sister made over her lovely cottage to you," she said, not moving.

"I knew then that Tatton had killed her," she said. "I had no proof, only that she would rather give it to me than let him have it. But then, when I was able to move here, back in the summer, I found her letter."

"There was a letter?" Abby's heart rate kicked up a beat. There was proof that Tatton was a murderer?

Yvonne sat on the bed, sending up a small cloud of dust from the patchwork quilt. It glittered in the low winter sunshine slanting in through the window.

"I'd been writing to her for a while," she said. "We were sisters and I wanted to put the past behind us, but it was obvious, when I read her letter, that she'd never got the ones I'd sent her."

There was no chair and Abby leaned against the windowsill. Her fingers strayed towards the bag slung over her shoulder and her mobile phone but Yvonne was watching her and Abby knew she would see the moment she went for it.

She had to keep her talking.

"Tatton had been intercepting her mail?" Abby asked as though she were having a normal conversation with a new acquaintance, and not a woman driven to murder.

266

"He must have been. If only I'd gone to the house and knocked on the door, but after all the things I'd said to her . . . I'd refused to go to her first wedding and I didn't get an invitation to the second."

"Did she know where you were?"

"She could have asked Susan . . ."

"Susan?"

"A distant cousin. She took care of us when our mother was ill, dying. I'd stayed in touch with her. Just Christmas and birthday cards." Yvonne couldn't hide the bitterness from her voice. "Elaine was always her favourite, which is why after her marriage, when Susan was in a bad place, she offered her this cottage at a peppercorn rent."

It was quiet in the little room while Yvonne remembered her sister, the missed chances to restore their broken relationship. Maybe to have saved her.

"Elaine hadn't got my letters, but when she was desperate, afraid, she wrote to me for help, but I never got the letter. I found it when I moved in over the summer."

Despite everything, Abby felt a pang of sympathy for this woman who had always come second best to her sister. The voice, the man, even the carer . . .

"She left it here?"

"She visited Susan regularly. I'm sure Tatton would have stopped her — he cut her off from all her other friends, as I discovered after she died — but it gave him a chance to keep an eye on a valuable piece of property that he already thought of as his own. She wouldn't have been able to ask Susan for my address with him there, so she wrote a letter and tucked it away where she could be sure Susan would find it and send it on.

"But she didn't find it . . . ?" Abby prompted.

"Susan phoned me, saying that she had something for me, but when I arrived she had no idea why I was there. She was already sliding into the early stages of Alzheimer's. I arranged for a carer, but we ended up having to move her into a home. When I moved in, I found Elaine's letter in the kitchen dresser, jumbled up with years of clutter. A small envelope with my name on it. I knew then, even before I opened it . . ."

"What was in the letter, Yvonne?"

"That she was sorry she'd hurt me. That Simon had done to her what he'd done to me, so he'd hurt us both. Well, I knew that . . . She said that she wasn't feeling well, was suffering from nausea and having dizzy spells. She wrote that she was certain that Gregory had somehow killed his first wife and was now poisoning her. It wasn't entirely coherent, she was rambling, clearly affected by whatever he was giving her . . ."

"I'm so sorry."

"The last thing she wrote was that she'd transferred the ownership of the cottage to me and she was enclosing a key."

"To the cottage?"

Abby had become so caught up in this tragedy that she'd forgotten the danger.

"What would have been the point of that?" Yvonne asked. "Susan was here . . . It was a key to River View."

"She wanted you to come and rescue her . . ."

"Why else would she give me the key?" Yvonne asked, as if she was slow-witted. "She was frightened. She had no one else to turn to and I wasn't there for her."

"You couldn't have known . . ."

"*She was my sister.*" Yvonne emphasized each word. "I *should* have known. I had my suspicions when she died, tried to get someone to listen to me when her lawyer explained about the cottage. Tatton asked about it when it wasn't included in her will. You should have seen his face . . ." She dwelt on the memory for a moment, a smile playing around her lips. Then she shook her head. "But I only discovered the truth when I read her letter."

Her voice was frighteningly calm, but her hands were clenched into fists. Abby tried to imagine what it must have been like to read that letter and discover what her sister had been going through. To know how frightened Elaine must have been.

"And that was when you decided to kill Gregory Tatton," she said. "How did you know about the castor oil plant, Yvonne?"

"I don't know what you're talking about."

"Did you look up poisonous plants on the web?" She'd told Iain Glover that anyone could find a list online. "You recognised one you had in your garden. What did you do? Dry the beans and powder them? Or did you grind them into a paste?"

"What would you do, Abby Finch?"

"I imagine the first thing you did was book that trip to follow in your sister's footsteps. It should be easy enough to check the dates."

She didn't wait for Yvonne to reply.

"The difficulty would be getting Tatton to take the poison. A capsule would be the safest way. You can pull them apart, empty out the contents and replace them with anything."

"It sounds as if you're the one planning a murder."

"You waited until he went out and then used the key to let yourself in. Most people of his age take a supplement of some sort. What was it? My grandmother took green-lipped mussel for her hips."

"Did it work?"

"Whatever you found, you refilled one of them with the ricin powder then pushed it to the bottom of the jar so that you'd be out of the country when he took it. Am I right?"

"You're the smart one, Abby Finch. You tell me." Yvonne was mocking her. "Oh, wait, there would only be one poison capsule. You wouldn't risk leaving another and giving the game away, would you, Abby? Ta-da! No evidence. You'll just have to—"

She was interrupted by a ring at the doorbell.

"Now who can that be? Someone else wanting to look at the house?" Yvonne suggested with a wry smile as she rose to her feet. "Or maybe it's someone worried about you, Abby. Did you leave a message to let your friend know where you were going?"

"Of course," Abby said, trying to remember exactly what she'd said in the message she'd left Megan.

Yvonne shook her head. "Never play poker . . ." Then as whoever it was put their thumb on the bell for the second time, she gestured to the door. "Let's go and see," she said, no longer smiling. "You first."

Abby felt herself propelled towards the bedroom door and knew she was running out of time. She slipped her hand into her bag and quickly activated her phone as she drew it out.

"Don't be stupid," Yvonne sneered, grabbing Abby's wrist in an iron grip. Wrenching her phone from her grasp, she flung it to the floor and stamped on it.

"Let's go answer the door, Abby," she said, manhandling her towards the landing.

Just as they reached the top step, Abby swung into Yvonne, giving her a hard push, and as she stumbled back, swearing, Abby bolted down the stairs and made a dash for the door.

The catch was stiff, and she was still struggling to open the door, shouting for help, as Yvonne hurtled down the stairs after her.

With a last-gasp wrench Abby finally flung open the door. Only to find her way blocked by Nigel Keane.

There was a single shocked moment as they confronted one another and then he surged forward. Without thinking, Abby flung up her fist, catching him hard on the nose just as his hands closed around her throat.

He released her with a grunt but, as Abby tried to knee him in the groin, Yvonne grabbed her by the hair and yanked her back.

CHAPTER FORTY-FIVE

There was blood trickling down Nigel Keane's nose as he loomed in the hallway, swaying slightly. Abby, her scalp on fire, opened her mouth to scream, but no sound emerged.

Yvonne, her mouth close to her ear, hissed, "He doesn't seem to like you, Abby. What have you done to him?"

"I—" Her throat was tight and the words wouldn't come. Yvonne tightened her grasp on Abby's hair and jerked her back before slapping her around the side of her head so that for a moment she saw stars.

"Tell me," she demanded.

"I rescued his wife," Abby gasped. "He's a controlling bastard. Just like Tatton . . ." she added, in the desperate hope that Yvonne would turn on him.

"She didn't need rescuing!" Keane howled his fury. "She didn't want to be rescued. She knows she's mine. She's *mine*," he repeated, angrily, "until death do us part, and you, evil woman, stole her from me. Where have you taken her? Tell me or I'll beat it out of you—"

"She's not your possession," Abby gasped. "Fiona found a man who loved her, who she wanted to be with . . ."

Yvonne loosened her grip and Abby dropped onto the stairs.

"No, no, no . . ." Keane's voice rose with every repeat of the word. "He was an adulterer, vile, tainted, and I'm glad he's dead. And you are a Jezebel, tempting her away . . ." He lurched towards her again, hands outstretched, hellbent on finishing what he'd started. "She is mine. She will come home . . ."

That was the point at which Yvonne hit him in the face with the crook of a walking stick she'd snatched from the hall stand.

He stood for a moment, stunned. Then sank to his knees and fell back against the wall.

"That's right," Yvonne said. "You just sit there and get your breath," she said, her voice all sympathy, "while I go and get something to make you feel better."

As she disappeared into the back of the house, Abby knew that she should run, but somehow she couldn't convince her body to move.

"This is what you need," Yvonne said, returning a few moments later with a steaming mug. "A nice cup of tea with lots of sugar . . ."

It was such a normal thing to offer in the circumstances that Abby scarcely registered what was happening until Nigel had raised the mug to his lips. Yvonne's words finally connected with what few brain cells were still functioning and she realised that Keane was holding the mug of tea that Yvonne had made for her.

"Don't drink that!" Abby lunged forward and knocked it out of his hand.

"What . . . ?"

"It's poisoned! She meant it for me."

Yvonne let out a shriek of frustration, turning again on Abby, but the adrenaline surge had got Abby to her feet and she pushed Yvonne back against the wall, pinning her there, her arm across Yvonne's chest.

"No, Yvonne!" she shouted, determined to get through to her. "No more killing! It's over!"

"Why? He's just another man who thinks he can do what he likes to women. He deserves to die." And she lashed out at him with her foot.

Keane roared, leaping to his feet, pushing Abby away. He made a grab for Yvonne, who brought up her knee sharply. He dropped with a howl of agony, rolling onto his side, clutching at his groin, and curled into a foetal ball.

She was still holding the walking stick, and raised it above her head. "I killed Tatton and I'll kill you."

As she brought the stick down, Abby threw herself against her so that it missed his head and they both fell against the wall.

Struggling to be the first to stand, Abby became conscious of the sound of an approaching police car.

"You called?" Dee said, a moment later, looking around her at Keane still groaning with pain, Yvonne weeping with frustration, Abby collapsed against the wall and the broken mug and the puddle of spilled tea staining the wooden floor.

"I hoped so," Abby told her, making an effort to get to her feet. "I really hoped I'd called someone, but five minutes earlier would have been helpful."

"You activated your emergency button and Megan, as your responder, dialled 999. We got here as fast as humanly possible," Dee replied. "Do you want to tell me what's going on?"

Yvonne looked at Dee and then at Abby. "You've got an emergency button?" she said. "Where?"

"Three quick presses on the side button of my phone sends an emergency alert with my location to someone I trust," Abby said, rubbing her wrist, twisted when Yvonne had wrenched it out of her hand.

A second police car arrived, followed by Megan's four-by-four. Megan beat the police officers up the path by yards.

"What on earth . . . !" she began and then just threw her arms around Abby and held her.

"I asked first," Dee said.

Abby turned, but Megan kept her arm around her as she said, "This is Yvonne Thompson, Dee. She killed Geoffrey Tatton, I suspect by filling one of his supplement capsules with ricin. She had a key to the house." Abby indicated the cup on the floor. "You might want to get forensics to take a look at that. I'm pretty sure it contains ricin. Yvonne made it for me, but decided that Nigel Keane deserved it more."

Dee turned to him, took in the tears of pain running into the blood from his nose. "What happened to you, Mr Keane?"

"These women tried to kill me."

"He was trying to strangle me," Abby said, and Megan gave a gasp.

"I stopped him," Yvonne pointed out.

Dee gave Yvonne a basilisk stare. "Was that before or after you attempted to poison Mrs Finch?" She didn't wait for a reply but clicked on her radio and said, "We need crime scene officers in Longbourne. And let DI Glover know that we're bringing in Tatton's murderer." She turned to the uniformed officers standing behind her. "One of you stay here until SOCO arrives, tell them we need samples of whatever was spilled here and to check the house for ricin." Then she turned to Abby. "I assume you'll be pressing charges for assault on the Reverend Keane, Abby?"

"I don't understand how he knew I was here," she said.

"I'm afraid Mrs Keane's cousin was in a rage after she spoke to him on the phone and learned how he'd kept his cards and gifts from her for years. He'd been getting thank-you cards, apologies for missing family gatherings — all of them sent by Mr Keane and he had no idea."

"He came to the vicarage," Keane said, "ranting and raving. He didn't mention your name, Abby Finch, but I knew it had to be you and I went to your house to make you tell me where Fiona was. Your daughter answered the door and told me that you'd just popped to the garden centre and I saw your van . . ."

Abby shivered. A vicar comes calling, looking for your mother. Why wouldn't you tell him where she was?

"Nigel Keane, I'm arresting you for assault—"

"She hit me!" He pointed at Abby, who was still shuddering as she imagined Lucy, always polite, asking him if he'd like to come and wait . . . "And so did that woman. With a walking stick. And then she tried to poison me. They're the ones you should be charging with assault."

"Your wife has made a statement about your coercive control, Mr Keane. We already have a warrant out for your arrest," she said, and continued with her caution. "Do you need to see a paramedic, Abby, or are you ready to come to the station and make a statement?"

"It's nothing that can't be sorted out by a couple of painkillers and a cup of tea, but I really need to get home." She needed to hug her children. And talk to Jake. And to hug Megan, who was the world's best friend.

Dee nodded. "You don't look all that hot. Tomorrow morning will do." Then, concerned, "Are you fit to drive?"

"I'll just go and get my handbag . . ." She looked up the stairs and thought better off it. "Actually, Megan, could you . . . ? My phone's up there too. The SIM card might be salvageable."

Megan retrieved her bag and the broken phone.

"Will you get someone to drive Abby's van back to Maybridge?" she asked, having fished the keys out of Abby's bag and handed them to Dee. "I'm going to take her home."

Five minutes later, having settled Abby into the passenger seat of her four-by-four and heading back towards Maybridge, Megan exploded. "What the hell did you think you were doing?"

"Being incredibly stupid?" she offered.

CHAPTER FORTY-SIX

"For heaven's sake, Abby. What the devil did you think you were doing?" Dee demanded when she called round first thing the following morning.

"You're not the first person to ask that." First Megan, then Jake, then Penny. Fortunately the children didn't know what had happened so she was saved a three-point lecture from them.

"You don't go questioning suspected murderers on your own. Or at all," she added quickly.

"She wasn't a suspect," Abby said. "Just a possibility that Megan and I were checking out. Being hauled in for a DNA swab gives you a strong incentive to find the real killer."

"That swab cleared you of any involvement," Dee said.

"Well, hooray. I suppose my DNA profile will now join my fingerprints on the police database." Then, more calmly, "Anyway, to get back to the murder. When Megan told Yvonne that Tatton was dead, she didn't ask when he died. She said that while she'd almost certainly get a visit from the police because of the way she'd reacted when her sister died, she had an alibi as she'd been away at the time."

"At which point you should have called me instead of going to have another go at her."

Abby, whose scalp was still a little tender, thought she might have a point.

"Megan found out that both Elaine and Yvonne had been in love with an actor, which made me wonder, so I checked with the actors' union and my hunch was right. They were a singing duet called the Thompson Sisters."

"Why was that important?"

"It wasn't. But the way Yvonne had invited her in, shared her life story . . . It seemed a little too easy."

"And knowing that, you decided to come and confront her on your own?"

"No . . . I was pretending to be interested in the house for a friend. I tried to contact Megan to let her know where I was going but my call went to voicemail so I left a message. I even sent her a photograph of the pair of them in their act."

"You should have sent it to me," Dee said, then drew in a deep breath. "You should have talked to me."

"Got it. Next time."

"There isn't going to be a next time!"

"No. Of course not. And you're right," Abby admitted. "I thought it was going so well, but she'd rumbled me straight away and Megan was with a prospective buyer who wanted a second look around Linton Lodge. She had no idea I was in trouble until she got my emergency alert."

She eased her wrist and Dee spotted the bruise. "Are you okay?"

"I'll live."

"Only just. That was a neat trick sending an emergency call."

"Eric Braithwaite set it up for me. He did it for his mother and he was concerned about me being alone — not just with Gregory Tatton but with any new client. I've set it up on the kid's phones too. My only mistake was thinking I had time and leaving it very nearly too late."

"You don't look that great."

"Give me a day." A day was all she had. She was going on her first ever date with Jake tomorrow . . . "I'd be happier if I knew my name wasn't going to be in the paper."

"The *Observer* will have more than enough to fill the paper this week, with the arrests of Fiona and Yvonne as well as a disgraced vicar. And unless you change your mind about not pressing charges against him for assault, there's no reason why your name should be mentioned."

Her sole reason for letting him off that particular hook.

"What will you tell the children?" Dee asked.

"Only that they shouldn't tell casual callers where I am."

"And Jake?"

"Jake?" She nodded. "I've already told him everything."

No more holding back. No more secrets . . .

* * *

When the doorbell rang promptly at seven thirty on Thursday evening, Abby was upstairs putting the finishing touches to her lipstick.

"Jake's here and he's wearing a suit," Tom called up. "And he's brought flowers."

"I hope you're taking notes," she called back, turning to check her reflection in the mirror before picking up her coat and walking down the stairs very carefully in the unaccustomed heels, and a dress she'd bought at least two years before but had never worn.

She accepted the flowers, a beautiful posy of Christmas roses, already arranged in a pretty green vase.

"These are beautiful. Thank you." She looked him up and down appraisingly. "The last time I saw you in a suit was the prom."

"I thought I was wearing one on Tuesday."

"Funerals don't count."

"If we're excluding funerals," he replied, "the prom was the last time I saw you in a dress. That was red too."

And for a moment they were eighteen again, on the brink of their lives and trembling with nerves and excitement as they'd taken a step into the unknown.

The children, who'd given permission for this date, had gathered around. "Mum thought the dress would match her hat," Tom interjected.

How to kill the moment.

"Mum," Lucy said, looking earnest — what was coming! "We've been talking and we thought that on Christmas Eve, after the panto . . ."

"Yes?"

"Well, it doesn't seem right that Jake should go back to the houseboat and wake up on his own on Christmas Day. We decided that he should stay here and be with us. For Christmas," she added.

"Now you're dating," Tom added. His cheeks went pink. "Officially."

"Sophie?" Abby prompted. "Do you have any thoughts about that?"

"He'll be coming here on Christmas Day anyway," Sophie said. "Izzy said that it was Jake who asked her to give me Daddy's phone."

Abby turned to him. "Your superpower in action?"

"It's not a superpower, I was just listening and I thought maybe that was the answer." He looked at Sophie. "Was it?"

Sophie gave him a smile that had been missing for a very long time. "I love it. Thank you."

"And thank you, all of you, for your kind invitation, but staying over has to be your mother's decision."

Jake had said that she'd been running from the past and Abby knew that he was right. Running all her life from the night of the prom, running from the career she'd envisaged for herself, running from making a commitment to him . . .

But she'd turned her career around, and if the last few days — seeing what a mess people could make of their lives — had taught her anything, it was that there was no time to waste being afraid.

If Edward and Fiona had run away, nothing Gregory Tatton or Nigel Keane could say would have hurt them.

If Trish and Sandra or any of the other people who'd lived in fear had publicly challenged Tatton, he would have been the one shamed.

Easy to say. She hadn't been put to that test . . . And now she had a much easier choice to make about changing the rest of her life.

She put out her hand and took Jake's.

"Actually, guys," she said, "I was thinking the same thing only a few days ago. About Jake waking up all alone on Christmas morning while we were here with our stockings, having breakfast together, opening presents. Thank all of you for being so thoughtful, so kind. I'm very proud of you. And Daddy would be proud of you too."

* * *

"No one said, 'Play it again, Sam . . .'" Jake said as they walked back to Mill Lane, stars glittering overhead on a clear, frosty night.

"No."

"And they didn't have a happy ending."

"They had a good ending," Abby said. "It was wartime and duty came first. Ingrid had to stay with her resistance leader husband, while Bogart's bitterness and cynicism was swept away when he learned why she hadn't turned up that day in Paris. He will fight and die a hero knowing that she loved him. Would always love him . . ." She looked at him. "But you know that."

"They had great hats."

"Loved the hats," Abby said, as they reached the gate. Then turning to him, "Are you going to come in?"

He grinned. "On a first date? If I'm lucky I'll get a kiss on the doorstep and float home thinking I'm the luckiest man alive." Then, suddenly serious, he said, "I know I may have taken this a little faster than you were ready for by asking your kids if I could date you, but don't let the sentimentality of Christmas push you beyond your comfort zone."

"It's your comfort you need to worry about, Jake Sullivan." And it was her turn to grin. "That sofa bed is like sleeping on a bed of nails."

THE END

THE JOFFE BOOKS STORY

We began in 2014 when Jasper agreed to publish his mum's much-rejected romance novel and it became a bestseller.

Since then we've grown into the largest independent publisher in the UK. We're extremely proud to publish some of the very best writers in the world, including Joy Ellis, Faith Martin, Caro Ramsay, Helen Forrester, Simon Brett and Robert Goddard. Everyone at Joffe Books loves reading and we never forget that it all begins with the magic of an author telling a story.

We are proud to publish talented first-time authors, as well as established writers whose books we love introducing to a new generation of readers.

We have been shortlisted for Independent Publisher of the Year at the British Book Awards three times, in 2020, 2021 and 2022, and for the Diversity and Inclusivity Award at the Independent Publishing Awards in 2022.

We built this company with your help, and we love to hear from you, so please email us about absolutely anything bookish at feedback@joffebooks.com

If you want to receive free books every Friday and hear about all our new releases, join our mailing list: www.joffebooks.com/contact

And when you tell your friends about us, just remember: it's pronounced Joffe as in coffee or toffee!

Made in the USA
Monee, IL
21 November 2023

47065080R00166